Pirate
Unmasked

Pirate Unmasked

Judie Kleng

Black Lyon Publishing, LLC

PIRATE UNMASKED
Copyright © 2011 by JUDIE KLENG

Our books may be ordered through your local bookstore or by visiting the publisher:

www.BlackLyonPublishing.com

Black Lyon Publishing, LLC
PO Box 567
Baker City, OR 97814

This is a work of fiction. All of the characters, names, events, organizations and conversations in this novel are either the products of the author's vivid imagination or are used in a fictitious way for the purposes of this story.

COVER MODEL: Jason Baca

ISBN-10:   1-934912-34-4
ISBN-13:   978-1-934912-34-8
Library of Congress Control Number: 2010941758

Written, published and printed in
the United States of America.

Black Lyon Historical Romance

For my captain.

Chapter One

The Island of Crete
Mediterranean Sea
April 4, 1850

It's gone! What will I do now? Julie's thoughts raced as she crested the hill and yanked her scarf tight to protect against the frigid wind. Ducking under a cypress tree, she searched the docks below. Most of the smaller boats were already long gone, sailing in the predawn hours to set their fishing nets. Two large cargo boats still bobbed side by side out a ways from shore, their anchors straining against the choppy waves in the sleepy little inlet.

Then she saw it, anchored farther out, the large sailing ship that had arrived last night before dusk. It rocked gently in the water while she tried to make out the name on the side, but it was too far away. Something about it gave her an uneasy feeling, dark and mysterious. She was desperate. There were few choices left to her now.

Trying to quell the knot in her stomach, she hurried down the sloping bank leading to the shore. A grizzled old man was hunkered down near a decrepit flatboat and was carving on a piece of old driftwood, a multicolored parrot perched on his shoulder.

As she walked up the parrot flapped a wing and cocked its head sideways. "Wanna cup a'coffee?"

The old man grinned at her puzzled look. "Yeah, that wuz 'im. But I'm a' feared we're fresh outta coffee."

Julie smiled despite her distressed mood. "He really talks plain. He sure fooled me." She pointed to the two closer ships. "Would you be from one of those boats out there?"

He straightened slowly, lifting a bushy white eyebrow at her. "What would ye be wantin' ta know?"

"T'would be passage I'm needing. I can pay well." This was an out and out fib. She hadn't a single coin to place next to another; but she did have an idea where she could get some.

He paused in his whittling and looked at the two big boats. "They be cargo ships an' they 'dinna carry passengers; and certainly ... no young gurls," he offered as his chapped lips parted in a toothless smile.

Her heart sank but she went on with desperation building in her voice. "Are you quite certain they wouldn't change their minds. Just this once?"

He spat on the boards at her feet, and then wiped a grimy sleeve across his mouth. "Nope, females are bad luck, always causin' fights and wantin' special favors." Looking toward the lone ship anchored off by itself he stated, "Don't know 'bout that big'un though. Ain't seen it 'round here b'fore."

Julie gazed at it. She had no way to get out to it and she certainly wouldn't ask the old man to row her there. He had already returned to the knife in his hand and was chipping away as though she wasn't there. She thanked him anyway.

Dejected she walked slowly up the shoreline, stopping to pick a Greek spider orchid looking much like a bumblebee rather than a native flower. Caches of white asphodel and tassel hyacinth were also in full bloom and she brought the orchid to her nose, smelling the sweet pungent aroma. She forced back tears while her thoughts returned to her wretched predicament.

Her mother had been buried only yesterday, and her stepfather—No! She refused to think of him as any kind of a father! He'd been her mother's husband and that was all. She cringed. He'd been lusting after her ever since she began blossoming into young womanhood. While her mother was alive she'd threatened telling her of his unwanted advances. But now that she was gone, what would she use as a deterrent?

There was no one to turn to in this small village on the island of Crete. He had never permitted her or her mother to have friends. Once she had tried to escape to another part of the island, but he had sent his obnoxious watchdogs after her and they'd brought her back. He was a misogynist one day and a womanizer the next.

Julie had pretended to get along with Henri when her mother got consumption, as she didn't want to worry her. She had planned to tell her when she got better but she'd grown steadily worse, never to recover. In the ground just yesterday and she was already having trouble just conjuring up her pale, tired face. Only forty years old and she had looked to be in her seventies. Death had been somewhat of a blessing for her. At least she had escaped Henri, hadn't she?

She was jerked back to reality by the sound of scraping in the sand. Turning, she saw a young man leap out of a small boat beaching on the shore behind her. He grinned at her and she couldn't help but smile back at his contagious friendliness as she took in the unruly mass of blonde hair and blue eyes, set in a lightly freckled face.

"Hello," he laughed. "Didn't mean to scare you. Looks like you were daydreamin' or somethin."

She didn't know what to say. She'd always found it difficult to talk with young men and hadn't been around many, so she couldn't really relate. Her mother had tutored her after her father died at sea and she'd been more or less sheltered ever since.

"Yes, I guess I was." Her shyness began to dissolve with his jovial manner and she gestured to the big ship still looking ominous. "Are you from that ship?"

His grin grew wider. "Yes'm. That's the Black Hornet, finest ship ever sailed these waters," he said proudly. Extending his hand, he grasped her fingers lightly. "My name's Jeremy O'Flanahan. Twenty and one years of age but mostly Irish with a lot of stubborn Norwegian thrown in." His eyes twinkled and she couldn't help but like him immediately. He was now walking with her back up the beach.

A sudden thought struck her. Trying to keep her voice steady, she asked, "Does your ship need any workers?"

He stopped, looking at her intently. "We do need a ..." His heart fell, picturing her with a young and eager husband. "Who is it that would be wantin' ta sign on?

"My brother," she stammered. A plan was rapidly taking shape and the excitement brought a quick rush of color to her cheeks and her eyes sparkled. Besides, she'd remembered the old man's theory of women bringing bad luck aboard ship just in time.

Jeremy liked this newfound feeling of importance. "Our first mate's ashore and he'd be the one to decide if we could use him or not. We sail with the first light in the morning, and could be, if'n he's a hard worker we could use him. How old is he?"

"Seventeen," she blurted. She was praying fervently that she hadn't blundered since seventeen might be too young. "He'd work hard and wouldn't get in anyone's way... or cause any trouble." Her pulse raced with excitement in this new dangerous plan.

"His name's Old Walters." At her puzzled expression, he laughed. "That's his name, Old Walters. Never did tell anyone all these years his whole name, so that's what we all call 'im. He's got a big ole white walrus mustache and limps with his right leg. If I run into him. I'll tell him your brother wants to talk to him." They had reached the warehouse where Jeremy was going to help load supplies.

Julie smiled gratefully, her mind still racing ahead making plans. "Thanks, Jeremy. He'll be ever so grateful." She left after telling him where she and her brother could be found later that evening.

Jeremy stared after her; thinking what a delectable young girl she was. Her long red hair glistened as the sun struck the long ends that swung below her bonnet. She was certainly a breathtaking beauty and he began to fantasize about seeing her again.

Julie's mind was swirling. She had a chance to escape from Henri Wellar! She shuddered, thinking of him. He had married her mother five years ago and promptly took over her pub and inn, the only means of supporting herself and her daughter.

She had lied about having a brother but she'd wished for a sibling many times over. Her mother had a sister in St. Louis, Missouri. If she could just get to America! Her mother had even hinted as much before she died—had she known?

As she neared the inn she took a deep breath and opened the big heavy side door that led to the staircase to their quarters upstairs, but instead went down the hall to the pub to ready it for the nightly crowd. She breathed a sigh when she saw no sign of Henri. Good, he was probably sleeping it off with one of the trollops he hung around with in the village.

The room was cold, so she picked up some kindling stacked near the potbellied stove to make a fire. Striking a flint, she worked until small amber flames began to lick at the small bits of wood and crumpled paper and gradually she was warmed. Looking around, she saw that the tables were still littered with the remnants of last night's drinking.

Shaking her head in disgust, she rolled up her sleeves after hanging her bonnet on a hook. He couldn't even tend to business! And now it was his business, built from her mother's meager savings. According to law everything now fell to his hands. The pub and inn and now even the raising of his "daughter." He was now her legal guardian since she was not yet eighteen. Her mother had never given this a thought when she'd married him. But, giving her mother credit when she'd married him, he'd been a different sort, not showing his true colors until sometime later.

When Julie had started to fill out into an appealing beauty he had began to follow her with his evil eyes, and then bumping into her with his disgusting, groping hands. More recently his attacks had begun to increase in frequency until she now found him harder and harder to dissuade. How could her mother have been so blind!

Julie shook it off and wiped down the tables and chairs and cleaned up the spilled ashes. She then set the taps for the evening's onslaught, trying to follow her daily regime as not to raise suspicions. With a seemingly lightheartedness she didn't really feel she climbed the stairs to the flat above. If Henri came near her—she tried not to dwell on it.

Letting herself in with her skeleton key, she was glad she'd stoked up the fire before she left. She now felt the warmth circulating the room. Henri was still out. It seemed unusually quiet now with her mother gone and, once again, she felt a great emptiness that was now growing familiar. She shook her long flowing hair back from her face and stepped out of her shoes. Unhooking her dress down the front, she let it drop to the floor. She stooped to pick it up and then went into the kitchen area to pick up her cup and saucer from the table and placed them both on the scarred and well-worn sideboard.

She poured some warm water left simmering on the back of the wood stove into a chipped crockery washbasin and quickly sponged herself. Clad only in her light shift, she passed the mirror on the back of the door then stopped and studied herself.

Could she possibly hope to pass herself off as a boy? There, the thought that had lurked in the far reaches of her mind this past hour suddenly burst forth. Her long slim legs, tiny waist, and trim girlish hips ... Would they give her away in some loose fitting baggy breeches?

Ah, but her breasts. She could never hide their fullness unless... She reached for a long strip of cloth and quickly bound it around her chest and turned sideways. In a loose-fitting shirt she just might pull it off.

Smiling at her reflection, her mind raced on. Maybe she could get away with it! At least until they were far enough out to sea they couldn't bring her back. She didn't even know where The Black Hornet was bound. They would have to let her off someplace. Surely they weren't barbarians! They couldn't just throw her overboard; but anything was better than this. Just as long as she could get off this island and away from Henri!

She rummaged around in a small drawer and found her parents' miniature and her aunt's letter. She tucked those, along with a few personal items and some of Henri's clothes, in a canvas reticule and stuffed it under the bed. She jerked open the closet and dug around until she found what she was looking for—a pair of brown sealskin boots. She sat down hard on the floor and jammed a small dainty foot into one and laughed out loud. That Henri was not a big man, she was grateful. They would fit with paper stuffed in the toes!

She sat them back in the closet, hiding them behind a box. Now to find Old Walters! Flushed and excited, she turned when she heard the door open.

"That pretty smile fer me?" Henri said drunkenly, closing the door behind him. He stumbled toward her, while holding a shaky hand out to grab her wrist.

She tried to twist away, fear washing over her. He was fumbling at the front of her shift, and tearing it in his haste. Feeling the swell of her breasts, he squeezed painfully causing her to cry out.

"Let me go! Get your filthy hands off me!"

His other arm came up to pin hard against her throat as she fought him. She sank her teeth into the side of his hand. He jerked and let her go; his dark eyes narrowing to dangerous slits as he came at her again.

"Come on now, honey. We don't have to worry about your

mama finding out about us anymore. You want me, you know you do," he slobbered as he fell against the wall. Julie moved backward, her heart thumping loudly in her chest.

He watched her for a long moment without moving, and she began to think he was having second thoughts when suddenly he dove for her, throwing her to the floor. Pinning her down under him, he grabbed a handful of hair and yanked her head back.

Clenching her teeth tightly, she fought the sickening smell of him as the bile rose in her chest to burn her throat. With a sudden burst of strength, she broke his hold and lifted a knee to catch him solidly in the groin.

He yelped in pain as she rolled away. Then she picked up a vase, which had fallen, and threw it with all her might as he lumbered again to his feet. It hit him forcefully on the side of his head and he brought up his hand and made a sweep alongside his head, staring in disbelief at the blood before he wiped it off on his pants.

"You dirty little—" he choked. "You'll pay for this. I was only funnin' before. Let's see just how tough you really are!" He took a short menacing step toward her.

Reaching the door in one leap, she smoothed her dress as she raced down the stairs. When she reached the bottom step, she stumbled and was grabbed around the waist by a tall figure with a black beard who had been leaning against the banister listening to the commotion upstairs. She was shaking so violently that she took several deep breaths before collapsing breathlessly against him.

"Holy Mary!" he warned. "You could break your damn fool neck coming down a stairway like that."

She peered back up the stairs, surprised Henri hadn't followed. Distraught, she began to laugh hysterically. She hadn't noticed the man that held her but this same observation was not being returned.

He couldn't see her face clearly as her wild mane of Titian hair hid the most part of her face. She felt as light as a feather in his arms, and he was overwhelmingly aware of the scent of a flowery exotic perfume. His arm was pressed tightly about her chest, forcing her half-exposed breasts to his unrestricted but very interested view.

By the state of her dress and uncontrollable laughter, his first thought was this was surely a cheap little trollop and no doubt for hire. His jaw tightened as he thought of the one that he'd left back home. She'd fooled him too.

Breathing easier now, Julie looked down for the first time at her torn bodice. She drew it quickly together and pulled away from the man with the brazen, penetrating eyes. "Thank you, I'm quite all right now."

She spoke in a tinkling, slightly accented voice, and her long hair spilled over her face as she had her head down and fussing with her torn dress. He was still trying to see her face when she jerked at the loud sound at the top of the stairs. She tossed her hair back in a swift motion and he found himself staring down into beautiful tear-filled emerald green eyes.

He sucked in his breath. She was astonishingly beautiful.

Her eyes locked with his for a long moment and then she jerked away and hurried down the hall to the pub.

"But wait," he called after her. "I would like—"

"Ask him," she said as she turned her head toward the man descending the stairs. Then she disappeared through the door.

•

A short while later, Julie was serving customers in the busy pub and trying to appear normal. The fishermen were returning ashore and the local crowd seemed to be in an especially rowdy mood this night, which was a little unusual for a weekday. The smoke hung low over the tables and Julie's eyes strained through the thick haze while keeping watch for the man with the walrus mustache and game leg.

She reasoned that he was bound to wander in some time this evening, as it was the only drinking establishment in the village. All the seamen she knew seemed to be notorious imbibers.

She hovered around the tables, overlong she sometimes feared, trying to listen to conversations for any information at all about the black ship and it's crew. Since it was leaving at dawn, she knew time was quickly running out. Her escape had to come tonight.

Several times she felt Henri's eyes on her, and once when she turned to face him, she detected a queer smirk on his face that left her frightened. His very presence grated on her, and when a boisterous fisherman jokingly pulled her into his lap, Henri was right there and jealously yanked her to her feet, causing her great embarrassment. Henri drew back as if to hit her when she heard a tankard of ale hit the table from a shadowy corner as a man rose to his feet.

It was the man with the black beard and Julie could see a vein raised rigidly across his forehead as he crossed the room in a flash and yanked Henri's arm back. His black eyes snapped as he sneered with contempt. "It's a small man indeed that would strike a woman. Let alone a small slip of a girl."

His voice was laced with sarcasm as he towered over a no-longer-brave bully, and Julie leaned against the table for support as her legs warned they were soon to give out. The room grew completely silent. Then just as suddenly as he had appeared, the stranger wheeled and left the room.

Julie was left to stare fearfully at Henri and she felt a small degree of comfort that he had been made to look foolish in front of his friends. The rest of the evening dragged by slowly, but when Walters didn't show she really started to worry. Now she knew she had no choice. She had to steal aboard the ship and take the consequences if she got caught.

Suddenly Henri was at her elbow. "There's an older gentleman wants to talk to you when you're finished here. He's got the room upstairs at the end of the hall." When she only stared blankly at him, he continued, "Maybe it's about your mother. He didn't say what he wanted."

Julie tried to look puzzled but she didn't know if she pulled it off or not. It had to be Old Walters! She let out her breath and tried to appear nonchalant as she left the pub and quickly climbed the stairs. She smoothed her skirt and paused at a mirror at the top of the stairs to straighten a flyaway curl.

Then, stopping at the last door, she knocked softly and was bade to enter by a low voice. As soon as she closed the door behind her, she realized her mistake.

This was not some harmless old gray-haired man of advancing years as she'd expected. In the dim moonlight streaming through the opened window, she saw the tall dark figure of a much younger, hard muscled man clad in an open-necked white shirt with dark close fitting trousers.

Black shiny Hessian boots turned toward her, and as her eyes quickly became accustomed to the darkness, she knew him to be the man she'd encountered earlier. She waited timidly for the man to speak.

"You came," he whispered huskily, and in one quick motion he reached for her.

She had no time to act as he caught her up in his strong arms and crushed his lips to hers in a hard searing kiss. Maneuvering her easily across the room, he deftly eased her down on the bed.

He held her so tightly she couldn't struggle or speak with his lips devouring hers completely. He kicked off his boots and before she knew what was happening, he straightened and skillfully removed her dress in one quick movement. She was left clad only in her chemise.

With a wave of despair she pushed at his chest, not surprised she could smell the strong odor of rum on his breath. Her eyes flew to the bed stand and she saw a nearly empty bottle of amber colored liquid and squeezed her eyes shut tightly. She wouldn't cry. She'd not give Henri the satisfaction, certain he was the one responsible for this.

In all this time his lips had never left hers, and he was pressing her so hard that she could scarcely draw a breath. She twisted her head and tried to explain but he seemed a wild man. Pushing her into the pillows, he yanked the coverlet aside. Still holding her in a vise-like grip, he rolled her onto her side facing him, and then grasped the back of her chemise and ripped it from her body.

Somehow she had lost her slippers and was aghast to find he was also amazingly free of his clothes. She pushed furiously at his chest when she felt his warm body pressing boldly into hers. *Oh, God! How could this happen twice in one day? Was it a dream?*

She could only moan with his hand clamped over her mouth. *Dreams don't smell like Haitian rum and imported tobacco*, she reminded herself.

"All right, missy. Stop your fighting! One of us is gonna get hurt and it sure as hell ain't gonna be me, seein' as how I'm at least twice your size." His eyes were black as soot with his hand still over her mouth. "He said you liked to fight for it, but enough's enough!"

He rolled her onto her back without giving her a chance to say a word, pinning her arms beneath her. Drawing back he stared fascinated at her quivering pink-tipped breasts, and then she died of shame when his admiring eyes swept down her length.

"Lovely," he murmured low in his throat as his mouth slid over her ear where she felt his warm breath.

"No," she whimpered. With one last desperate shove, she tore her lips away. "I'm not what you think! You've been tricked!" He drew back a couple inches and stared down into her face as she took a short breath and gasped, "I've never lain with a man before."

He released her instantly. With the unmistakable fear in her voice and the look on her face, he was brought abruptly to his senses. Then with a low curse he rolled to the edge of the bed.

She grabbed for the sheet to cover her, drawing it up to her chin as she sat up on her knees.

"Are you kidding me?" he whispered raggedly.

"No, God's truth! I'm a virgin."

With a yank, he drug the blanket from her, forcing her to leap from the bed. Sinking back against the pillows, he watched her in screaming silence.

"The day is yet to come I would stoop so low as to pluck a blooming flower or ravish an unwilling maid." His head hurt mightily and the room was spinning before his eyes. He was damnably tired. Too tired to try and explain himself.

She leaned back against the wall and slid noiselessly to the floor. She kept her eyes riveted to the bed and then leaned her head back against the wall and tried to think. Henri was to blame for this, he must be laughing his insane head off by now!

The dark head on the pillow turned and their eyes locked together for what seemed an eternity before he turned away to study a spot on the ceiling. After another abominable amount of time, she heard him snoring softly.

With a last look over her shoulder at the dark figure in the bed, she opened the door and closed it softly behind her.

Chapter Two

When the man with the black beard opened his eyes the next morning, he had for one long moment forgotten everything but his pounding headache. Disoriented, his eyes swept the room, quickly coming to rest on the little table by his bed and the chipped water pitcher. He started to reach for it when he spied a crumpled garment under his elbow. Only when he pulled it free did he remember the girl.

He fell back against the iron grill-work bumping his head, and then gave a low groan. *God Almighty! All I'd wanted was a room and bath last night.* The proprietor had been all too eager to procure a lady of the evening to keep him company last night and said he'd not be disappointed. He said she was a wild thing and would give him his money's worth.

But she had left in the night, and his mind was hazy as to what had really gone on. He sat up with a start. Maybe this had been a ruse. Maybe they'd had a plan to pick him clean! He grabbed his pants and quickly went through the pockets. No, everything was as he'd left it. His money, and he had quite a large roll with him, was still there.

All of it.

•

While she thought she'd had the courage before; now she was frightened nearly out of her wits. How could she possibly hope to get away with this? Somehow she'd managed to climb into a longboat heading out to the big black ship and had crouched down among the yawning crew managing to look inconspicuous.

One man, slightly more sober than the rest, asked her what she was doing there. She told him she was the new cabin boy, hired earlier that day by Old Walters. Satisfied, he'd had no further questions, much to her great relief. Now, stepping aboard the polished decks, she remembered to hunch her shoulders and keep her eyes downcast, trying not to bring attention to herself.

She kept her fingers crossed that they would be well out to sea before she ran into Walters and her plans went awry. Following the men down into their quarters, she congratulated herself on her success when one pointed to an empty bunk in a narrow cubbyhole near the stairwell. It was small, but private. She was hungry, but knew it was better to be this than chance discovery.

The men were all tired. Some were noisy, and a few little tipsy, but she hurriedly climbed into her bunk. Letting out her breath, she bunched up her pillow and lay back, kicking her knapsack to the foot of her bunk. She'd done it! And better still, no one suspected! Pulling off her overlarge boots, she reached over the side and let them fall softly to the floor. She couldn't risk undressing, so she would sleep in her clothes. Such as they were.

Reaching up, she pulled off her stocking cap and ran her fingers through her hair. It certainly felt different. She hadn't had much time, but the deed was done. Her hair was cut ragged and inept, and in much haste. But it was short.

Now she was a boy.

Almost.

·

A loud whistle blasted her awake. She sat up quickly and bumped her head a good whack. Sinking back down on her rough ticked pillow, she rubbed vigorously where she felt a small bump beginning to raise and tried to get her bearings. A second blast and she could tell they were getting underway. Jumping to her knees, she peered out a small opening in the curtain, seeing nothing but lots of brass, assorted ropes and storage boxes.

There was a rocking lurch and soon she heard sails slapping the wind. She lay back down and felt a swell of sadness, leaving her mother to rest forgotten on the island while she sailed farther and farther away. She pulled her stocking cap back on her head as tears streamed down her cheeks. Memories flitted behind her closed eyes before she finally drifted off to sleep again.

The next time she awoke, she was staring into the freckled face of Jeremy O'Flanahan. He was grinning down at her from the ladder with his wide friendly grin. "I see they hired ya on after all. Wasn't sure Old Walters would take a young boy from his family. I tried to meet up with your sister last night, but the place was dark. I guess I missed her." His gaze fell instinctively to her ragged shirtsleeves gripping the blanket tight to her chin. Then they traveled up to the top of her head where the cap covered her hair. "You sure look like her. What's your name, boy?"

Julie struggled to maintain her confidence and to muster a masculine sounding voice. "M'name's Jack. Jack Sinclair," she stuttered.

"Jack," he repeated. "Okay, Jack. Let's go eat." He handed her boots to her when she climbed down the ladder, smiling when she leaned clumsily against the wall to pull them on.

Following him down the narrow passageway and into the galley, as he referred to it, the aroma of salt pork and fresh coffee assailed her starving nostrils, making her stomach growl.

There had been a hushed silence when they'd first walked in and Julie's heart was pounding so hard in her chest, she'd feared it would stop. Trying to quell her fear, she glanced around the rough-hewn table, dreading to see Old Walters, or even the captain. But all she saw were two rows of friendly faces staring back at her and not one of them had a white mustache. She let out her breath and took a seat next to Jeremy.

When Jeremy asked someone about Walters, Julie learned he was at the helm as the captain was under the weather. She let out her breath. Luck was with her! Not that she wanted him to be sick, but another day or so could make a big difference in her escape.

Jeremy made introductions. "This here's our new cabin boy. His name is Jack Sinclair. He's young n' more refined than all of you, so watch your manners." The men all guffawed and returned to their meal.

A crockery mug of steaming coffee was shoved in front of her, followed by a tin plate of salt pork, two greasy eggs, some sort of beans, along with a large twist of hard bread. Picking up a fork with a wooden handle, she bent her head and began to eat hungrily. Their curiosity now appeased, the men all resumed eating.

The man across from her raised his head. He had a long salt-and-pepper beard and was sopping up juice with his hunk of bread. He grinned over at her and showed a missing a front tooth.

"The bread's hard as a rock, only way to tolerate it," he said, juice dripping down his chin. "Ever been to sea before?" He waited for her to speak.

Julie took the bull by the horns and hoped to put some gravel in her voice. She prayed she wouldn't give herself away. "Yeah, I have." Not a lie, she had sailed with her folks. She turned to Jeremy. "Walters didn't really get a chance to tell me what my duties are. Could you tell me what a cabin boy is expected to do?" She was determined to jump right in and earn her keep.

"Mostly, you're a 'fetch-it' boy, a 'help out everyone' type. You're expected to mop floors, help out in the galley, wash dishes, wash clothes, polish brass and keep the lamps filled with whale oil." He gave her such a friendly look he instantly claimed her trust. "The captain likes things neat and orderly. He's strict, but always fair, 'n likes everything shining like a new coin." He looked down at her empty plate. "You musta been starving. Want some more?"

"No thanks," she murmured, still keeping her face downcast as much as possible.

"I'll warn you," Jeremy continued as he poured her another cup of coffee, "the Cap'n keeps mostly to hisself. He's moody but the crew is fiercely devoted to him. Most of us have been with him a long time."

She nodded her understanding and sipped at her hot coffee. It was very strong and the food could use a lot of help in the taste department she thought to herself as she stole a look at the grouchy-faced cook. She wondered how he'd managed to keep this crew happy. He was a wiry little man, not even five feet tall. Stealing another look at Jeremy, she wondered what he would think if he knew that she was the girl from the island.

Immediately after eating, Jeremy told her he was going to give her a tour of the boat before she started her duties. They walked down the companionway and climbed the steps up to the deck. She noted the clean polished wood with shiny brass fixtures, and neatly coiled ropes of all sizes. Huge sails cupped and popped with the wind. There was a great deal of pride on the men's faces she noted as they moved among them. She met carpenters, riggers, caulkers and assorted deckhands. Each one was skilled in their specific tasks. It was a huge boat. The gleaming decks and wood were black, hence the name, The Black Hornet.

She looked beyond the bow and saw only whitecaps and endless horizon all around them. No shore, no other ships around them, and no ... Henri. Now she felt free! The feeling was almost overwhelming. Tears welled up in her eyes and she kept her face averted. For the first time, she learned their destination. They would cross the Atlantic Ocean and make their way to America. Julie, new at mastering deception, hid her outward excitement. But inside, she was a quivering mass of varying conflicts. She suddenly felt a little faint.

Jeremy tapped her elbow. "Next, I'll show you the cargo hold, where we keep supplies and how we catch rainwater for baths and cooking. Then I'll show you where the captain's quarters are." But, before they got any farther, Julie began to feel really ill.

She hadn't given it a thought, but she felt certain now she was growing seasick. Nausea had washed over her when they were down in the hold. The pungent smell of spices, coffee beans, stale seawater, along with the putrid smell of fish and garbage, quickly turned her face white, evidence of her plight.

Jeremy recognized the look. With a friendly slap on her back he returned her to her bunk. For the next four days she left it only to use the chamberpot. She didn't want anything to eat since just the smell produced another round of wild retching. She was so miserable she was afraid she wouldn't live.

After three days Jeremy was finally able to make her drink some tepid water, then some broth and weak Chinese tea. Finally she was able to wash down a small piece of dry bread.

She was mortified and loath to face anyone. Then, by the fourth morning, she decided she wanted to live. When she climbed down her ladder, and to her astonishment, she came face to face with Old Walters. She knew him instantly. But instead of reproach, his merry eyes twinkled down at her. Jeremy was standing just behind him.

"Thought we were going to lose our cabin boy," he declared. Her mouth dropped in astonishment. He went on. "But then, you had warned me you'd never been to sea before." He grinned back at Jeremy when he fell behind them. Walters leaned and whispered in her ear when they turned the corner. "How do you think I got here when I was just a lad like you?"

She put a hand on his elbow, her voice low. "Thank you, sir. I didn't know of any other way since I didn't have much time. I did have a good reason for getting off the island. One day soon I'll tell you." She wasn't quite up to letting out her secret just yet, just a little longer, then she'd take whatever punishment was doled out. Right now there were too many men about and she felt threatened. She'd wait until she knew them all better.

After they had been at sea for six days, she began her duties. She worked hard and never complained, and was often found humming while she labored. She scrubbed floors on her hands and knees, washed clothes and bedding, then hung them to dry on lines stretched on the end of the deck where they dried quickly in the wind.

She washed dishes, peeled fruit and vegetables, made sure the flour, sugar and spices were kept full, kept the water pails full and warm water always simmering on the big cast-iron wood stove. There were endless chores to do, and at night she fell asleep quickly and learned to wake up at dawn the next morning.

The crew seemed to like her but they often had a habit of telling ribald jokes, and then heehawing and slapping their knees when she blushed. Still she relaxed by slow degrees and began to laugh a lot more, mostly at the funny way they told their stories. Not so much at the ofttimes colorful content.

She had yet to see the captain who she learned came out only at night. She could sometimes hear him walk up and down the deck, long after everyone was supposed to be asleep. Jeremy told her he'd been under the weather for several days after leaving Crete and that he liked to eat, bathe and work on his books in solitude.

Once, she peeked out at the top of the stairs and saw his dark form standing near the rail, looking out over the water. He seemed to be a mysterious sort, but his men didn't seem to think his manner strange. If anything, they rarely mentioned him.

A week later they reached the Strait of Gibraltar. Originally she had planned to leave the ship at her first opportunity, but quickly concluded that since she had no money she was better off to stay put. Since they were headed to America anyway, she reasoned she might just as well stay on the boat.

They docked at Tangier, the last stop before they reached open seas. They stocked more fresh water, eggs, salted pork and beef, fruit and vegetables, even some live chickens in wire cages, all for eating at some later date.

Julie had no desire to go ashore, but when Thaddious the cook returned, he reached in his hind pocket and offered her a pouch of Spanish tobacco. He shoved it in her pants pocket when she started backing up. He laughed out loud, "Most boys yer age would have been chawin' on that stuff an' spittin' up a storm."

"Thank you, Thaddious," she sputtered, still learning to play the part. "I best wait. Make sure t'won't make me sick again." Ducking her head, she quickly made to flee the room.

"Suit yer'self, boy. But it'll put a little hair on yer chest." There was something about that boy that made him feel sorry for him. He couldn't quite put his finger on it but maybe the boy just needed time to adjust. This was no place for a tenderfoot. He'd have to learn to hold his own.

There were two men Julie couldn't quite let down her guard with. They talked constantly of bawdy women and made crude jokes, demeaning them and putting them down in a way that made her uncomfortable. The other men's stories were mostly funny and they made fun of themselves and didn't just talk about women.

Julie was always careful with her mannerisms and voice and she practiced constantly in order not to give herself away.

The men she didn't trust was a big Swede named Samuel Mallory, and the other was a small cocky man named simply Bracken. She never felt at ease with either and they took profound pleasure in poking fun and teasing her every chance they got. They tried several times to get her to drink rum with them, and with her increasing rebuffs, they only seemed to pick on her more.

It was while they were still docked at Tangier that Julie began to take a wider interest in the galley of the big ship. With a crew of twenty, she'd noticed from the beginning that their appetites were sometimes lacking. With Thaddious' increasing warming up to her, she began to make subtle hints about adding more flavor to dishes. With plenty of spices at their disposal, it was simply a matter of blending and experimenting.

When they tried some and then seeing the men's pleased reaction, he praised her in front of the men, giving her the credit. In the weeks that followed she was quickly eased into more cooking and Walters delegated someone else to take over the heavier labor.

One night after leaving the Strait, and two days after entering the open sea, she and Thaddious presented the crew with a zesty stew. It was swimming with tender chunks of meat and tasty vegetables. One could have heard a pin hit the floor when she walked to the table, holding two large trays of cornbread biscuits.

For one long wordless minute, she almost wished she hadn't gone so far. It was beyond their comprehension, a lad making biscuits. With an embarrassed drop of her chin, she set the trays down and stepped back. It became way too quiet. She raised her eyes, meeting their astonished stares, and then they all dove at once.

Thaddious shoved a tray in her hand and told her to take it to the captain. Her heart hammered loudly in her ears as she left the room. She had done her best to avoid him, and had no real reason to fear meeting him, it was just a nagging gut feeling.

As she neared his cabin, she stopped at the door, stalling for time. Taking a deep breath, she knocked softly but there was no answer. She rapped again, and then a little louder. Finally she slowly opened the door and tiptoed in. She realized she was holding her breath and let it out. He must be out on the bridge.

Setting the tray on a small table bolted to the floor, she looked around her. It was definitely a masculine room. A large bunk was against the outer wall on a swing-down platform which could then be bolted back flush to the wall. A roll-top mahogany desk was also bolted to the floor, adjacent from the bunk and on the opposite wall.

There was a black leather oversized chair next to the ship's only porthole. Papers and parchments were strewn about on the bed and clothing was piled recklessly in a heap at the foot. An empty bottle of rum was gently rolling back in forth on the floor in rhythm with the rock of the ship. She bent down and picked it up.

Humph! And they said he was meticulous? He was obviously a drinking man such as the two she'd escaped from the island. She wondered now what Henri and the man in the room had said about her when next they'd met. Lest the captain should return, she hurried back to the galley where most of the men were just finishing up.

She sat down next to Jeremy to finish her dinner. He was drinking his coffee and smiled warmly at her.

"Bet your sister cooks good too, or did your mother teach

you?"

"Both," she murmured, then thought it best to explain. "At first I thought it was sissy, but 'twas better that than clean and scale fish all day." Then, sounding as gruff as she possibly could, she offered more. "How was I 'ta know I'd be cookin' fer a bunch of horny ole toads like youse guys."

She looked braver than she felt down the double row of faces. With a hearty laugh, she was slapped on the back from both sides. She was one of them.

•

Donning her secondary pair of baggy breeches and a scratchy wool shirt the next morning, she raced down to the galley to help Thaddious with breakfast. She had gotten in the habit of washing herself in sections after everyone left her alone each night after supper and she had high hopes for a real bath soon. Her head itched from constantly wearing the cap and she scratched it, then pulled it down over her ears as she hurried along.

This morning she'd prepared potato pancakes with molasses, thick sliced pork bacon, and the men all hungrily chowed down. Afterward, she washed and dried the dishes, while marveling at the way they all ate. On deck, she could hear chains grating over the sides and the never-ending slap of canvas cupping the wind. She could tell they'd stepped it up a few knots.

She refilled the water barrels and washed the table down, then picked up a bucket and some cleaning rags and went to the captain's room. Jeremy had told her before he left that the captain was up on the bridge. She let herself in and quickly tore into his bunk, stripping his bed and gathered up his dirty laundry. She found fresh bedding and remade his bed. She then carried the soiled laundry back to the galley, filled a bucket with warm water and returned to scrub the floors.

When she'd finished, she waxed all the tables and chairs. Also the desk and headboard, until they shined. On the night table, she discovered several rings from drinking mugs and made a mental note to try and find some walnut oil to try and capture the original luster.

She returned to the galley where the water was hot enough for suds, located the scrub board and washed his clothes as well as hers. With the gentle breeze of the hot July sunshine, they would be dry in less than two hours. The captain was still gone when she returned to hang up his clothes and restock his linens.

There was no time to sit down and relax before it was time to start fixing dinner. As usual, the meal was the time for the men to catch up. They solved the day's problems with rounds of off-color stories. She was relieved the labors of the day were drawing to a close since she was bone tired. She was sweaty and felt restricted with the tight binding around her chest.

This night she was able to find privacy after her chores were done, so she quickly took a sponge bath and headed for her bunk. After tossing and turning, unable to sleep after her hectic day, she decided a walk in the fresh air might be what she needed. Donning her still damp shirt and breeches, she was barefoot and enjoying her freedom. She tiptoed quietly out on deck.

It was a glorious moonlit night, and after a slow turn around the entire ship, she still didn't feel sleepy. She sat down and leaned back against the wall under the stairway to the bridge. The moonlight was shining out over the water and she raised her eyes to the yellow full moon and searched for the North Star. When she found it, her eyes traveled on across the gigantic cluster of the Milky Way and searched for the two dippers.

She had only been there about five minutes when footsteps sounded overhead and she saw the tall figure of a man slowly descending the stairs. She pulled herself back to stay hidden and watched as he stopped and looked out over the water. As the moonlight illuminated his face, she sucked in her breath with a deep gasp.

Black beard, dark hard eyes, and the unmistakable chest. It was him, the man from the inn! *Oh, Good Lord! How could this be so?* He was the captain? Her heart was hammering so loud in her ears, she feared he could hear it. Now what was she to do? She would have to continue this charade all the way to America. He must never know it was she! Jeremy knowing wouldn't be bad, but this man?

She waited and watched, barely breathing. He stood there for a very long time, staring out over the water until she thought she'd go mad. He was so close she could see the flaring of his nostrils and the hard line of his jaw, clenching and unclenching angrily. Whatever he was thinking, she could see it was not pleasant. There was a frequent red glow when he drew in on the cheroot he held between his teeth.

Then, with the swiftness of movements, he brought up his hand and tossed it angrily into the sea, then moved off down the deck. She waited a few minutes until she felt she could move her trembling legs, and then scurried back to the safety of her bunk and another sleepless two hours.

After that, she was more determined than ever to stay out of his way. But it seemed the more she tried, the more inevitable it became they would meet. He had begun asking questions about the elusive cabin boy who had turned his crew into ravenous eaters. He wanted to know about this young boy that made biscuits, even properly washing clothes and bedding.

She neatly dodged him a couple more days until her luck finally ran out.

She was elbow-deep in flour and lard, and bending over the sideboard in the galley, when she swung around at a loud footstep and stepped right into a hard chest. Arms flew out and caught her when she tripped and she nearly fell over his boots. A hand came up, and before she could think, she had smacked him none too gently on his cheek. Her face flamed when she saw the flour all over the side of his face. She didn't know whether to laugh or run.

"Whoa there, lad! Are we working you so hard, you've no time to slow down a minute so I can have a word with you?" He reached for a cloth to wipe off the flour. "I just thought I'd like to see this boy wonder who's making fat and lazy members of my crew."

"Sorry, sir. About the flour, I mean."

She struggled to keep the tremor from her voice but found it still easy keeping her voice boyish. She didn't have to be reminded to keep her shoulders hunched since she was ever aware of the tight breast binder. Quaking from head to toe, she turned quickly and began to knead the flour on the sideboard, seeing nothing.

"How is it that a boy such as you should be able to cook?" he asked as he slowly moved around the table, trying to get a closer look at her. He got a puzzled look on his face when he saw her trembling and frowned.

Still keeping her head down, she muttered, "S'no big thing. I was jes' sickly a lot at home, n' hung 'round the kitchen. Guess yer bound to pick up a few things, here n' there."

Leaning back on the sideboard next to her, he crossed his booted feet at the ankles. She started with his black leather boots, highly polished and stopping just below his knees. From there, she went on up his tight black trousers, to a black leather belt with a shiny gold buckle, then up to an immaculate white linen shirt, opened carelessly at the neck. When she got to the dark curly hair on his chest, she quickly dropped her eyes again.

She wished he would leave, and when he spoke again she jumped.

"They said your name was Jack. Where did you sign on at?"

He would surely guess! But she knew she had to tell the truth. She couldn't take the chance that Walters or one of the men hadn't told him any different.

"I came aboard at Crete." There, it was said. And if this finished her, she would just have to confess and hope for the best.

His hand went to the bridge of his nose and he grimaced. That had been a lost weekend for him. He'd gotten drunk on some bad ale on the island, and for the next couple of weeks, anything could have happened. When Walters had finally gotten him back to the ship, he had been so sick he'd not ventured out of his cabin.

That it was Crete the boy hired on at meant nothing to him.

A few minutes later Thaddious came into the galley. He had passed the captain in the passageway and had stood thoughtfully a moment watching the lad kneading the dough furiously. He was surely an odd sort of young man, keeping mostly to himself and always wearing that grotesque stocking cap. He couldn't find fault though. The lad was worth his weight in ambition and he'd never heard him complain about anything.

Upon seeing Thaddious, Julie's curiosity got the better of her. "What's the Cap'n's name, Thad?" She had starting using the nickname most of the crew used.

"Challenger. Cap'n Daine Challenger," he answered.

It had a menacing ring to it, but then he was a challenging man. She remembered his black piercing eyes and shuddered. Resolving to keep out of his way, she returned to her assault on the dough, punching it with her balled up fists. The innocent receiver of her discord.

•

Late that afternoon Jeremy came and got her to watch a school of porpoises frolicking alongside the boat. They dove, then burst up out of the water, twisting and diving again, only to corkscrew back to cut the water in graceful precision, works of art as they performed for their audience on the ship.

Fascinating creatures, Julie thought, beginning to relax and feeling the salt spray on her face. She leaned against the rail and enjoyed the bright sunny day. She felt almost happy now with this new peace and it's promise of a new and exciting life in store for her somewhere. That's if she could keep up this ruse.

Hearing the sound of metal upon metal, she turned and looked back down the deck and saw two men fencing. One moved awkwardly while the other more lithe form moved more gracefully and seemed more adept. She recognized the big Swede, Mallory, and the captain. Most of the crew had gathered and were enjoying the jousting.

Julie was not a stranger to the sport. She had watched her father many times in Ireland and he had shown her the basics though she had only been a child. She watched the quick thrusts and parrying, acknowledging their training yet individual expertise. Slowly they worked their way closer to her and Jeremy. The late afternoon sun was warm and soon the sweat was rolling down their faces.

Mallory seemed to be tiring first, stumbling several times and Julie saw a trickle of sweat run down the captain's chin and down onto his chest. Then with a quick movement of his left hand Daine freed his damp shirt and tossed it aside. The muscles rippled across his shoulders and she stared transfixed.

Her gaze traveled again to his beard. He was no doubt a handsome man under all that hair on his face. Dropping to the dark hair on his chest, it seemed to leap out at her. She quickly turned away but not before Jeremy saw the pink flush that traveled up her neck and lit her face scarlet.

"Somethin' wrong, Jack? They ain't gonna hurt each other, they're only sparrin'. We all practice." Seeing her lip tremble, he went on. "We gotta keep up our skills. If yer gonna keep to the sea, you'd best learn too." Could this boy be a sissy?

"It's just … They're going at it like it's life or death." Even as she spoke, the captain suddenly backed Mallory up against the stairwell, catching the fabric with the tip of his blade and pinning his shirt to the rail.

With a devilish grin, Daine yanked out his sword with a swift flick of his wrist, shoved it into the scabbard at his waist and offered his hand. With a big round of applause, the men all cheered. Then, with the swiftness of an eye's blink, Julie saw a flash of hatred in Mallory's face just before he offered his hand to his captain in a seeming gesture of fair play.

Daine turned and gazed down at Julie, seeing her still flushed face. "Looks like we have a pansy on board," he quipped, talking to Jeremy. Then he looked back down at Julie. "You'd best take up the sport if you're to be at my back in battle."

Her mouth flew open with an unuttered retort, then she just as quickly clamped her mouth shut. Did he think her a coward? She hated him with all her soul at that moment. She reached up and yanked her cap even farther down over her ears and haughtily stalked away.

"Jack," Daine said in an authoritative voice, "I'll be needing a bath. See that it's ready in twenty minutes."

She had turned when he spoke and now watched as he walked off, leaving her staring at his bronzed back. *Ooh! The nerve of the man! Who did he think he was?*

But she knew who he was and had just been reminded of her place.

In twenty minutes she rapped on his cabin door. When there was no answer at three knocks, she stepped inside with two large buckets carried on a yoke across her shoulders. She saw the brass tub already set out for her as she set the buckets down. Quickly she set out clean towels and some scented soap along with cologne from his dresser.

How she longed for a real bath and to once again don a dress! Let her hair blow free in the wind, instead of crammed into this grimy cap and wearing these sloppy fitting clothes. The breast binder was very uncomfortable and chaffed her tender skin.

Stopping to look in the mirror, what she saw shocked her. She truly did look like a boy! Her face was reddened and rough from the salt water and her hands felt like sandpaper. Her hair was limp and dry and she feared that now she had a permanent cowlick.

She started when Daine walked in the room and he grinned sarcastically when he caught her looking in the mirror.

"Wouldn't hurt you to wash your dirty self either," he snapped rudely.

She turned her back huffily, but not before he saw her scowl. She had caught herself in time before she'd let loose with any unladylike words she'd grown accustomed to hearing aboard ship. She dumped both buckets, and then without another glance left to get another two.

He was still standing in the center of the room with his hands on his hips when she returned panting and set them down hard on the floor. She dumped them both.

Another trip ought to do it, she thought as she measured the water with her eyes and was aghast when she returned and backed into the room to find him already deposited in the tub. He eyed her with an amused grin on his face as she set the heavy buckets down. He was waist deep in suds but looked harmless enough.

"Come on, boy. Don't just stand there gawking."

She started forward.

"Just one, save the last for rinse."

She set one down, and then dumped the other in his lap with her eyes closed tightly. He sucked in his breath and stood up quickly, bellowing at her.

"Dammit! Since these buckets were on the stove longer than the first two, wouldn't they be hotter?" It was apparent he had been nearly scalded.

She had a terrible time trying to keep her eyes on his face, thankfully soapsuds covered a strategic area. She struggled to find her suddenly evasive mannish voice.

"I'm sorry. T'won't happen again," she stammered. She made to leave when he again stopped her.

"Wait a minute! You're always in a hurry! I'm sorry I yelled at you, but what in the hell's the matter with you? You're either throwing flour in my face, walking all over my feet, hiding someplace when I send for you, now burning me. You shake to death when I'm near and you must be afraid of your own shadow." He motioned for her to sit. "As far as I know, I've never horsewhipped a child or been caught thrashing any old women." He was studying her very intently. "I can see right now, I'm going to have my hands full, making a man out of you."

If he only knew! What would he think if he knew that he was staring at the girl he'd almost raped in Crete? Just the thought of her secret caused the lightest of smiles to pass over her lips. She could almost picture his face.

His sooty eyes were fixed on her lips. Had he seen?

She quickly sobered when he asked, "Just how old are you?"

"Ah … seven—eighteen." In another month anyway.

"Well, which is it?" His narrowed gaze doubted even the first number.

"Eighteen," she stated flatly, her chin rising defiantly.

Her eyes suddenly became fascinated with the towel he had thrown over the edge of the tub. His presence was so overwhelming that she suddenly felt suffocated. Dropping her eyes to stare at her toes, her breathing grew ragged.

"Jack?" she heard through the buzzing in her ears. Her head jerked up and her hands automatically caught the dripping sponge when it landed against her chest. "Get my back, will you?"

The rest of the blood drained from her face.

"Hellfire! I can't reach back there," his voice snapped at her. "What's the matter with you?" His dark eyes swept over her as she stumbled forward and knelt at his back. Dipping the sponge in the water, she swiped at his back in light, timid strokes and then they steadily became angry, rebellious ones.

His muscles rippled across his shoulders as he flexed his arms and she was reminded again of his rugged strength and undaunted masculinity. She already knew how he could overpower her if he chose. She quickly lessened her pressure, lest he become angered.

Set this coiled predatory animal in motion and there would be no stopping him once he became aware of her secret.

The hackles rose behind her neck, hating him for intimidating her this way with his mocking arrogance. She was feeling a giant urge to throw the sponge in his face. This deep enmity froze her into stillness.

Then, before she had time to react, he rose and stood dripping before her, waiting to be rinsed with the final bucket.

Her mouth dropped open, then she was gone like a flash. Out the door without a word.

Chapter Three

Daine stared at the door a moment after Jack's hasty departure, and then reached for the bucket of water and poured it over his own head. He dried himself briskly with a fluffy towel while he puzzled over his cabin boy's strange behavior.

There was something about the boy that reminded him of his younger brother, Darold. When their father died suddenly some ten years previous, Daine had found himself at the head of a household that had been run exclusively by his father's iron hand. He had stepped in to make all the decisions in raising crops for shipping abroad. He ran the household while overseeing their large plantation, the family's sawmill, all the while taking care of his ailing mother, younger sister Dayna and brother Darold until they gradually assumed their own duties.

Home was in New Orleans. There they raised cotton, pecans, sugar cane and lumber cut and processed in their own mills. The Challenger family shipped many products abroad and brought back spices, olives, coffee beans and French silks to sell in their homeland.

He had every reason to be proud of what he had done with the family business. Becoming the head of the family after his father's death had made him grow up in a way he had not thought possible. He had only been twenty-two when it all fell in his lap. Somewhat of a hell raiser in his younger days, his world up to then had alternated between fast horses and faster women.

Darold was eight years his junior, along with his twin, Dayna. Their mother had retreated into her room upon her husband's untimely death and left all the problems of her world to her children. Inactivity and her refusal to face reality had eventually taken its toll, eventually leaving their mother a frail reflection of her former self. Her children all doted on her.

Now the plantation was prospering even more with Darold overseeing the lumber business. With Daine's broadening knowledge of shipping, which he owed to Old Walters, Dayna had eventually stepped in and taken over the running of the plantation house. She handled the books and accounts, as well as their mother's care.

Walters had worked for their father and was now a loyal employee to his children. It was all a well-oiled wheel and everything seemed to be running smoothly.

Daine's thoughts quickly returned to this strange boy. The lad may just have to be shown the hard way that life's no easy ride. He had to grow himself some balls.

When he stepped into the galley a few minutes later, he was greeted with an icy stare from Jack. He flounced saucily over to the big iron stove, picked up a mug and filled it with steaming coffee. Turning, he scooted it across the table in front of him.

Silently, he took a sip but his eyes never left her face. He spoke first.

"Not that I can find fault with your culinary skills, Jack, but if you are to stay a member of my crew, a few lessons in self-preservation and useful defense could have far-reaching value to you and some other stricken member of my crew should the need arise. You do get my meaning, don't you?" At his puzzled look, he continued. "What I mean to say is, we've been attacked before by pirates. They mean to steal our cargo and whatever else they can get their thieving hands on." His eyes squinted angrily. "You must be able to protect yourself and lend defense to the ship. I'm not saying we will be attacked, but it's a moderately safe bet we could."

Clearing his throat Jack finally muttered, "I've picked up some things here and there." Then lifting his chin proudly, he went on, "My father was a very brave and fearless man, having at one time served under Her Majesty's colors. He never ran from a fight, nor will I." His eyes sparkled in barely contained anger at this undeserved insinuation as to his lack of fortitude. The full potency of his resentment crackled the air around them.

"Do go on." Daine grinned, suddenly enjoying the young man's obvious building tirade.

Dangerously, he blurted, "Now, aside from scrubbing your already spotless decks, toting your bath water and filling the bellies of your horny crew, what is it about me that really irks you so?" He was treading on cracking ice, but with his nerves finally unstrung he rasped hotly, "If it's my size that troubles you, then let me assure you that a swift kick to the groin from someone closer to the floor has surer aim than a swing from where he is expecting it!"

Daine's black eyebrows drew together in an amused frown and he stared down at the feisty boy with the spicy voice before he smiled wide at the sudden rash of temper. His English had been flawless with no hint of the cockney accent he had detected earlier. He let it pass.

"Sounds like you've kicked your share. It's comforting to know you can be riled to a challenge." He took another sip. "Good, I don't need any weak knees aboard."

Of course Julie had kneed someone before, but he didn't know about Henri.

•

They continued to stare at each other in stony silence before Daine let his eyes drop slowly down the length of her, barely suppressing a smile when he reached her feet. Embarrassment formed a thin white line around her lips while she gritted her teeth at his rude appraisal of her ill-fitting clothes. Her pants bagged loosely around her ankles and her scuffed and scarred boots with the too long size curling up at the toes, looked clumsy and sadly woebegone.

"If yer done wit' yer coffee, Cap'n, I need ta wash yer cup," she said acidly as she reached for it.

His lips curled in an infuriating smile as he left her angrily chipping soap slivers into the big dishpan, filled high with dirty dishes.

He was disgusting! Her slicing stopped as she leaned against the sideboard where plates were stacked upside down to dry. She suddenly laughed out loud as if demented. So, he thought she was planning to stay on with his crew. Ha! She'd show him when they got to America! She could almost picture his face when she stepped off his ship and told him just who she was, and right under his egotistical nose all the time!

Tidying up the galley for the night, she quickly sponged herself as clean as could be done with all her clothes intact, then slipped down the narrow passageway to the bunks. She would have liked a quiet stroll on deck but dismissed it for fear of running into the captain. Some of the men were playing cards and she decided to stay and watch a bit before turning in. Since she rose so much earlier than the others, in no time at all she had fallen asleep.

Walters watched her for a little while, her head bobbing up and down, then limped over to pick her up easily. She weighed naught he mused as he lifted her into the bunk. She smiled dreamily, mumbled something unintelligible softly and then rolled over onto her stomach.

He stood silent a long moment, looking at the back of her head.

After breakfast the next morning, Julie went down into the hold for a check of the spices. She gathered cinnamon, oregano leaves, sage and nutmeg, grinding them for future use. She took some sage leaves for tea and ground some coffee beans while she was at it.

She was still helping with the cooking, but just this morning Walters told her another crew-member was to take over the decks and floor scrubbing. She wondered if it was the captain's idea following her outburst yesterday, or if it came from Walters.

She was still busy enough with the numerous minute details men seemed to overlook. They tended to let their bedding go and always cringed when she asked for their dirty clothes. She'd had to search among the bunks for their wadded up soiled clothes, and hold them up to the light just to see if they could get one more day out of them. If it resembled wearing apparel, she'd wash it and wait for someone to claim it. She quickly became their 'mother-hen'.

"Land, ho!" she heard as she stepped out into the bright sunlight from below deck. Off in the distance she could see the jagged outline of an island.

"Where are we?" she asked Jeremy excitedly.

"This is the last place to get firewood and perishables. It's the island of Madeira. We'll spend about two days here."

Her arms full of tins, she flew into the galley. She crammed them into a cupboard and raced back outside in time for them to drop the anchor. With a big splash, it lowered into the watery depths below, the crank slowing, then it caught. Already men were loading axes and wedges into the longboats while Thaddious and Jeremy brought baskets of food and water for lunch on the island. Soon they were lowered with ropes to the workers below.

Walters was suddenly beside her.

"Come on, lad. Yer wantin' to feel solid ground beneath yer feet and not rockin' slipp'rey wood, eh?"

Doing her best to hide her excitement, she asked excitedly. "I get to go?"

Grinning happily, she scrambled down the rope ladder and plopped down awkwardly in the skiff. When they beached in the sand some fifteen minutes later, she yanked off her boots. Ragged or not, they were all she had and she didn't want to get them wet.

Sliding over the side of the boat, she dropped into the water and felt sandy ground for the first time in six weeks. The sand on shore was warm on the soles of her feet and it felt so wonderful it made her a little giddy. She quickly brushed the sand from her wet feet and crammed them back into her boots, and then hurried off down the path.

•

In the boat beaching behind her, Daine watched as Jack gaily ran up the shoreline. He stopped and lifted his face to the sun, breathed deep and then took off again. He felt a sudden strange compassion for the lonely lad and resolved to try and be more patient with him in the future.

•

While the men chopped wood, Julie stacked it in neat little piles. The sweat rolled as they all toiled with the sun beating mercilessly down on them. Soon many of the shirts were yanked off and tied in knots around their waists.

Pausing to wipe her sleeve across her forehead, Julie had her arms full and failed to see a stick someone had dropped. It rolled beneath her feet and sent her sprawling, and she lost her load in the process. She was roughly yanked back up to her feet and groaned audibly when she looked up into the amused eyes of the captain.

The top of her head barely came to his shoulders and she found herself loath to meet his eyes. Without a word, he swung her around and brushed the sand from her bottom before walking away.

She hated him and his smug know-it-all ways with all her heart at that moment. When he turned once to look at her, she was quick to look the other way.

After eating a lunch of hard tack biscuits, boiled goat meat and dried raisins chased with tepid water, everyone took a break from the sun to rest up. Julie found a big tree and lay back in its shade. She closed her eyes and promptly fell asleep.

Two low flying gulls flapping their wings only inches from her head, startled her awake. Rising to a sitting position, she was soon aware of the sound of splashing and hollering.

Horrified, she watched a man close to her unbuckle his belt, allowing his pants to fall to the sand. He wore nothing underneath, and with a long running jump, dove naked into the water. Piles of clothes and discarded boots lay strewn across the beach. Everyone was in the water except for her.

Loud laughter and playful roughhousing eased the tensions of a long confinement aboard the ship, combined with their leaving families behind when they sailed. This was exercise they all relished, albeit infrequent.

Seeing her awake, they began waving at her to join them.

She had an overwhelming wish for the earth to open up and quickly swallow her.

The sun was stifling and her back and neck was wet with sweat. Even Daine had joined them. She could see his arms skim through the water effortlessly, his hard muscles bunching across his back. She felt a keen admiration for the rapport he had with his crew and grudgingly admitted he worked just as hard, if not more so, than his crew.

Red-faced, she kept her eyes trained on the horizon as he swam closer to the bank. When he motioned her in, she turned her head while avoiding looking at him, and pleaded she was a little nauseated from the heat. Also, blaming her fall, she didn't feel up to a swim. He gave her that familiar knowing smile and turned away to rejoin his men.

As if to prove her weariness, she lay back down, flinging her arm across her eyes. She would lie thus until they were all dressed again. Five minutes passed, ten minutes, then fifteen.

"Guess I was right in thinking you and a bath being strangers after all. Or could it be it's just you and a bar of soap not on speaking terms?"

Recognizing the captain's voice, she staggered to her feet in a snit while the color drained from her face. Thankfully, he was now partially dressed, although his chest was still bare as she confronted him. Her hands were on her hips and her hot Irish temper again burst forth.

"Yeah, that's it! Why take a bath wit you old toads? You've no modesty, none a' ya! I prefer ta take me bath by me'self, and not in the same water wi't scurvy an' pox. Yer all braggarts and … and … foulmouthed! None a'ya 'ppreciates a body's privacy!"

His eyes were so blue-black she could hardly see the pupils. And when he broke out into a rolling laugh, they took on a glint of barely concealed devilish mischief. His white teeth sparkled in his tanned face and the urge to kill him was quickly fanned.

"They are, no doubt, all of that," he laughed. "They hit shore and everyone's baying at the moon, rearing to take on a hot and willing woman, a cold bottle of rum, and some generally spoilin' for a fight." Sobering, he added, albeit somewhat rebuking, "But scurvy and pox … never! We may be uncouth louts and half of them unkempt, but they would never forgive you for accusing them of being taken in by a marked woman."

Stepping closer, he looked closely down at her face, reading the strange combination of rage and uncertainty. "A woman with pox is not hard to spot by observing the company she keeps. It wouldn't hurt for you to keep your own ears and eyes open, you could learn a lot from them." A strange look crossed his face as if remembering something he might have forgotten.

With a loud snort, she whirled and fled. When she saw the men returning to their wood gathering, she was careful to keep her eyes averted from him the rest of the afternoon. She took an early boat back to the ship to help with dinner.

After dinner was over, and the dishes done and put away by her new helper, Julie stayed in the galley to clean and peel vegetables, soaking them in salt water for a stew the next day. She wrenched open a big wooden barrel and removed a piece of salted burlap, peeling it off a hunk of aging mutton.

Taking a sharp knife from the big tin containing the cutlery, she sat down on a stool to cut off mold forming on the ends. When that was done, she covered it with a clean cloth and then decided to join the men in the commons.

She was relaxed and watching the men play cards when Mallory and Bracken began taking jabs at her for her refusal to join them in their swim that day. She ignored them until they began getting drunk, and then seeing their barbs were getting out of hand, she rose to her feet and started to leave.

Bracken reached out suddenly and shoved her roughly to the floor. She hit hard on her shoulder, but rolled quickly to her feet and stood crouched as he slowly advanced on her. She wasn't too scared of him until he reached for a scabbard on the wall and withdrew a sword. When someone slipped one into her hand, she suddenly realized they were testing her.

Walters was nowhere to be seen and Jeremy only smiled weakly at her as he moved around the table to stand by the door.

Bracken came closer and she saw him raise his arm. She sidestepped neatly and twisted back around to face him. Keeping her eyes glued to his face, she could see out of the corner of her eye, the men backing away to give them room.

"So yer too good for the likes of us riff-raff? Too high and mighty to swim or 'ssociate with us heathens, always hidin' yerself off in a corner."

He glowered at her all the while moving closer. "Too good to take a drink with us, or talk about yer wimmen. Ain't ya ever had any tail, boy?" He was slobbering all over himself and all at once she thought of Henri. Was she never to get away from his kind?

"Nay, mate," she heard near her, "leave the lad be, he's just a young'un." The voice was Thad.

Then, like a flash, he struck at her and she dodged, turning full circle only to have him pass his blade under the soft flesh at her elbow.

Her mind seemed to snap, and she thrust at him with one quick swipe and then another. He stumbled and caught himself and then came at her like a mad dog. She had drawn blood across the back of his hand and he paused long enough to stare down at it, and then he aimed his sword at her chest.

"I'll fix that foppish face of yer's!" he croaked.

She dodged and he caught her cap with the tip of his blade and yanked it off her head. There were a few gasps as her bright red hair was exposed for the first time. It was short and curled tightly around her face. A bright trickle of blood rolled down her cheek from the cut along her temple. Out of the corner of her eye she saw his sword rise again.

With a sudden pivot, she stepped aside and ran her sword clean through his arm. He shrieked in pain, then was pushed roughly against the wall by a powerful arm and held there, the arm cutting off his wind as it threatened to choke the life out of him.

Julie teetered back and forth on her feet when she saw Bracken released and sliding like a limp rag to the floor.

Daine turned and stared down at the carrot-topped creature standing small and shaking before him and opened his arms to catch her as she fell into them. His shirtfront was smeared with blood and he bellowed loudly.

"You men! You allowed this to happen? You know this boy's just a greenhorn! If he's hurt, I'll have all your asses!"

He scooped her up and deposited her on the table.

Brushing back the curly red hair, he let out his breath when he saw it was only a superficial wound. Soon he had more help than he needed as the crew came alive and were falling all over themselves trying to help. Thank God, Jeremy had come running for him!

Daine was handed a damp cloth and he draped it over her forehead. Her eyelids fluttered open, then she sat up quickly. They had all been so busy with her, no one had seemed to notice the slight bulge in her chest while she had lain prone on the table.

She didn't remember taking off her boots, but she was barefoot.

Daine threw her a dark look and continued to dress the wound on the side of her head, brushing her hand away when she tried to scoot away from him. Rolling up her sleeve, he took her slender arm and dabbed at the wound above her elbow.

His beard was ticklish and she shifted uncomfortably, causing him to stop once and look down at her with questioning eyes. She quickly ducked her chin and he resumed his ministrations.

Satisfied at last, he stepped back.

Julie slid off the table and stood quietly before him.

"You could have been hurt badly, you know. Thankfully he was in his cups, or who knows what I would have found if Jeremy hadn't come for me," he murmured gently.

Julie started to turn away, but then swung back to look him full

in the face. Her chin lifted defiantly and her green eyes glittered.
"T'would take more than a drunken sot to lay me low."

That out of the way, she smiled sweetly and showed him a trim
heel as she pivoted and walked away.

He stared at her retreating back a minute and a dim recollection
streaked across his mind. Of what?

It had something to do with the eyes.

•

The next day went by without incident. More wood was
gathered and most of the crew had apologized to her, saying simply
they didn't know she would get hurt and thought she had needed
the practice and didn't know it would get out of hand. Bracken had
been reprimanded, though she didn't know in what kind of way.

The next morning they were already at full sail by the time she
woke. As she scanned the water on her way to the galley, she could
see choppy seas and big breakers along the faint horizon. Keeping
busy, she still kept returning to the deck to watch the darkening
sky. She knew this was a sturdy ship and Walters had already told
her the wood was a combination of Virginia cedar and Carolina
mahogany and she could tell the craftsmanship was first class.

Everything that was moveable was tied or nailed down, checked
and double-checked. Moving up alongside her, Walters suddenly
ordered her below. He had been hovering around her the past
couple of days and was beginning to grate sorely on her nerves.
With a last worried look around, she obeyed him and grudgingly
went below.

She lay in her bunk for a while and then unable to keep from
knowing what was going on, crept up the stairway and looked
out over the port cathead. All she could see was large foaming
whitecaps, which looked bigger and still ominous, doing little to
quell her rising anxiety. The wind howled outside and she could
hear the topsails whipping and snapping overhead.

After what seemed like hours, Walters appeared and told her
the worst seemed to be over. It wasn't as bad as he'd anticipated.

Not long after he left, she fell into an exhausted sleep. Her
dreams were filled with men with no faces and ships that flew
instead of skimming across the water.

She slept well into the afternoon and woke to a much calmer
sea. Climbing down from her bunk, she sat down on the rough

planking of the floor and pulled on her awkward fitting boots. She started to pull on her cap and then decided against it. Fluffing the short curls with her fingers, she peered into the small cracked mirror she kept under her pillow. With her rough complexion and close-cropped hair, she still looked like a boy and felt like one.

She walked into the galley and saw that Thaddious had dinner nearly prepared. She helped dish up steaming bowls of rice, plates of thick sliced goat meat and some tasty sprouts he had gathered on the island, setting them down on the long table. The men filed in, filled with raucous good humor and glad the storm had dissipated.

Bracken brushed by her, careful not to look at her or sit too near.

There seemed to be no end to the jokes and comments about her red hair. She took it all good-naturedly enough, even when Jeremy, sitting next to her, whispered, "I should have been prepared for the hair, seein' as how you take after your sister and all." He raised a knowing eyebrow. "She looked to be a mite younger than you and certainly easier on the eyes."

She surprised herself by not being offended. "Yeah, 'bout a year or so, but she's a bossy one. She's never had a boyfriend though. We were like twins, we were so close."

"When we get back to Crete, I'm going to look her up. She might change her mind about a boyfriend. You must miss her."

The pain that crossed over her face was not for an imaginary sister but for the mother she hadn't thought of in several weeks. He mistook it for his bringing up painful memories, which was true.

"Never can tell," she said low. "It seems like it's been a long time ago."

She finished her meal in a hurry and then went out on deck, leaning over the rail and watching the bow cut the water below. The salt spray was misty on her face as she lifted her face to the horizon. She was now even farther away from home. Closing her eyes and breathing deeply, she didn't hear the footsteps until they stopped beside her.

"It's like a faithless woman. She'll have you under her thumb until she's ready to cast you aside."

Startled, she looked up into steely dark eyes. "You mean the sea?"

"Yes, the sea. Men will leave their homes and families to chase her their entire lives and never really tame her."

How could he have read her mood? He seemed in an unusually subdued mood too. She suddenly asked, "Where do we stop next?"

"In about two weeks, we'll stop at the Azores Islands. We'll take on more supplies and deliver the Greek olives, cheeses, raisins and herbs we purchased in Greece."

She had seen the huge olive barrels in the hold with their thick wax seals.

"It sounds like a very exotic and romantic place," she said without thinking. At her blush, his white teeth flashed in the moonlight.

"Don't tell me there's hope for you after all," he laughed as he turned and slapped her on the back. "I'll take you ashore and find us some girls. They are never hard to find."

Damn him! Why did he always rub her the wrong way? Yes, without a doubt he could find all the women he wanted! She bit her lip as she once more pictured that scene back home at the inn. And she had almost liked him!

Suddenly he took on a different form in her eyes. She could almost see the horns growing out of the top of his head. With a cool smile, she wordlessly took her leave, leaving him to look puzzled after her. She returned to the galley to clean up.

A little later she gathered the bedding left to flap in the breeze near the fife rail and let herself into the captain's cabin. She made up his bed and tidied up the room. Folding his clean white shirts neatly, she placed them in the mahogany chest and pressed it shut. Her green eyes stared back at her in the mirror and she was lost in reverie when the door opened and the captain walked in.

He strode easily across the room and stopped behind her where their eyes met in the mirror. Then he reached up with his tanned hand and ran it along her cheekbone without taking his eyes away from hers. Feeling nothing but smooth skin where beard stubble should have been, his brow crinkled in wonder.

Julie's heart pounded furiously. She was shocked at his familiarity and couldn't have explained the quickening of her pulse. His fingertips felt like fire and her knees went weak. She closed her eyes to gain control, then Daine suddenly stepped back.

"The men in your family must take late to a razor."

He had felt strangely moved by something he couldn't quite put his finger on, and then he gruffly told her to fix his bathwater.

She nearly tripped over his boots in her haste to leave.

When she returned with the first two buckets, a scant half-hour later, she stopped outside his door and gazed up at the darkening sky. Could there be another storm brewing? Steeling herself, she backed in the room to see he had already set the brass tub in the middle of the floor.

When she poured the two buckets in the tub, it all sloshed to one side, nearly spilling over onto the polished planks. Daine was removing his shirt and didn't look her way. With a shrug, she left to get the other two.

With this next trip, she'd had to dance her way down the companionway to keep her balance. Daine was looking out his parted curtain as she moved across the floor when the door suddenly burst open and Jeremy rushed in.

"Walters said you'd best come! We've got another squall coming quick and he said it looks like it might be a dandy!"

Daine grabbed for his shirt, stuffed it into his trousers, and started out the door. He looked back over his shoulder. "Might as well dump the water. It looks like I won't be back for awhile." Then he was gone.

She picked up a bucket, started to dip it into the water and stopped. *What a waste!* Her mind worked. He won't be back for some time, why not take advantage of it? She had dreamed of a real bath for weeks. Besides, who would know?

She tugged off her boots and dropped them with a plunk on the floor. Straightening, she stepped out of her breeches and quickly unbuttoned her shirt. Next, she loosened the hated breast binder and her breasts bounced free. Slipping into the water, she sighed deeply in long awaited pleasure.

Wasting no time, she grabbed for the sponge and lathered herself from her neck to her toes, then worked the suds into her short hair, working quickly. Her nostrils flared as she took in the lavender scent of soap that wafted the air before she sank down under the water to rinse herself all over.

As she rose back up to the surface, she shook her hair and reached for the towel and stood up. Still toweling her head and face, she opened her eyes and looked straight into angry black ones.

His gaze fell to her wet glistening breasts, then back up to her face. "A woman! God, what fools we all must seem to you!"

He'd returned for his pea coat and had opened the door just when she sank down in the water. He'd watched a goddess emerge from his tub, mesmerized when she'd lifted her arms to towel her hair. Rivulets of water had run down her neck and across her naked breasts to drip off the tips of her rosy nipples. He watched the tiny paths run down her creamy golden skin, over her small waist and flat stomach, then past that secret place and on down to end at her tiny bare feet.

He had recognized her immediately. The girl from the inn had duped him. She'd butchered her long red hair, but he had never forgotten that perfectly formed body. The boyish face and frumpy clothes had completely fooled him.

She couldn't think of a thing to say, she just stared at him dumbly as he reached for his coat hung on a peg behind the door. "You will stay here until I know what's to be done with you!" he shouted at her before opening the door, stopping long enough to blow out the two flickering candles on the wall and plunging the room into darkness.

Then he locked the door firmly behind him.

Chapter Four

This storm was much worse than the one before. The Hornet dipped nose-first, then bucked like a wild mustang, rolling and pitching while the wind howled and scattered everything that wasn't nailed down.

Julie had no time to empty the water and most of it had splashed over the sides, sloshing back and forth on the floor and soaking everything.

Her clothes were drenched and she had felt around in the darkness, finally finding a large shirt from one of the drawers and slipping it on. It hung almost to her knees and she'd had to roll up the sleeves several times in order to move freely. She fell several times while trying to sop up the water, and then wound up crawling back to the bunk and lay there shaking.

After a while she heard loud yelling and more crashing from above and fresh fear consumed her. What if the crew was swept overboard? She'd be trapped here in this cabin. And, even worse … what if it sank? *No, don't think of that!*

She made her way over to the door again and banged on it. She yelled as loudly as she could, even though she knew her voice couldn't possibly be heard above the thunderous wind; unless someone happened to be on the other side.

Another giant lurch shook the boat and she was thrown across the room, banging her hip painfully against the desk in the dark. She felt her way back to the bunk, wrapped herself up in a blanket, and decided she'd be safer to stay put.

Time stood still while the wind whistled outside.

◆

Above, the crew was fighting hard for the ship. The wind

whipped the torn and tangled sails, where earlier in a desperate attempt to lower them, Daine had picked up a cutlass and cut the taut ropes. It had helped considerably.

Now there was even more trouble. He made his way back to the foredeck, and leaned back against the bulwark, trying his best to steady himself. Above, he could see where the topsail was tangled around the mast, the canvas cupping too much wind and listing the ship dangerously.

He started for the upper deck.

Walters grabbed his arm, afraid for his safety. "No, let a smaller man do it," he yelled. "You're needed down here."

"The topsail's catching too much wind and three of the stay-sails are tangled!" Pointing upward, he shook his head and jerked himself free. "That mainsail's gonna snap the mast!"

Walters knew it was useless to argue. The captain would never permit any of his crew to risk their lives doing what he could do himself.

"Stand back!" he snarled, "just steady this pole so I can shinny up! I needn't climb far, fifteen feet or so." He'd already begun his climb.

The ship was listing toward the starboard side, and while Walters nervously watched, the captain slowly made headway. Then he heard his loud shout to stand clear.

A large piece of canvas and part of the broken mast crashed to the deck, bringing a twisted and crumpled Challenger with it. His heart in his throat, Walters yelled for help where they soon had him lifted free of the debris.

Daine was still breathing, but unconscious. There was matted blood in his hair but it didn't look like he had suffered any broken bones.

The ship had straightened itself out with the heavy sails down and now they had some control of their direction. It was drifting with the waves, and not fighting against them.

Walters and another man carried Daine back to his quarters. When they found his door locked, they steadied him against the wall and slid open the deadbolt. Walters took the still unconscious form and told his mate to leave.

When Julie saw a dark form moving toward her, she sat up on her knees and shrank into the corner as a limp object was laid on the bed. Walters picked up a flint and lit the candle. As her eyes became accustomed to the faint light, Walters seemed not to be surprised to see her on the bed.

"Is he hurt bad?" she asked anxiously, concern in her voice.

Walters tried to keep the worry out of his.

"Got to git his clothes off, so's I kin tell."

Julie was already working to remove his shirt, and then pulled off his boots and breeches. Demurely she pulled the blanket back up to his waist. She could see fresh blood smeared across his shoulder but they only found one nasty gash on his head. There were no broken bones but found a purple bruise on his shin along with a minor scrape across his thigh.

They dressed the wound on the back of his head, and then Julie had to ask. "You didn't seem surprised when you saw me. You knew?"

Walters smiled kindly back at her. "I've known ever since the night I put you to bed."

His face reddened somewhat. "Your shirt didn't hide all that much when I carried you to your bunk that night. Since you seemed to want to keep it a secret, I went along with you. I figured you had a good reason." He patted her arm. "I have to get back up on deck. Are you going to be all right here? He's had quite a fall and he needs to be watched closely. Can you stay here with him?"

She was under orders to stay there anyway but said nothing, nodding mutely when he left. Earlier she'd discovered a chamberpot in a curtained section of the room for her abolitions and had helped herself to it.

She watched the rise and fall of his chest for a long time after Walters left. He would no doubt sleep the whole night through, or what was left of it. When she was sure there was no more danger of fever, she pulled up a chair beside the bed and draped a blanket around her.

The ship had ceased most of it's wild pitching, but was still showing it's superiority. She was feeling strangely safe with the captain here, even if he was asleep. Her eyelids drooped before she jerked her head back up.

When it bobbed again, the back of her neck began to ache as she looked longingly at the bed. It was chilly, and the cold leather of the chair seemed to draw the dampness of the room. The floor was still wet and the only other chairs were straight-backed ones with hard wooden slats.

Finally, she stood up and looked down at the bunk where Daine lay. She made a sudden decision, and then crawled over him and lay down on the top. With the sheet between them, she felt he wouldn't object. After all, hadn't he locked her up in here with him?

Her eyes flew to the door. It wasn't locked! But then, she reasoned, she had promised Walters to stay and look after him. The bed was now warm with his body heat, and drawing the blankets up to her chin, and with the comforting knowledge of his presence, she was soon fast asleep.

•

She felt warm breath on her face and her eyes shot open. She tried to pull away but found herself caught tightly in the sheet. He was scowling down at her, and she tried again to pull away. Daylight streamed through the transom and she knew she'd slept the night away.

"Ah, the little rabbit's caught in a trap. How is it you fought me on land, then followed me to sea?"

"Followed you? I didn't follow you! I didn't even know this was your ship!" Her eyes snapped fire. "If I had, t'would be the last ship I'd stow away on." She had reverted back to her native brogue.

"Stowaway?" he frowned at her. "You mean you stowed away?" With this new knowledge, he rolled over on his back and laughed uproariously. "And I thought you were a green lad with no guts." Remembering the swim on the island, he roared all the harder. "Now I know why you wouldn't join our swim when we were getting wood."

Struck by her hot blushing face, he raised again to his elbow. Quickly sobering, he asked, "Why did you run away? Why would you want to leave Crete?"

She had nothing more to lose so she haltingly told him of her mother's death and Henri's unfatherly treatment of her. She saw his eyes darken in anger as he finally grasped her stepfather's trickery. He fought new emotions that were both foreign and agonizing to him. Suddenly silent in his own thinking, he struggled to make sense of it all.

Then, remembering her brave fight with Bracken, he shuddered.

She'd not be safe with the likes of Bracken now. His mind a jumble of confused thoughts, he reached up and touched the bandage on his head. "Is it deep?"

"No, but Walters said you need to take it easy. You took quite a fall."

Suddenly he was standing, dragging the sheet with him. He made a hasty grab for it when it started to fall away, drawing it back up around his middle.

Julie ignored him and scampered off the bed, crossed to a chest and removed a clean shirt, trousers and socks.

He admired the trim legs peeking out from under his shirt before he looked guiltily away. She handed them to him with an unreadable expression, and then turned her back to him to make up the bunk while he dressed.

She picked up her discarded clothes from the night before and found they were still wet. Starting to put them on anyway, she hoped he'd let her get back to her own quarters but he'd already crossed to a chest and drew out a pair of cotton breeches and a small long-sleeved pullover cotton shirt.

"They belonged to my last cabin boy. He outgrew them so you can have them." She silently reached for them and was about to thank him, when he crossed to the door. "You will stay here until I return. Then I'll decide what's to be done with you."

With a bang, he shut the door and locked it.

She stared at the door. Just who did he think he was? Locking her up like a child? Furious with him and with herself for talking nicely to him, she flung out her arm in an angry swipe across the table and tin cups and plates with dried food went flying.

She was still cleaning up the mess when Walters brought her a hastily prepared breakfast a short while later. He set down the tray, and when he saw her on her hands and knees and read her mutinous look, he departed in haste.

At first she was too angry to eat but soon the tantalizing aroma brought forth a betraying rumble from her stomach. There was a thick slice of smoked ham, steaming hot coffee in a tin carafe, and a toasted piece of fried corn bread.

She didn't see Daine for most of the day while he directed the cleanup on the ship. All day long she could hear shouting and loud bumps and bangs from above. When he did come in at dusk, she kept her back to him and sulked.

Good, he thought. *If she wants to act like a child, I'll treat her like one!* He ignored her.

When Walters brought in their dinner and set it on the table, she made a bolt for the door. Two steel bands caught her around the waist and swung her around to face him. His face was dark with anger.

"When I give an order on my ship, it better damn well be obeyed!" He hissed. "You are to stay in this room where you will be safe from a crew of men who haven't had a woman in months, and aren't likely to for some time. Do you get my meaning?"

"Safe? Do you mean to tell me that I will be safe here alone with the likes of you?" she spat at him incredulously. "Do you get my meaning?"

She was a sight to behold. Her eyes glittered like green pools and her heart-shaped face was bright red, her pink lips trembling in fury.

"Better to be watchful of one man, instead of fighting off twenty, barring Walters of course. Don't worry, you still look like a boy to me."

She moved away from him. During the altercation, Walters had slipped out but not before casting a sheepish look her way. She was too angry and prideful to eat, so she turned the back of the chair toward him and sulked in silence.

He watched her stiff back while he ate ravenously. He spoke to her once to come eat but she ignored him so he shrugged and continued eating. In a half-hour, Walters showed back up with two buckets of water.

After Walters left with the tray, Julie could hear Daine moving about, then the splashing of water as he bathed. She still kept her profile to him and was shocked at his audacity when he spoke.

"Would you like to wash my back? Seems like you weren't so bashful before."

She gnashed her teeth, refusing to rise to his baiting. Out of the corner of her eye, she could see him stand up and towel his hair and body, then move to his dresser and comb his hair, clad only in a towel draped loosely around his waist. He then walked to the bunk and drew the covers back.

"Since there's only one bed, we'll just have to share it," he said roguishly as he slid beneath the covers, a self-assured smile curling his lips.

She was livid. "Well, you're going to have to wait 'til hell freezes over for that privilege from me, sir!" She leaped up and grabbed a blanket from the bed and flounced back to the chair and dropped down in it. Since the floor was still damp the chair would have to do.

He turned his back and before long, and she could hear his deep breathing and knew he was fast asleep. In truth, he was exhausted and had quickly succumbed to the blessedness of sleep.

She drew her legs up under her, and before long one had fallen asleep with the circulation cut off. Stretching it out painfully, she shifted around uncomfortably, changing position for the dozenth time. The cold leather of the chair brought another round of shivers but she toughed it out. After another sleepless hour, her reservations all evaporated.

Creeping over to the bed, she stared down at the pile of warm blankets and pillows piled there. He was sound asleep and looked harmless enough. With a sigh, she gently climbed over to the backside against the wall, careful not to touch him. She reasoned to herself that she would waken before he did and he'd never know the difference. Carefully, she drew the covers up to her chin and basked in his body warmth awhile, then fell quickly asleep.

When she woke the next morning he was gone. She seethed in anger, and could just picture his look of triumph when he'd seen her there. She jumped out of bed and was just stuffing her shirt in her pants when the door opened and Walters backed in with a tray.

"Mornin' Jack, don't know what ta' call ya' now," he went on. "Ya' gonna tell me the truth now, lass?"

"It's Julie, Julie Sinclair. There is no Jack, and I don't even have a brother. In fact, I've no kin at all, 'cept'n an aunt I've never met."

His kindly eyes surveyed her as he set the dish of hot fried potatoes and onions and crisp bacon in front of her. The enticing smell enveloped her and she grabbed up a fork and began to eat hungrily.

In between bites, she filled him in. "I haven't thanked you properly for protecting me. When I first got on the boat, and when you found out I was a girl."

He grinned as he dragged out a chair and sat down across from her. "That's not necessary. Like I said before, I ran away from home when I was fourteen. My dad was a drunk and beat me regular. I had to either run or die. I chose to run and live. I stowed away on this very ship, only it was the 'old' captain, Damien Challenger who took me in. He gave me a job and watched over me. He was a kind honest man who eventually became my best friend. Daine is cut from the same cloth."

Julie only blinked, wondering what he'd say if he knew what he'd tried to do to her.

Walters went on. "They's French. Damien died years ago, but his mom is still alive and well back home in New Orleans."

She sucked in her breath. New Orleans? That wasn't far from where she was going, St. Louis, Missouri. Her mother had drawn her a map of the Mississippi River where paddle wheels navigated up and down the river. Then she shivered, thinking of being confined in this cabin with this lecherous rake for several months.

Walters looked at her oddly.

She asked him to be sure, "So, that's where we're headed, New Orleans?"

"That's where we'll end up in the fall. We sell abroad then we pick up more cargo on our return trip to sell back home." He rose to leave.

"Can't I leave this cabin?" she questioned imploringly. "I've proved myself with the blade, surely I could defend myself."

"It's not for me to say. And there are those on board who would be looking at you now in a whole new way." He limped to the door, and paused. "At least you don't have to scrub floors and wrestle all that bedding around anymore, washing and drying them." He winked before he closed the door, "I'm sure the Cap'n is only lookin' out for you."

She heard the lock slide before he walked away. Slumping in her chair, her mind raced. *Damn! I'd rather be busy than stare at these wooden walls all day.*

She busied herself straightening the cabin and even found a dog-eared book on American history to read and was just plumping up a pillow on top of the bunk to read it when she heard Daine opening the door. She buried her face in it.

He walked straight to a cupboard and took down an amber filled bottle. He twisted out the cork and poured a glass full, tipped it up and drank it down. Then reaching up, he took down another glass and poured a small amount into it. He walked to her and extended his hand.

"What is it?" she asked, determined to be nice if it killed her.

"Brandy. A little sip might do you good," he murmured, his eyes shuttered.

She brought it to her lips and sipped. It had a strong biting taste, but she arrogantly swallowed the rest in one gulp. She hiccuped and saw he was grinning at her.

He's testing me, she thought.

Smiling back demurely she returned to her book.

"Can't you read?" he asked.

"Yes, I can read quite well, thank you."

"Then why don't you turn the book around so that the words are right side up?"

Julie threw down the book and glared at him. She was about to say something nasty, when he offered, "Would you like to go out on deck for a while?"

Her face lit up then she bounded off the bed.

"Oh yes!" She reacted like a child given a sweet tart for being good and she felt a burst of anger, but she would keep smiling at him until her face froze. She remembered her mother telling her it was easier to catch flies with honey than it was with vinegar, and that old wives tale just might prove true.

If it's the last thing I do, I'll make him sorry for treating me this way.

She quietly followed him up the narrow companionway and into the bright sunlight. She could see they were still repairing the damage from the storm, and looking up could see they were only running on two sails and moving quite slowly in the water.

Canvas was strewn along the deck and men were repairing tears and threading new rope from big spools. Hot tar was warming in the sun in big oak barrels. Brass cannons gleamed while ammunition and soaked boxes of non-perishables dried on pallets.

As she trailed along after the captain, Julie noticed all eyes watching her. Most looked surprised yet she was quickly becoming aware of this new type of danger. She trusted most of them but there were still three or four she'd have to keep up her guard with. Mallory, Bracken, a man called Sal, and a tall wiry, arrogant Italian, named Tonio, one of the rowdiest and lewdest talkers of the bunch.

As they moved by Bracken, Julie saw his look of total surprise when he recognized her. Then the faces of the other men went from complete shock to puzzlement. She realized then that none of them knew, except for Walters and the captain.

They stopped at the forecastle next to where Jeremy stood silent, his face drained of all color.

"You," he managed, his eyes traveling down her length. "I should'a knew you was that girl. We were told you was injured, n' re'cupin' in the captain's quarters."

Suddenly she was grabbed by her elbow as the captain yanked her back the way they'd come, not stopping until they reached his cabin again. She'd had a hard time keeping up with his long strides. When she'd stumbled, he'd just kept on.

At his door, she screamed at him, "You beast, what's the matter with you? Are you crazy? Let me go!" She tried to yank away but he held firm.

He shoved her inside and she could see a tight muscle along his jaw from his clenched teeth.

Suddenly her fear was renewed. He could be capable of anything! She ceased struggling when he closed the door and marched her straight over to the mirror.

"If that's the way you're going to strut around my men, with your tits bouncing every which way, then don't come hollering to me when one of them gets you alone and has their way with you!"

He had her by the nape of her neck, drawing her shirt even more tightly across her chest. Her nipples were outlined plainly against the thin fabric as she strained away from him. Trying to shake loose, she felt his other hand on the small of her back as he caught her to him. Her face was only inches from his.

His look was thunderous and her heart skipped erratically with what he might do. Their eyes were glued together.

He had thought he was in control, but gazing into the green fathomless eyes swimming with unshed tears, he found he had no control at all. Her pink lips trembled, and just for an instant his eyes softened as he bent toward her. She swayed as she read his intent.

When her eyes suddenly closed, he regained his senses and let her go.

She was left to stare stupidly at him, and then turned blindly away. What was the matter with her? She had mentally accepted that he was going to kiss her.

Turning away she walked to the bed and sat down, her chin dropping to her chest. She picked up the book and thumbed unseeing through the pages, feeling his eyes still on her. Then he moved and headed for the door, his boots sounding like gunshots on the wood floor as he left.

That night she thought she'd turn the tables somewhat. After a nearly wordless dinner, she waited until he went out to the bridge and then hurried to bed. She meticulously rolled up a blanket and placed it between them as a barrier, turned her face to the wall and pretended to be asleep. If he chose the chair instead of the bed, then let it be his discomfort.

But when he did come in she was disappointed when he climbed in beside her, saying nothing about the blanket between them. She was also certain he knew she wasn't asleep.

They both tossed and turned, and with the moonlight night shining through the transom, she could make out his faint outline. He was lying on his back with one arm resting across his waist. The other was thrown back above his head on the pillow.

A strange tremor shook her body, then was still. She turned her back to him and willed herself to sleep.

•

She was warm and snuggled closer to the source. Her face was pressed against a furry chest and her legs were entwined with muscular ones. She smiled dreamily and pressed even closer, then was instantly alert, pushing herself quickly away.

Her eyes flew open wide and she saw he was smiling at her. She glowered and rolled away, sitting up on her knees. His bold eyes dropped to her gaping shirt, and red-faced, she jerked it shut. The blanket that had been between them was kicked to the foot of the bed.

"You … you …*pirate*! And you insist I'm safe with you! Ha! My dear old grandmother, would that she lived to be ninety, wouldn't even be safe with the likes of you. A rapist!"

At that word, he grabbed her wrist tightly, snarling at her,

"Rapist, you say? I paid good money for what I thought was a willing woman. A rapist, nay, but a fool, yay!"

Again two sets of eyes dared the other but she was the first to look away. She was tired of all this fighting, tired of being locked up and tired of always having to defend her actions.

He felt her change of mood and was again hypnotized by her limpid eyes. Noting her chaffed skin, he murmured softly, "What's the matter with your face?"

She brought up her other hand to her cheek and then daringly ran a finger down his prickly beard. "If you insist on my sharing your bed, then kindly stay on your own side."

She was actually smiling at him. He let her go and she straightened out her shirt. A bare thigh was showing under her blanket and he felt himself responding to her. Lest she notice his predicament, he slipped out of bed and grabbed for his trousers.

"If you think you can behave yourself on deck, we can try again." He flashed her a smile, as he continued, "I suggest you do to yourself whatever you managed to do before, so you don't tempt the crew beyond their limitations."

She understood, and began to look for the binder.

After wandering around a couple hours doing nothing worthwhile, she thankfully admitted to herself that Daine was right. With no further display of her female charms, the men paid little attention to her and went on about their duties. She decided to head to the galley and hopefully get back to work. She hated being idle.

Thaddious was glad to see her and set her straight to work peeling vegetables. She had her head down cutting up potatoes when she heard, "I don't know quite how to greet you." She looked up into the grinning freckled face of Jeremy.

"Well, it's not Jack," she laughed. "It's Julie—but without the long hair." Running her fingers through the short curls emphasized the latter. "You weren't too hard to fool either," she grinned. "And you had even talked to me before."

He was really studying her now, wondering how he could have missed it. "Guess I was taken in just like the others. You really pulled it off." Her voice had now returned to normal and he recognized the girl he'd met before. "Except the girl I met on the island was much prettier than you."

She burst out laughing, "You big tease. You didn't suspect a thing."

Daine walked in the door and was struck at once by a strange sensation. Julie's hand was resting on Jeremy's arm and she was laughing merrily while Jeremy's eyes never left her face.

They were deeply absorbed in conversation and he was unprepared for the jealous spark that ignited and spread through his body. He fought for control of his wicked temper and had just succeeded when Julie turned, feeling his dark eyes fastened on her.

For some unknown reason, she felt guilty but didn't know why. When he beckoned that she follow him, she gave Jeremy a wan smile and made her exit. Upon reaching the cabin, she was surprised to see the tub in the center of the room, ready and waiting.

"I find it's safer knowing you're to take a bath, than to show up unannounced."

At his insinuation, she blushed hotly. She watched as he crossed the room, pulled out a drawer and removed a bottle and crystal pewter of sweet smelling cream. He removed the cap on the bottle and let her sniff it.

"It's jasmine," he offered. "And the cream is for your face where it's taken the weather, and … other things."

She knew what he meant.

He stood very close, then raised his hand and rubbed a finger lightly along her cheek and down her pointed chin where it stopped in the pulsing hollow of her throat. Her skin burned where he'd touched. Then he whirled and left the room.

She quickly stripped and sank down into the deliciously warm water. Soaping her body she rubbed it until it tingled, then she washed her hair. When she finished, she rinsed herself then stepped out of the tub, vigorously rubbing the pungent cream into her skin.

She fluffed her hair dry and trimmed her nails where they'd split on the night of the storm. Donning a clean shirt, she shrugged in distaste as she pulled on the old baggy breeches. At least they were clean.

Walters rapped on the door to see if she was decent, then set about emptying the water and refilling it again for the captain. When Daine entered a little later, Julie paid scant attention to him.

Walters, who had been in and out, winked once at her and smiled, then shrugged his shoulders. Julie was left confused.

When he winked a third time she looked from him to Daine.

She nearly dropped the brush in her hand, for she found herself staring at a beardless, smooth-cheeked man. He was incredibly handsome and looked much younger than she had imagined.

His teeth flashed white when he caught her staring and found it was now his turn to be flustered. She saw a flush slowly creep up his neck and color his cheeks.

"I see 'tis a week for changes all around," she said.

Chapter Five

Julie left Daine to take his bath to go stroll along the deck. It was almost dusk and she could hear the laughter below as the men played cards, slinging their ale and telling their raucous jokes.

The stars were out and she stopped midway down the deck, tipped her head back and picked out familiar stars and objects in the solar system. The azure water was vast, endless rolling swells as far as the eye could see.

Standing at the rail a while, she wondered about St Louis. What was it like? She'd been too little when she and her family left Ireland, which was several years before her dad died, to even remember sailing to Crete. Admitting now that she loved sailing on the Hornet, she knew she would be sorry to have to leave it.

She never heard a sound as she was grabbed around the waist with a strong arm, then a hand clamped down hard on her mouth, nearly suffocating her. She was yanked roughly across the deck, her boots dragging on the floor. Twisting, she tried to get away and pulled at the hand over her mouth, but it held firm.

Smelling stale tobacco smoke and rank ale, she twisted her head as far away from him as she could and was rewarded with the sickening smell of a sweaty armpit. The rough thumb dropped from over her nose but the hand still clamped against her teeth. Her first clue was the voice.

"Well now, I can hardly believe my luck. All this time you was really a girl," said Bracken. "Just give me a little lovin' and maybe I'll forget you tried to chop off my arm."

His sand-papery hand was still clamped over her mouth, and she kicked back at him wildly and tried to jerk away, but he bent her arm sharply behind her back. She sucked in her breath with the excruciating pain and pulled him down with her when she slumped onto the deck. They rolled over a couple times before coming to a stop up against a huge pile of rope.

He reached up under her shirt and jerked the binder free. Finding a soft breast, he kneaded it roughly and began to writhe in ecstasy. He freed her mouth to kiss her, but she sank her teeth in his bottom lip. Jerking away from her, he slapped her face hard. She felt blood running from her nose and dimly heard his threatening voice.

"Okay, if a rough piece of tail is what you want sweetheart, that's just the way you'll get it!" He was unhooking his pants with one hand as he held her down with the other. "Nobody'll know what happened to you, they'll just think you fell overboard." He yanked her breeches down and placed a hand on her most private place.

She was sobbing and knew for certain death would be her choice if he proved successful in taking her.

"You're beautiful," he rasped. "Much more than I even imagined." His eyes looked glassy as he stroked her. He bent to part her legs with his knee and then suddenly he was flying through the air, a look of total surprise on his face.

Daine's face bent down to assess her and it was contorted with rage. The cords in his neck were drawn tight and his teeth were bared like a stalking tiger. Lightning fast, he grabbed the now prone man by the hair and yanked him back up on his feet.

"You mangy bastard! I'd kill you this very minute, but that would be too good for the likes of you. When I get through with you, I guarantee you'll wish I had." Shoving him to the second mate Lucas who had come up behind him, he snarled, "Put him in irons!"

Bending down, he pulled Julie's breeches back up and yanked her shirt over her exposed breasts, and then he lifted her up easily, cradling her gently against his chest. She brought her arms up to circle his neck, and laid her head on his chest. His chin rested on the top of her head while he prayed silently he had got there in time.

Vividly aware of feeling safe in his arms, she trembled uncontrollably. Then choking back a sob, she hiccuped, "He didn't ... do anything." She would wonder later why it was important he know this.

When he lowered her to the bunk, she clung to him in a death-grip until he sat down on the edge of the blankets. Walters bustled in with an assortment of bandages and ointments. Daine disentangled himself from her clutches and together he and Walters administered to her.

Walters raised an eyebrow in silent question and Daine shook his head. The older man gratefully crossed himself then poured a small draught of laudanum in a tin cup and forced her to swallow it.

"It should help her sleep the night through," he smiled earnestly at Daine before walking to the door. "We can't let Bracken at her again. We'll get rid of him at Ponta Delgada."

Daine nodded his agreement. He stood near the bed a long moment and watched Julie toss fitfully, torn between wanting to deal with Bracken right now or stay close to her.

He chose the latter and climbed into bed with the now sleeping Julie. After gazing a long moment at the rolled up blanket she had put back between them when she'd made the bed, he shoved it to the bottom of the bed with his foot. He took her into his arms and she came willingly.

Slender arms slid around his neck when she pressed full against him. Though she was in a deep sleep, in her subconscious she felt warm and protected. She was as good as drunk. Lifting her face to his, she smiled dreamily and he could see her long lashes still damp from crying.

He stared down at her face, then at her soft innocent lips, and shuddered. With a pent-up groan, he lowered his lips and pressed them softly against hers. He wasn't prepared for the effect it had on him or to the passion that responded back as he held her close to him. Moist lips parted under his and he felt himself falling into a bottomless whirlpool.

His head was spinning, and not from drink as she clung tight to him. Knowing he had to let her go, he knew he couldn't take her like this, not without her consent. He wanted her more than he had ever wanted anyone before, but she had to be willing. It shocked him to know, that suddenly and without any doubts, he loved her.

With a control he never knew he possessed, he rolled her over onto her back, and then did the same. He wasn't a bit sleepy, so he got back up and walked over to the cupboard and poured himself a snifter of cognac. One wasn't enough, so he had two. When at last he felt like he could sleep, he crawled back into the warm sheets, and reaching down, placed the rolled up barricade back safely between them.

When Julie wakened in the morning, she was embarrassed to find she was once again pressed close to the captain. His back was to her and she was molded close against him, one bare ankle resting familiarly atop his.

The barrier was in a heap behind her, where she'd no doubt thrown it.

She tried to ease away from him, but couldn't move since he was lying on the tail of her shirt. It was bunched around her waist, leaving her lower half nude and covered only by the thin sheet. At her gentle tug, he rolled onto his back and looked up into her blushing face while she smoothed the shirt back down over her hips.

His eyes twinkled, and his handsome face once again struck her. Turning scarlet, she ducked her face.

"I like you better with green eyes," he teased. "Purple and green tend to clash."

She raised her hand to feel her still warm cheek. "You always seem to be in the right place at the right time," she murmured.

"And you seem to have a penchant for trouble," he answered dryly.

She only smiled.

He was suddenly at a loss for words.

•

After a leisurely breakfast she sat on the edge of the bed and watched him dress. The muscles rippled along his back as he bent to pull on the black knee-boots, tugging them on over the mauve colored breeches. Rising to his feet, he fastened the cuffs of his shirt, stuffing in lastly the tail of his shirt. His cream-colored shirt was open to the waist and the dark hair on his chest curled over the top of his belt.

There was a tap at the door and Daine bade enter.

"We're ready, sir," said Jeremy. He was speaking to the captain, but his eyes were focused on Julie who was still resting on her knees on the bed. Daine turned to see what he was looking at, taking it in. He felt a small surge of something he couldn't define.

His voice sounded a little gruff. "I'll be there in a minute. You're dismissed."

With an anxious look her way again, Jeremy turned to go.

"What are they ready for?" she asked.

Without a glance her way, Daine took down a strap made of usu, with nine long strands of knotted twine, and a short wooden handle.

She stared fascinated as he flicked it back and forth against his leg, and only when he left did she fathom what it was for.

Cat-o'-nine tails. They could lash a man to pieces!

•

Ten minutes later she rushed up the stairs to the upper deck. Standing a minute, she looked up and down the deck, not knowing quite what to do. She knew what was going to happen. Then hearing distant footsteps she jumped in fright when she heard the first scream, then another and another. Putting her hands over her ears to shut out the sound, she shook her head from side to side.

No matter how much she hated the man, no human being deserved this. All thoughts vanished as to the cause as she started running toward the sounds.

She saw Daine facing a man tied to a mast, and then she ran up and started pummeling his back with her small fists. "Stop! Damn you. Stop ... Stop!"

He twisted around in surprise, but her flailing arms kept striking him. Grabbing her wrists he swung her around roughly to face him. She was babbling and sobbing then looked down at the inert bloodied form of Bracken being unleashed from the mast. He was conscious, but staring at her with hatred in his eyes.

She stopped fighting and leaned weakly against Daine. He took her by her shoulders and pushed her away.

"Julie, go back to the cabin," he gritted, "and stay there!"

Spinning on her heel after throwing him a mutinous look, she obeyed. What manner of man was this? To be so gentle one minute and then calmly thrash a man half to death in the next. If she displeased him, would he be compelled to do the same thing to her?

Reaching the quiet of the cabin, she threw herself down on the bed and cried about everything that had happened to her these past few months and the unknown of soon entering a new land to live with complete strangers.

Daine stayed clear of the cabin for the rest of the afternoon but did send Walters to check on her. He reported back that she had seemed all right but had refused to speak to him and her tray still remained untouched.

"She's making too much of it," Daine snapped.

"It's not all Bracken," Walters tried to smooth over. "It's just all caught up with her. She's blocked him out of her mind, forgetting the weasel even tried to force himself on her."

Daine blanched. Sweeping his hand through his hair, he took a deep breath, and then let it out raggedly. "She's just a child." His face a mask of warring emotions, Walters had to strain to hear his next words. "I guess I never really thought about what she's gone through and why she even felt she'd had to hide her femininity. And some, I'm responsible for."

Walters pondered his meaning, but still left puzzled.

She was sound asleep as he hoped when he entered his quarters close to midnight. A glance at the bed revealed the rolled up blanket again as her feeble attempt at protection. He condescended and climbed in the bed and was asleep in no time at all.

•

"Please no! Henri! Bracken! Oh God, help me!"

It took a few seconds for Daine's eyes to become accustomed to the darkness, and then he could see Julie was sitting up on her knees, her eyes wide with fright. He reached for her, but she pushed back at him and then upon recognizing him, collapsed in his arms. He pitched the blanket to the foot, and then laid back, pulling her down with him. Holding her close, he felt wet tears as she quietly sobbed.

"I'm sorry, Julie."

She stilled and he had to strain to hear her. "For what?"

"My part in this. When I took a room at the inn that night I was approached by the innkeeper. He offered me a 'beautiful bonus', a young woman who enjoyed 'a roll in the hay' and would certainly make my stay quite enjoyable. For a fee, of course."

He felt her stiffen, but she remained silent.

He went on. "I'm not a celibate … and he made it sound you were more than willing."

She grated her teeth it was so ... Henri. If he couldn't have her then he'd teach her a lesson. However, she was still confused. "Why would you take a room on land when you have—" She swept her arm in an arc. "—all this?"

"I was to meet a buyer there but we somehow missed each other. I don't know if he ever showed, but by then I was too sick to care." He grinned down at her. "It may interest you to know that the last time I saw that innkeeper, he was missing quite a few of his teeth."

Julie clapped her hand over her mouth and laughed with glee. "That would be Henri, the stepfather from hell."

They both laid there, each lost in their own thoughts. He was thinking he'd love to kiss her senseless right then and there. She was wondering now if he ever would.

Shame enveloped her. Of course he'd never kiss her. How could he even desire her? Why would anyone want a boy-girl who dressed in rags and strutted about like a man?

This would never do! she mused. She was beginning to look at him in a whole different light. When had the fear stopped and trust began? He had saved her life twice and once tried to rape her. *No*, she corrected herself. He had thought she was a trollop. *Not his doing.*

"You do understand why Bracken must be kept from you, at least until we reach land, don't you?" he asked suddenly, breaking her reverie.

"Yes," she murmured, bringing her thoughts back from her physical awareness of him and not finding the thought all that unpleasant. She felt herself growing sleepy again and she had no idea what time it was.

He was just content with his nose pressed into her fragrant smelling hair, his arm still encircling her shoulder.

"Go back to sleep," he said huskily, fighting a raging tiger within. He was shocked at the potent rush of protectiveness he felt. He had wronged her once and vowed he wouldn't again, not if he could help it.

The next day they reached the Azores Islands.

She leaned on the rail while they dropped anchor, watching the colorful brown skinned people milling about. Most of them were watching the big black ship. It was the biggest ship docked in the bay and it quickly drew a curious crowd.

Julie had moved down the deck when she saw Daine talking with one of the crew. She was again struck by how handsome he was when he turned and smiled lazily down at her when she stopped near him. He was wearing fawn colored breeches and a cream silk shirt, open at the neck. He wore a hammerlock pistol tucked in his belt, ever diligent.

When the mate took his leave, he turned his attention to her. "We'll be here a couple days in cargo exchange and repair some of the damage we sustained in the storm. I have to tend to my prisoner. If you like, perhaps in an hour or so, I'll show you around the island."

She looked down at her ragged clothes and then curtsied, "I'm ready when you are, m'lord. Pardon me if I don't press my clothes or coiffure my hair first, I'm kinda traveling light."

"I hardly noticed," he laughed, then made a playful slap at her; causing all eyes to look their way.

All the rest of the day they walked around the village. They followed the shoreline and then visited a blacksmith where the captain bought some tools. They ended up at a little pub where they met up with some of their crew, as well as some local whalers and fishermen. She was singing loudly along with them when the crew returned to the ship; sometime after midnight.

Julie quickly undressed in the semi darkness and tumbled into bed. When Daine reached for the coverlet, Julie beat him to it and drew it back, inviting him in. For all his resolutions he bent close and cupped her chin in his palm, drawing his face close on a level with hers.

She misread his smile as mockery and ducked her head in frustration before he drew away in silence, turning their backs to one another. Sleep was a long time coming for them both.

•

Julie slept late the next morning while Daine saw to the restocking of his vessel. She was surprised when he returned in the early afternoon and hurried her off the boat. No idea where he was taking her, she was stunned when he took her into a little shop where he said he had ordered some ready-made clothes for her the day before. There was a three-fold Bamboo-dressing screen in a corner she was told she could try them on in privacy.

Daine sat down on a chair on the other side of it and handed clothing over the top. A blue and yellow print dress, lavender colored skirt and an off-white blouse, then a small strip of fabric with hooks and eyes. It was her first real breast support that wasn't a binder. It felt uncomfortable at first, but it fit her and she deemed to get used to it.

Before Daine was through, she had two pairs of breeches, a button up sweater and three more pullover shirts, all in appropriate feminine sizes.

When she stepped around the partition, she was instantly dismayed at the giggle that escaped from beneath the clerk's fingers as she bent toward her and whispered in her ear.

"But miss, your dress is on backward."

To his everlasting credit; Daine turned and pretended to be engrossed in a length of fabric as a deep chuckle rumbled up from his chest.

Julie looked quickly in his direction and was relieved he hadn't seemed to notice her ignorance, missing completely the smile that tugged at his mouth. She'd never owned a grown up dress as her clothing had barely been fit for a quickly growing girl such as she was. In total dismay, she retreated back behind the screen.

"Sir?" asked the clerk as she moved to the tacit man fingering still more items on the table. "Your wife has such a lovely figure. She's very pretty, you are a lucky man, yes?"

Daine glanced back at Julie, who was just emerging again and this time dressed correctly. He sucked in his breath, hearing the clerk put into words his own thoughts.

"Yes to both. Any man would be lucky to have her." He murmured for her ears only.

Julie stopped, meeting Daine's smoky gaze as the clerk walked off unaware of her presumption. She suddenly yelped as a pin stuck her under an arm.

Daine was at her side instantly, and focusing his eyes only on the target of her distress, placed a finger under the fabric beneath her arm and gently removed the culprit. His eyes were drawn to the soft swell of her breasts, unrestricted now without the binder and he found his breathing seemed labored. Gruffly he told her to return behind the screen to await her final sizing.

At last the clerk returned for the final measurements. At his urging, Julie picked out two new chemises, a pair of soft dainty slippers, and a pair of comfortable black leather walking shoes.

When she protested at what he was spending, he dismissed her and walked over to the clerk. He whispered something in her ear.

The clerk returned with some nightgowns across her arm, and when Julie picked out a flannel one with a high neck, she barely hid her disapproval. When Julie returned to the changing screen, Daine pointed to a silky green one and indicated she include it along with the flannel one.

He seemed rather quiet after they left the shop to return to the boat, while Julie felt strangely giddy. When they reached the cabin, she laid the packages on the bed and wondered aloud, "I hope dinner arrives soon. I'm famished."

It arrived a half-hour later and she ate everything on her plate.

"Hope you didn't underestimate the size of your clothes. You keep eating like that and the two of us won't fit in yonder bunk."

Her stomach lurched; she would never learn to be a lady! Why did he always see her at her worst? Her cheeks turned as red as the roots of her hair and she didn't question why it even mattered. Looking over at him with lowered lashes, he seemingly had dismissed her, and absorbed now with something else.

Jeremy came in shortly for their trays and Daine ordered a bath for Julie. When he brought the buckets of water a short while later, the captain made no move to leave. Julie fumed quietly. Just because he'd bought her clothes; did that give him the right to stay there and humiliate her? He picked up his parchments from the desk and crossed to the table and spread them out to study, paying no attention to her.

Julie stood a moment in a quandary and then turning her back to him, kicked her boots off and undid her breeches and let them fall to the floor. Unfastening her shirt, she laid it aside. Testing the water with her toe, she stepped in quickly and began soaping herself. When it came time to wash her hair she did so quickly. She heard him come up behind her before he spoke.

"I'll rinse you. Tell me when."

She nodded wordlessly and then he poured the bucket over her head. Picking up the second bucket, she kept her back to him as he poured it down her length and then handed her a towel.

Wrapping it around her, she stepped out onto the polished

floor. He turned away to cross to the bunk and returned again with the green gown dangling from his finger. There was an unreadable look on his face.

She froze. "This is not the gown I picked out!" she gasped.

He didn't bat an eye as he turned away and answered, "The clerk must have made a mistake. Let's see if she put in the other one." He made a show of opening the package again. "Ah yes, here it is. Much more suited to you." He picked up the high-necked flannel one.

Chagrined at his insult she took the gown and turned her back to him again, slipping it over her head.

The door opened upon Daine's acknowledgment and Jeremy came in to dip the empty buckets and empty the bath water. She could feel his inquisitive eyes on her but she avoided looking at him, and was still standing when he returned with fresh water for the captain's bath. She was in front of the mirror toweling her hair, which was quickly growing out, and her skin was much softer, all thanks to the creams she'd been using. He left quietly.

Daine was already in his bath when she turned away from the mirror. He certainly wasn't shy about displaying his body, she thought as she climbed into bed. She rolled up the blanket again and turned her face to the wall.

To her chagrin, he began to whistle a lilting version of *Row Row Row Your Boat*. She could hear him splashing around awhile, and then the sound of his stepping out of the tub when Jeremy returned again. She heard him make several trips to empty the water then heard him hang up the tub before he left. When Daine blew out the candles she pretended sleep.

When she wakened the next morning Daine was long gone. The crew was scurrying about making ready to sail when she walked out on deck. She didn't see the captain for a while but soon he appeared on shore and was talking to an unfamiliar man. She could see he was obviously irritated about something. Then he walked up the gangplank to the ship carrying a package under his arm.

•

On shore and out of sight, Bracken watched as his former ship made ready to sail. He could see the captain approach the ship and then when he stopped to talk with Julie. With sudden hatred in his eyes, he turned his face away from the constable standing next to him. He spoke too low to for the man to hear, but the other man that just joined him did.

"I'll get 'em if it's the last thing I do. They'll both pay for this, especially Challenger, leaving me here in this stinking hellhole." He looked at the new arrival. "What will he think when he finds out you jumped ship, Mallory?"

"Who gives a big-assed damn?" he laughed. "Soon as the Hornet leaves port you're free. Bet Challenger didn't take to that too kindly, seein' as how his orders have no jurisdiction here." They both continued to watch as the big black ship pulled its anchor and was towed out a safe distance to hoist its sails.

A sleek Baltimore clipper suddenly caught Bracken's eye, tied to the wharf a hundred yards away. A slow wide grin eased his usual homely features and Mallory turned his head to see what had pleased his friend.

A smartly dressed man of apparent means had just appeared topside and Bracken said, barely above a whisper, "For once it seems our luck is about to change"

•

With the Azores islands a tiny speck in the distance Daine asked Julie to come below. She followed quietly, and upon reaching the cabin, Daine took down the package he'd had under his arm earlier. He opened it and handed her the altered dress, then a mauve colored balloon sleeve shirt and a darker brown pair of doeskin breeches. Next he brought out a pair of gray sealskin ankle boots and told her to try them on.

Somewhat reluctant, she turned her back to him and tried them all on. Everything fit. Turning to him, she asked a burning question. "How did you know ... what sizes?"

He only looked pleased with himself. "I was pretty sure about the clothes. I used my palm to measure your feet while you slept."

She felt embarrassed and angry he'd taken such liberties while she was indisposed. "Please don't buy me anything more. I'll never be able to repay you."

He looked stricken. He'd only wanted to please her and now she was feeling beholden.

"I can't have you traipsing around the ship in dresses, that was meant for the privacy of my cabin and when we go ashore. I'm sure you'll find the breeches less cumbersome and we'll discuss wages later."

Neither brought up the fact that now she seemed to be just a passenger rather then working off her passage. This was a fact that now stuck in her craw as she'd never intended to have free passage. She'd never been afraid of work and inactivity was foreign to her.

When she grew silent his mouth curled in disdain before he headed for the door.

Julie stared after him knowing she'd managed to anger him again. Stooping, she picked up her ragged clothes and threw them in with the cleaning rags. A good place for them!

Unable to resist a look in the mirror, she smiled back at herself. If he thinks she would be too tempting to the crew in a dress, then he'd better take another look she thought defiantly. The shirt molded to her body and her feminine curves would not be denied.

The air was heavy when she went back out on deck. The ship had slowed, only to about eight knots, until they seemed to be barely moving. Feeling rising apprehension, she approached Walters who was scanning the horizon with a big brass telescope on a tripod.

"What is it?" she asked. "Why is it so muggy?"

He didn't take his eye from the scope. "Those dark clouds came up very sudden, I don't like the looks of it. Hope it's just a little storm kickin' up." He cleared his throat, but she could hear the worry. "Could even be a hurricane, they can start quickly like this. The Chinese call it a typhoon, but it's really the same thing." His voice trailed off, "June's a little early though."

Julie scanned the horizon nervously, seeing the dark clouds still building to their left. The sky was no longer azure blue, as it had quickly turned dark and threatening. The crew all waited and watched for another twenty minutes. Then Lucas, the friendly Hungarian, climbed to the crow's nest for a better view. She could tell the rest of the crew was steadily growing uneasy and she still hadn't seen Daine.

Suddenly, she heard a shout from up above. "Swell! It must be sixty feet!"

Everyone scattered.

Julie stood rooted to the spot as though paralyzed. Great drops of water began to fall from out of nowhere and gusting wind rocked the ship. She was suddenly grabbed and slammed to the deck, and then jerked back to her feet and drug along behind the captain. Rain pelted the rocking ship.

"There's no time to get you below! I have to get up to the bridge!" he shouted, and then all was lost in the huge roar of the wind. She hung onto his belt as he dragged her up the stairs behind him. Then he grabbed the helm from Walters, taking over and ordering him below.

His orders seemed lost on his coxswain. "You may know a lot about sailing Cap'n, but you ain't doin' this one alone!" He had already lashed himself to a mast just as Daine grabbed a rope and tied he and Julie to a yardarm, and then grabbed the wheel again just as the monster wave raised up on its haunches to strike.

Daine had managed to turn the buffeted ship fore-and-aft just before it rose high on her stern end in his attempt to ride it out above the deck. He brought the rudder up as far as it would go and hoped the fore-topmast staysail eased the pressure on the helm. Partly deflected, Daine managed to set the head slowly around and into the main wave again.

Julie's face had been pressed hard into the captain's back and she breathlessly kissed his wet shirt. With a swift and positive realization, she knew now she loved him. He would never know for they would both surely die. For how long or even why, she couldn't begin to rationalize it.

She felt the Hornet rise high in the air where it seemed to perch forever in space, then nose down crazily again. All hell seemed to break loose. Her neck snapped and she was again drenched with water.

Huge swooshes of water rolled back away from the ship, and then it shuddered and crashed back into it again. Julie could hear wood snapping and men hollering, then the crash of thunder all around them as the sky was alight with bolts of lightning streaking across the sky.

The ship listed and then righted itself as the wave passed. They had survived the wave but the wind had now turned into a raging fury.

"It must be close to eighty miles a hour!" Walters shouted.

Daine leaned down to the binnacle and rubbed the dome of the compass. "The needle says southeast."

"Cut to the north!" Walters yelled.

The Hornet swung slowly and searched for a path to lead them into calmer waters. Daine fretted about his men but was helpless to go to their aid. He was most needed right where he was. He quietly thanked God he knew where Julie was.

The wind continued to tear at them unmercifully. Great torrents of water washed over the decks and the frigid wind was chilling. Daine could see torn canvas whipping in the wind and broken masts were jutting dangerously in the air and some lying about on the deck.

With a loud crack, a wooden beam broke loose and fell, landing on Walters and pinning him against a yardarm.

Daine jerked his rope free and rushed to help his friend, tugging futilely at the beam. Unable to budge it, he shaded his eyes from the rain to look up at what was holding it. The cracked top of it was still being held firm by a rope. He shouted at Julie to keep the wheel as level as she could, then started up the rope ladder that was swaying in the wind, inching his way up slowly.

Julie watched Daine, shifting often to look at Walter's face, seeing him grimace with pain as she tried her best to steer the floundering ship. When he reached the top, she saw Daine take his knife and begin to cut through the thick braided rope. One twine snapped, and then another. The wind caught a broken piece of sail and snapped it aside, knocking a large roped pulley loose. He dropped the knife and it clattered to the deck. He was tangled tight in it!

Julie had no time for fear. A picture of her father falling to his death flashed in front of her eyes but she closed her mind to it. She loosened her rope and lashed it tight to the wheel while judging her direction. She hoped it would hold until she returned. If she returned!

Darting for the knife she placed the cold steel between her teeth and started up the ladder. Walters was hollering something but she couldn't make it out. She quickly reached Daine's feet and eased up alongside of him.

The look on his face was one of absolute horror. Gingerly taking the knife from her teeth, she slashed at the rope, felt it give and then pulled on the sail where it fell free. With a cocky wink at his astonished face, she placed the knife back in her bared teeth and quickly descended, jumping lightly to the deck only an instant before Daine.

They both hurried to Walters and lifted the broken mast off him. He was only semi-conscious and they could see he had a broken leg.

Daine straightened and hugged Julie to him. "And you called me a pirate? You should have seen yourself with that knife stuck between your teeth. You took ten years off my life when I saw you!"

With a smile on his face he released her and turned to the wheel while noting she had even had the presence of mind to tie it down. He also knew what the climb had cost her, remembering what she had told him of her father's death.

There was much to learn about this red-haired girl that had captured his heart. With a shudder he knew he would remember this day all the rest of his life.

Chapter Six

The damage was devastating. The last storm seemed only a breeze compared to this one.

This time they had a few men injured besides Walters, and a lot of damage scattered throughout the ship. Sails were down and some torn, with broken masts, broken doors and splintered rails and walls, along with numerous supplies that had to be thrown away. Dry goods were spilled in the hold and most had massive water damage.

Walters' leg had to be set, but he kept saying it was his game leg and would hardly be noticed at all. His bravado ended abruptly however, when Sal had to sit on him allowing Lars and Daine free rein in setting his leg. Julie sat at his side and wiped the sweat that ran profusely down his forehead.

"Give him a swig out 'a that jug," Daine told her as he loosened the fist clamped on his arm. It started back and he grabbed it again and then rested his knee down on it as Julie rose and grabbed a blanket to use as a pillow. When she squatted down next to Walters again, she raised his head up and let him drink. He managed a few swallows of the biting rye whiskey and then he dropped his head back down. He turned several shades of green before quickly fading to an ashen gray.

Julie squeezed his shoulder. "Sorry mate, but right now I wish you were roaring drunk."

"Not half as much as I do, lass," he grimaced at her. His eyes swung back to Daine. "Get it done, boy."

Reaching for the thin cut boards that would serve as a splint, Daine laid them on either side of his leg then nodded to Sal. At his signal, they both yanked quickly on his leg in one swift, numbing motion.

They were all grateful when he chose unconsciousness over enduring more torture.

After Walters had been carried back to his bunk for the night, and all other injuries tended to, Julie scrounged what food she could find for supper for the crew. A fire in the galley would not be wise until the smokestack could be checked out. She found some cold goat meat, sea biscuits, and some hard Swiss cheese in the galley and set about making sure everyone had something to eat.

The wind was still blowing at a good clip when Julie and Daine finally went below, leaving Lucas at the wheel. Since lighting a candle could have spelled disaster, they instead stumbled around in the dark. She heard a low curse when Daine stubbed his toe on a chair.

"Hellfire!" he groaned.

"Here ... Give me your hand and I'll guide you to the bunk."

She felt for his hand and it clasped around her wrist pulling him in her direction. He let go, then pulled back the covers allowing her first entry. They were both exhausted and she fell asleep almost immediately. But Daine tossed and turned, fretting about his injured crew and damaged ship.

After another half-hour of thrashing around, he got up and dressed, and then lit a lantern and returned topside.

Jeremy had joined Lucas, also unable to sleep, feeling relief when he saw the dark form of the captain walk up to them. In the faint moonlight, they could see his haggard face before he took a long drag from his cheroot.

They all stood silent for a long while, and then realizing there was nothing he could do tonight that couldn't wait until morning, Daine dashed his cheroot and moved back down the quarterdeck. Letting himself in the cabin, he closed the door quietly being careful not to wake the sleeping girl.

Julie had awakened to find him gone. She was wondering whether or not to get back up, when she saw the faint crack as the door opened and he stepped back in. Her eyes had adjusted to the darkness, and she could see him moving about while he shed his clothes again.

Relieved at his return, she lay back and soon drifted off again. She slept fitfully, and when the boat made a sharp dip, she rolled into him. Her eyes flew open to stare into smoky black ones, and their lips met, parted, and then met again. Sliding her arms around his neck, she pressed closer.

He was instantly aware of her smooth, warm skin. His passion flared instantly and he pushed her away, but she resisted, moving even closer to his length. Shaken to his depths, he reached over and kissed her deeply.

It was the most natural place in the world to be, she thought breathlessly, as a golden ache spread through her like wildfire. She was oblivious to the torment she had thrust unwittingly on him, and then he pulled away again, whispering huskily, "If you don't move over to your side of the bed, then don't hold me responsible for what likely could happen."

She could feel his maleness against her leg and that alone should have given a clue to his meaning, but she made no move to pull away. No longer was she in control of her own body as his invading kisses unleashed unborn desires spilling out of every pore. His hands moved up her spine in a slow caress, blazing a fiery trail throughout her entire being.

"Make love to me," she begged to her astonishment.

His mouth, hot and demanding, closed over hers while drawing her tight against him. She filled his heart as no one had ever done before, nor ever would again. This he knew. He ached with it, but was justifiably wary. Was he dreaming?

"If this be no dream," he said huskily, "then I would advise you one more time to move over and leave things as they were. But, know this well. If instead you turn away, I will abide with your decision, and I swear to God I'll sleep on the floor the rest of the way."

Rising up on one elbow she placed her other palm on his chest. She knew nothing of the way a man made love to a woman, only what her mother had told her of her happy years with her father. At that moment she was ignorant of what that entailed. She only knew how she felt about him now and knew he desired her.

"Yes, I'm sure." And she was.

He reached to kiss her again and was lost. His free hand deftly removed her gown then traveled back down her silky skin as he rolled her onto her back. She flinched for only a second as the back of his hand brushed over a sensitive nipple, then cupped over a breast.

It was a slow, weightless descent into a never-land that pulled deliciously at her. Her reservations, if she had any left, melted away in her complete trust and finally placing herself in his capable hands.

His lips left hers to travel down her neck to the gentle swell of her breasts. His other hand moved lower, over her tight belly and she felt deft fingers caressing, then growing bolder, finding places she alone knew of, and was hers alone to give. And she was gladly giving ... to him.

His breathing grew labored, and then it was she who pulled him back down to kiss her again. Her body had begun moving in a slow sensuous rhythm all its own, seeking an end to this tremendous ache that was now totally consuming her.

She was barely aware of his knee slowly parting her legs as he lowered himself into her. She felt a small thrust, and then a sharp searing pain and it shocked her. Crying out as they joined together at last, she pressed her face into his shoulder, and he stilled, gathering her close. Very tenderly he kissed her, and unbidden she began to slowly move with him.

Increasing, resilient desire enveloped her anew, then soon a piercing sweet ecstasy lifted her up higher and higher. Time stood still and she could scarcely breathe.

With a careening, earth shattering jolt, they reached that highest peak together.

A bewildered cry at this new experience gripped her body, and she opened her eyes in panic, still clutching his shoulders. He gave a reassuring hug before burying his face in her hair and settled her down to enjoy this new sensation as it slowly ebbed away. A feeling of complete contentment and wonder washed over her.

Daine had never felt such fierce possessiveness. It was startlingly unsettling since he hadn't been prepared for such powerful desires this bewitching creature had just invoked. When she had first cried out it had tore at his soul, but blind passion and need had all but smothered that. He burned with this need for her.

He studied her now intently, experiencing a new pang of guilt and finding it totally unexpected. She had been a virgin, but then he had known it since that night in the inn. Now that it was over, would she chastise him, berate him, or even worse, would she cry?

She only smiled kittenish up at him as they rolled to their sides, still facing each other. Brushing his lips softly with hers, and then kissing her again firmly, he finally released her to roll over onto his back.

Her eyes wandered over the rugged virile features of his face. He had enjoyed her; she had no misconceptions about that.

He began to talk. "You know, I don't even know where you were headed when you stole aboard my ship."

For some reason she didn't want to tell him just yet about her aunt in St Louis. Right now all she wanted to do was follow him around the seas and everything else now seemed unimportant. Just to be with him, right here, right now, was all she wanted to think about.

"Just away from Crete. Maybe I'll go back to Ireland. Or maybe," she said impishly, "I'll turn into a pirate." That garnered her a laugh.

"Yeah, and maybe you'd make a fierce looking one at that. The way you carry knives in your teeth and that hidden cutthroat nature."

She giggled, and then quickly sobered. He hadn't said a thing about we. Just where was she going? She forced calmness in her voice. "What's our next stop?"

"The Cape Verde Islands. We need a lot of repairs and supplies before sailing across the Atlantic Ocean. It's about 2500 miles to the Bahamas, and then on through the Gulf of Mexico. We should end up at my home port in New Orleans. And if all goes well, we should make it home in about four months."

He had said "his home" and the "we" was his crew and it wasn't lost on Julie. She felt a small twinge of fear but no regret at what had just happened between them. She closed her eyes to relive again the last few minutes.

He took her silence for being sleepy. He'd been thinking of his family and what they would all think of her. His urge to protect and care for her was suddenly great. For the first time in a long while, he missed home and solid ground. He hoped they were all okay back there.

They each had no idea the other was still awake. After a short time, and lost in their own thoughts, they both drifted off to sleep.

In the early morning Daine awakened, and just for a few seconds he thought he had dreamed the whole thing. But when he rolled over, and he saw dark stains on the sheets, he knew it had not been his imagination at all.

He studied her long lashes and pert lips in deep sleep while marveling at her quiet beauty, and then he quietly got up to dress and check out the rest of the damage. They always carried some lumber in the hold but a good part of the rebuilding would have to wait until they reached the Cape Verde islands.

When Julie woke a scant half-hour later, she stretched and saw his pillow still held the indention of his head. She found she was still naked, so she hopped out of bed and hurriedly got dressed. Attending to her toilette in front of the mirror, she seemed surprised she didn't look any different. But she knew she was different.

She hurried to the galley, finding she was hungrier than she thought. Thaddious still had some warm porridge and he sliced some hardtack sea biscuits for browning on top of the stove. Most of the crew had already left when Daine ambled in.

Julie couldn't help the slight blush but she still looked him squarely in the eyes and even managed an enticing smile. "Have you eaten yet?" she asked as she poured him a cup of coffee.

"No, but I could eat a—seahorse," he laughed, flashing a smile as he took the cup from her.

She bent close so only he could hear. "Thad's porridge is thick enough to glue some of the ship's broken boards back together. Want I should fry you a piece of pork and an egg?"

He chuckled at her. "Thad, would we happen to have any eggs that aren't scrambled already?" Julie hadn't thought of that.

"Not unless you can go below and stare down a hen," he laughed. "There's porridge and some salt pork in the barrel over there." Julie had already pried open the top and was slicing off a chunk, then rinsed off some of the dried salt.

Thaddious left to get water and Julie placed the pork on the stove to heat and began stacking dishes and cleaning up before he returned. The men had surprised her when she'd first came in, thanking her for her part in saving the ship and helping their captain. She hadn't thought herself a hero, but it was very obvious that they all did.

Daine watched her quietly working around the kitchen while she fixed his breakfast. It was a feeling of domesticity he'd never experienced before and it felt natural. He was certain he could get used to it.

After he left, Julie went back out on deck and helped roll tarps and torn sails and try to salvage what ropes they had left. In the hold, each barrel and carton was checked for leaks. She worked late into the afternoon, only catching quick glimpses of the captain.

Lunch had consisted of something cold and quick since everyone ate at different times. There was always someone taking turns standing watch and also at the wheel, so eating was almost always staggered between the crew.

She'd missed seeing Jeremy at breakfast but he'd walked in while she was finishing cleaning up the galley after a late supper. He moved to her and picked up her hand.

"Julie, I haven't had a chance to talk to you alone, Challenger always seems to be hanging around." His serious blue eyes bored inquiringly into hers.

"Is he treating you all right?"

She looked at him, unsure how to answer with these new developments. "Yes," she stuttered.   As he continued, she realized she was mistaken in his meaning.

"I know how you hate him for making you share his quarters, it's not right. Maybe I can think of something to get you out of his room and back in your bunk where you belong. Is he making you sleep in his bed?"

She blushed hotly and started to say something when his arm shot out and grabbed her, kissing her before she could draw a breath. Neither heard the footsteps behind them in the doorway until they heard the cutting voice.

"If I'm interrupting anything, I'll take but a minute."

She stepped back quickly and her eyes met dark scowling ones.

For Daine, it was the straw that sent the camel to its knees. His afternoon had been stressful enough but this was a kick in the gut, however innocent on Julie's part. To have seen her in the arms of another brought back the memory of once before being cuckolded by another man. Was a kiss just a kiss?

With an effort he brought his voice under control. "I've decided, along with Walters, that we would be smart in returning to the Azores. It's only a little more than two days backtracking, but we have much more damage than we can repair at sea."   He kept his eyes averted from Julie's and she was devastated. What must he think of her? He addressed Jeremy, "You're needed topside," adding an emphasis, "pronto." Then he turned and strode away.

"I'll think of something, Julie," Jeremy whispered as he turned to follow the captain.

Julie hurried back down the companionway leading to the cabin. Once inside, she moved about listlessly, running her fingertips over the polished desk. Then, folding his discarded shirt, she put it away and kept busy doing some general cleaning.

She heard a sound at the door and waited with her heart hammering, but it was only Walters. He was leaning on a makeshift pair of crutches and when he saw her, he grinned.

"Sal will be bringing yer bathwater in a bit. I needed to git some air, ain't used ta' bein' idle," he said. "Thanks be to ya fer all ya did the night of the storm."

"It was nothing. I'm hardly paying for my passage as it stands now." She tried to sound jovial but failed. It didn't go unnoticed.

Walters tried to assess her mood but it wasn't his nature to pry in personal things. He decided to let it pass for now, perhaps she was just tired. She was happy to take another bath since she'd worked up a sweat with all her activity and greeted Sal with a warm smile.

After closing the door behind him a short while later, she undressed and slipped into the warm water. Lathering her body with the lavender scented soap; she dunked her head and soaped her hair. She had just completed her rinse when she opened her eyes and saw Daine staring down at her.

He was standing in the exact spot he had stood on the night he'd discovered her secret, which now seemed eons ago. Stepping closer, he reached out a hand to brush a damp tendril of hair out of her eyes.

She blushed and found she'd folded her arms across her chest to block his view. But he had noticed, and frowning, had stepped away and crossed to his liquor cupboard. It seemed an affront to hide what he had already so admired.

With his back to her she dried herself hurriedly, and watching from the corner of her eye, she wrapped the towel around her. Then she stood wondering what she should say if he asked about

Jeremy's kiss.

He took down two snifters and poured amber liquid in them, and then casually walked to her and handed her one.

"What is it?" she murmured.

"Madeira," he answered softly, studying her face as she brought the wine to her lips. Was she in love with Jeremy? What did he mean to her? His thoughts were in turmoil as he tried to read her thoughts. He was totally bewitched by her fathomless green eyes.

She sipped the wine slowly. Would he even believe me? Perhaps I've read too much into this? Maybe I'm just a plaything on this voyage. She swooned remembering last night. He probably thinks I'm just a brazen hussy! She had to explain.

"I know what you must think, about Jeremy and me. I don't know why he kissed me." She felt like a fool, but went on, "I'm sure he just forgot himself for a minute, I had no idea."

His eyes widened in mock surprise. "Do say, and you didn't see the wisdom in locking you away from the crew? You would rather have taken your chances with a knife-happy cutthroat and his less than lecherous ship-jumping partner, and now a lovesick greenhorn? Tell me, is there not one member of my crew who's not besotted with you?"

She slammed her drink down on the table, spilling what was left.

"Yes, that's it! While you're at it, tell me just how safe I was with you! Oh, ravager of maidens!" She was suddenly trembling with rage. "Tell me just how safe you kept me from rapists and knife happy cutthroats. I've seen only two such characters on board, and they have since left your employ!"

He blanched with anger. "Anytime you want to leave my undesirable company, it's a big ship, so feel free!" He headed back toward the door.

The wine had made her giddy and she didn't want to fight with him, much less want him to leave. She was suddenly insane with the urge to have him hold her, and kiss her tears away while he calmed her fears.

When he reached the door, he turned at her low sob.

"Please, Daine. Stay here with me." She had dropped the towel and stood unashamedly naked before him.

His pulse quickened at the ravishing sight before him and he couldn't find words, nor believe what she said next. "I haven't forgotten that last night, t'was I that raped you."

In two long strides she was in his arms. Their eyes met in quiet soul searching, and then his head descended where his lips crushed hers. Her breasts flattened against his chest while her fingers dug into his back. She clung to him before he effortlessly lifted her and carried her over to the bunk.

Laying her down, he pulled off his boots and she saw his eyes sweep her length, then return to the firm drawn-up breasts as she leaned back with her weight on her elbows. In seconds, he was free of his clothes and when he slid into bed, she came willingly into his arms.

His warm seeking mouth closed over hers again and she felt the taut muscles relax in his back as he moved slowly over her, and then she went limp as she succumbed to the pleasures coursing throughout her body.

With a gentle pry, he parted her lips and kissed her in a thrilling way she'd never known before. Then he rubbed his thumb over a nipple where it hardened instantly and a deep ache coursed over her. He tantalized and teased while she shuddered, aching for this new torment to end, but he only prolonged that elusive frenzied longing that gripped and took her breath away.

Suddenly, he wedged himself between her legs in a breathtaking swiftness that stunned her. She sucked in a sharp breath as he penetrated, then they both began to move together in a slow sensuous rocking, complete molding of bodies.

Her mouth opened again to his probing tongue and the promise of pleasure far outweighed any soreness left from the previous night. Too soon, a long shattering free-fall swept over them in unison. He held her close to his chest as their passion slowly subsided, and then they moved apart but still remained entwined.

She stared into his eyes, noticing for the first time the golden flecks that flickered in their depths. Right now, he looked not unlike a Cheshire cat toying with a mouse before he ate it. He was gentle as a kitten when making love and as protective as a mother lion with two unruly cubs, when called upon.

Feeling an overwhelming rush of love, she suddenly squelched it back. The first declaration would not be hers.

They slept then, entwined in each others arms as though it were an everyday routine.

•

They approached the Azores islands late on the second day after the storm. The island had also sustained much damage and some of the ships standing at anchor had their crews busily repairing sails and dumping what damaged cargo they could onto flatboats for disposal at sea. Water-soaked boxes were stacked several feet high on the banks where people were picking through them like vultures while they salvaged everything they could.

The Hornet eased her way as close as it could before finally dropping anchor. Running out the wide planking for the gangway, Sal and Lars threw out the thick ropes and tied the bow snugly to the pier. They were in dire need of fittings, running rigging, and halyard rope for hoisting spars with attached sails. The captain feared these would be in short supply with all the ships in various states of disrepair clambering for all they could buy.

Even though they carried some lumber in the hold, they still needed large trees from the island for the three tall masts, new block and tackle, and the good thing was they had plenty of supplies left for trade. The captain and two of his crew went ashore right away, intent on procuring what they had urgent need of before supplies ran out. Three hours later, they were back. They had been successful in the most needed items. Tomorrow would be a long day and they would need every hand. And, if more workers were needed, they'd been told help could be hired from the island.

Early the next morning the Hornet became a beehive of activity. Julie was working in the galley and glad to be back at work. After a couple of hours, Daine showed up smiling that devastatingly handsome smile that never failed to make her heart skip a beat.

"Could you go ashore and buy some supplies? I've listed some things, but we need all the guys here and I could really use your help. Don't worry about fixing a big meal, they can grab something as they need it."

She was delighted he had asked her. "Yes, I can do it. Do you want me to go now?"

"Yes, but you need to take Cyrus with you for protection. I don't want you wandering around alone." He gave her the list and some signed bank notes that she tucked in her blouse under her new breast holder.

Cyrus was a big Swede, in his early fifties with straw-white hair and several cowlicks from cutting his own hair with a knife. She found him to be a very pleasant fellow. He was waiting for her at the pier.

Soon they were poking around in huge piles of boxes and stacks of soggy clothes and Cyrus was surprised at the haggling Julie was doing. They found medicinal supplies, sacks of potatoes and onions, apples, oranges and flour, most without weevils. A newly arrived ship was unloading waxed blocks of rendered lard, burlap bags of wheat, and they even found a barrel of grease which could be used for protecting new wood and moving parts.

Julie also bought several bolts of linen and ticking for new pillows. She had been aware of the crew's tacky pillows and most were in a sad state. Finding thread and needles, she made plans to make them all new ones. Cyrus told her there were several sacks of feathers already aboard, saved for such a future project.

Pleased with herself, she and Cyrus returned to the Hornet.

Once, she had an odd sensation of being watched, but when she turned to look around, she could see nothing. Feeling somewhat uneasy, she hurried along with both arms full.

•

Only a few feet away, Bracken and Mallory watched her trim figure climb the gangplank and disappear out of sight. They had hidden behind some large crates they had just helped unload tp make themselves drinking money.

"Well, if that just don't beat all. Here we's a'wonderin' if we was gonna catch up with 'em and they come sailin' right back," Bracken said with a scornful sneer. "Talk about Ladyluck."

Mallory cleared his throat, pulled his soiled hanky out of his back pocket and wiped his sweaty face. "How we gonna git her away from Challenger? He's about as watchful as a long-tailed cat in a roomful a' rockin' chairs."

"Don't worry, we'll git her. And Jerico's gonna help us," he said, nodding toward the Baltimore clipper still sitting at anchor. On the bow in big letters were the word, *Ladyluck*.

"It's an omen."

•

Julie leaned against the rail, shading her eyes with one hand, while she looked up at Daine outlined against the bright sun. The dark clouds of the last few days had disappeared and the day had now turned into a scorcher. It seemed everyone around her had a job to do.

Daine looked down at her from the platform in the crow's nest from time to time. The sun shone on her tawny red hair and he suppressed the urge to climb down and run to her, and take her in his arms. She was very different from any other girl he'd ever met. She rotated from loving and feminine one minute, to saucy and opinionated the next.

He was holding the rope on the cable as the main mast was raised in place. The other two would be rigged tomorrow and then they would raise the newly repaired sails when they returned to the sea, possibly the day after tomorrow. The bulwarks and foredecks were being repainted and the ten-foot long distinguishing figurehead of a hornet, with a yellow stinger and tucked in wings, was also getting a fresh coat of black paint. Daine's shirt had come off and his sun bronzed skin glistened with sweat. He pulled on the rope to signal, then when he was satisfied all was in place, he shinnied down the rope. He walked to Julie and put his arms around her waist, his first public show of affection to his crew.

Walters saw and was glad. He had guessed as much when Julie threw all caution to the wind and raced to help him the night of the storm. He loved them both and was doubly glad they now acknowledged those feelings he had only guessed at.

Then, in front of his astonished crew, he dipped his head and kissed his former cabin boy on the mouth, forgetting everything but the ravishing girl in his arms. Neither saw Jeremy slip away to ponder this surprising and unexpected event.

After supper that night, and long after dark, Daine consumed three glasses of brandy and was feeling a little light-headed, while Julie folded their clothes and plumped their pillows to make ready for bed. She picked up the near empty decanter and put it away, and then she donned the green gauzy gown for the first time.

Daine let out a long low whistle, quickly draining his glass. "You're almost as lovely in that gown, as out of it," he teased.

Demurely she sat down at the table next to where he sat, whereupon he leaned back and stretched his long legs out before him. Julie's eyes stayed fastened on him as she sipped at her first glass of Madeira.

So engrossed were they in each other, neither heard the door slowly open behind them. Daine had overlooked locking the door after Sal left with the trays.

The captain felt the touch of cold metal against his temple and froze. Julie leaped up, twisting to look into the evil face of Bracken, then Mallory's.

"What do you want?" croaked Julie.

"Just you, honey. Just you," Bracken leered. Raking his eyes over over her attire, he hissed nastily, "Get some more clothes. You're coming with us."

The captain started to rise, but was shoved back down hard. "No," he groaned.

Bracken pulled back the hammer for emphasis, keeping it pointed straight at Daine. He jerked his head at Julie. "Better get a move on or I'll blow his brains to kingdom come!"

She yanked open a closet and grabbed a yellow dress, slippers and some undergarments, her eyes never leaving Daine.

"Put 'em on and make it snappy! If you scream or if somebody comes, I'll shoot him first... then you! Ha!" Bracken spat, "and all the time you was sleepin' with him. I should'a knew it!"

Daine tried to stand, seeing where this was all leading. "Leave her alone! I'll give you anything. If it's money, I'll get it from the safe and you can take it all. She's done nothing, only defended herself!" he choked. He was grossly outnumbered. Dammit! Why had he downed so many drinks? It was hard to think.

He stared down the barrels of two flintlock pistols but still continued to bargain. "I've got gold coins, banknotes ..."

"Shut the hell up!" Bracken hissed but considered. They hadn't come to rob him, but this was sounding better and better, the girl *and* the money?

Her back to them, Julie pulled the dress on over her head. She hadn't tried this one on, only the green one. This one pushed her breasts up to dangerous limits in the low-scooped neck. Mallory yanked her back around.

Daine's face mirrored his misery as his eyes took in her garment. She'd never be safe now.

Bracken saw the look that passed between them. "Give us the money and we'll turn her loose on shore." But his eyes lied as he leered over at Julie.

"Raise the bunk and hook it to the wall. There's a safe under there and it opens with a key."

"Where's the key?"

"In my back pocket." As he stood, he suddenly turned and lunged at Bracken. With a loud explosion, the gun went off and Daine was thrown back by the concussion and fell heavily against the wall, then slid slowly to the floor. Blood oozed from his head.

Julie screamed and tried to get to him but was caught and dragged to the door.

"We've no time for the money! The crew will be here in seconds!"

Then they were running with her and she heard two more loud shots. They shoved her down the gangway to the wharf then she fell, landing hard on her knees. She was yanked back up and they dragged her between them again. Minutes later they shoved her down into a small boat where she went sprawling. They were moving before she had even hit the deck.

She was roughly hoisted to her feet again and strained to see as they shoved away from the docks. She could see the Hornet but all she could make out was people running about and lots of far-off yelling. Totally numb, she continued to search as they pushed past the wharf and out toward the open sea. In what seemed like only a few minutes, they pulled around to the other side of a much larger boat, anchored a ways offshore and then they all quickly climbed aboard and were moving again.

Dead! He has to be dead! No one could survive a shot like that to the head.

From on deck she watched as the Hornet grew smaller and smaller in the distance, then realized that someone was still holding on to her. She looked up into Bracken's triumphant face, and then she took a deep breath and spit into it.

He drew back as if to hit her and he would have if over her head he hadn't caught sight of two slitted eyes in the doorway, daring him. He let her go, then pulled a dingy rag out of his vest to wipe the spittle. "Now, who's to come to your rescue with your captain lover shot?" he said just low enough for her to hear. "Mallory checked him out, he's dead."

Chapter Seven

Julie looked around the spacious room at the soft feather-type bed, two plush captain's chairs, and a small cherry-wood square table with two wooden chairs. There was a chamberpot and a metal pitcher of water, a washbasin, towels and an assortment of cookies.

She sat in a state of shock with her mind going over and over the events on the Black Hornet. Too numb to cry, she was too traumatized to even grasp the gravity of her own situation. A huge knot in her chest hung there.

At the same time, Bracken was making his way to Jerico's stateroom while growing increasingly worried. He hadn't meant to kill Challenger, but the man had left him no choice. If he'd just let him take the girl ... now he had to contend with Jerico. He wasn't going to like it.

Rapping softly on his door, he was told to enter.

Jerico sat back with his feet propped up on the desk in front of him. He'd already been apprised of the situation by the skiff's operator that had brought them all aboard.

Bracken swallowed nervously, reading the condemnation on his angry face.

Swiftly removing his feet from the desk, Jerico leaned forward, "All right, you bastard! Let's hear what really happened back there!"

Pulling the black stocking cap from his head, Bracken twisted it nervously in his hands. "She was going to come with me but Challenger tried to stop her. He pulled a gun on me and I had to shoot 'im. That's all there is to it."

"That don't add up, you're lying. I've seen Challenger; he's a very handsome man. Why would this girl suddenly leave him for a lowlife like you?"

Bracken ignored the insult and went on, hoping to plead his case. "It's true. She hates the man. I was only trying to help her get away. I had to shoot 'im."

Jerico stared hard at the man. This was not the story he'd been told when they'd boarded and he'd seen her spit in his face. Bracken had told him the day before he was rescuing a girl held captive, a former girlfriend of sorts. He didn't know then that the captain of the Hornet was even involved. He knew Challenger and he had a fair and honest reputation.

Jerico stood up and pushed aside his chair with the back of his knees and crossed to a cabinet   set in the wall. He took out a bottle and two snifters and returned indolently, handing one to Bracken. Lighting up a cigar, he puffed a moment all the while thinking how he could rid himself of Bracken and Mallory. He didn't think he wanted them on the island of Martinique. Besides, Bracken knew too much.

·

Julie stayed curled up on the bunk, staring at the opposite wall. There were gold sconces with flickering candles, but her eyes could only see images of the man she had come to love and had been taken from her. She still couldn't cry. She was too numb and heartsick. Drawing the blanket up to her chin, she pressed it to her lips, certain the pain she felt was a shattered heart.

He had tried to save her, but one man against two armed men? Why oh why had he jumped Bracken? He had to know he couldn't fight them both. She was wracked with a new wave of guilt, but still she couldn't cry.

She was still lying there staring at the wall when the door opened and a young brown-skinned boy stepped in. He placed a tray on the table, looking meekly over at her. She sat up with a jerk and sent the tray and it's contents crashing to the floor. Silently he bent down and picked it all up and left without a backward glance.

Lying back down, she pulled the coverlet back over her. She wanted to be left alone in her misery and she made a solemn vow. If Bracken came near her, and even if he didn't, she'd kill him. There were many ways she could do it.

The next morning she did the same thing when a tray was

brought to her. Her stomach growled with hunger but she'd be hanged if she ate anything on this ship. There was a small porthole for her to look out of, but she could see nothing but miles of blue rolling seas. Sensing this ship was made for speed, she could see the low sided, sharp bowed upward curve to the hull and felt sure it was a clipper of some sort.

Still standing there when she heard the door open, she didn't turn around until she heard a new voice. "Empty the chamberpot, Seeka."

She swung around to see a tall, medium built man of middle years with a disgusted expression on his face. "Maybe she's too stubborn to even use it. Check it out," he said to the young island boy. He continued to stare hard at her. "Okay miss carrot-top, I guarantee you'll be crawling on your hands and knees for favors before this week is out. Your choice if you want to eat or not." He waited a minute and turned and left behind the boy.

Rushing to the door when she failed to hear the lock slide she opened it to see him still standing on the other side. He pursed his lips together in a malevolent smile, which stayed there while she looked him over.

He was impeccably groomed with chestnut brown hair, and was gray around the temples with a sharp-featured nose. He had the air of a man of means. Some might even consider him nice looking.

Eyes dropping to her heaving chest, he took in her womanly curves. She was indeed a beautiful girl but much too young for his taste. Still, he'd been married three times and he knew women. Perhaps younger was the wiser way to go. That he had failed three times was of no consequence to him.

Just then Seeka returned with the chamberpot and it had a clean white linen draped over it. In his other hand he carried a fresh pitcher of water.

Jerico finally spoke. "Are you going to eat something now or are you just going to sulk and make yourself sick?"

"Sulk!" she shrieked. "Bracken shot the captain for trying to protect me! So where do you get sulk?"

"Challenger had a gun didn't he?"

She answered incredulously, "No! He didn't have anything to protect himself with! But he did try to get Bracken's away from him."

Just as he'd thought. But he didn't tip his hand. "Now are you going to eat?"

"No! So don't bother bringing me anything."

"As you wish." With that he firmly pushed her back inside and locked the door. The boy's footsteps echoed his as he followed him back down the deck.

When Seeka unlocked the door the next morning, a now docile Julie told him she was ready to eat. He returned a few minutes later with a tray of buttery scones, a thick slice of sweet ham and scrambled eggs. There was a carafe of hot Russian tea and six lumps of sugar. She was now ravenous and ate every bite. If she was going to kill somebody, she thought under her breath, she didn't want to be the one to die first.

She stared out the porthole the rest of the morning and wondered where they were headed. Right after lunch Seeka told her she was allowed to go out on deck for some fresh air and exercise her legs. She was surprised, but took a light shawl with her, wrapping it around her bare arms to ward off the chill of the water's spray.

The ship was only half as big as the Hornet. Her thoughts had been right on, this was a clipper built for speed and it seemed they were barely skimming the top of the water. It looked to be only about sixty-five feet long and doing at least 18 knots. Overhead the sails billowed as they cupped huge pockets of wind.

She followed Seeka down the deck and wrinkled her nose at the peculiar smell that floated from the bowels of the vessel. The dank boards were slick from the elements and there was a strong scent of what she guessed was mildew. It didn't look like a cargo ship, but more like a pleasure vessel.

She decided to question Seeka.

"Who is the man that came in my room and where are we going?"

"This boat belongs to Jerico Trouchet. He be a trader, a gambler and has a big house on Martinique. That's where we're going." He looked at her proudly. His English had been perfect!

Julie was horrified. "Martinique? I don't even know where that is! I don't want to go there!"

Without a word he turned and led her to Jerico's private quarters. He seemed not at all surprised to see her and would have been disappointed had she not.

She stood sober-faced and declined his offer to sit while she fought the impulse to strike him across the face for being a party to this whole thing. "Why did you help Bracken and Mallory with this abduction?" she spat. "Return me at once to the Hornet!"

He eyed her with interest. She was indeed a pretty little twit.

"I merely provided the means for escape and am not to blame for what transpired before that. Why do you want to return to the Hornet?"

"I must see to it that Captain Challenger is returned to his family in New Orleans." Seeing his eyebrows raise sharply, she asked, "Why are you looking at me like that?"

"Mademoiselle, you are naive indeed. It would be quite impossible to return the captain's body back to the states. Granting the speed the Hornet is capable of traveling it would take four or five months to even get there. Wouldn't it make more sense to either bury him on the island or even at sea? His wishes would be noted in his ship's log in either case."

She hadn't thought of that and shivered. She sank into a red velvet chair, her eyes filling with her first tears. It all seemed final now.

Trouchet could see the truth. She'd been in love with the man and Bracken had indeed been lying. "What's your name?" he asked her softly.

"Julie Sinclair," she answered, loathe looking at him.

"Well, Julie," he echoed, leaning back in his chair. "What part did Bracken really play in all this?"

A look of pure hatred contorted her otherwise beautiful face. "He had tried to rape me after goading me into a sword fight and then was thrown off the Hornet at the Azores islands. His friend Mallory is no better and neither should be trusted out of any 'honest' mans sight."

He flinched at this.

"I gathered as much, but I assure you I'll be dealing with them." He walked her to the door as she stood up to leave. "Trust me, I'll not let either man near you."

•

She had been wrong in thinking the Ladyluck carried no cargo. The warm climate had permeated the odor more and more each day, and this was what she had smelled earlier. It was that very cargo Bracken was holding over Jerico's head.

Trouchet now pondered how to rid himself of his two unwanted passengers. He was hauling illegal cargo while carefully doctoring the manifest. He had first met Bracken when he was negotiating with Challenger while the Hornet was docked at the Greek fishing port of Piraeus.

The black ship was in port trading cotton and sugar cane for Greek olives, goat cheeses and fine aged wine. The Ladyluck had just arrived from Turkey with many barrels of poppy seeds. When finely ground, they produced the black-market opium and heroin. He was contracted to sell half his shipment among the opium dens in Morocco, along with the coveted fine Jamaican rum he'd transported for open trade.

Once back in Jamaica, Jerico had the advantage over larger ships. He could travel in half the time around the Horn, and from there on to California. He could capture an even higher price for the rest of the seeds in San Francisco's untamed frontier. Chinatown.

Jerico had approached Challenger while at Piraeus, offering to split hefty profits if Daine would try to garner a market in his home base of New Orleans.

He'd been quickly rebuffed, but unfortunately Bracken had overheard their conversation. Either help him get the girl away from Challenger or the authorities would be checking Jerico's cargo. An easy enough request, and he didn't really feel he owed Challenger anything any longer.

But he hadn't counted on murder. Now he was certain to have the authorities on his trail anyway.

Jerico kept his promise of seeing to it that Bracken and Mallory stayed clear of her.

Soon her cabin began to stifle her as they moved closer to the equator, and her only relief was sitting near the rail and collecting the fine spray from the boat's wake. It didn't last long before she suffered sunburn and was forced to cover all of her exposed skin.

The next day she sat on a bench near the rail and Seeka sat down next to her and pulled out a Jew's harp, stuck it in his mouth and began to play. He hummed as he plucked it and Julie found herself also humming and tapping her foot.

"What's the name of that song? It sounds like one I've heard before," she questioned, intrigued by the sound and melody.

He pulled the instrument, a curved flexible wire of sorts, from his mouth and smiled shyly.

"It's called 'lady in waiting' and it was one of Trouchet's wife's favorite, she played it on her harpsichord." He had an islander accent but she had no difficulty in understanding him. "She was his last wife, she was from Boll Weevil, or something like that."

Julie's eyebrows knitted together in puzzlement before a chuckle escaped her. "You must mean Bolivia?"

He grinned, "That's it." Then looking closely at her, he thrust the harp into the waistband of the long wraparound skirt he wore, and bent down to look closely at her face.

"Stay here. Your lips and nose are red and chapped. I'll go get some salve for you."

With that he hurried off.

Jerico spied her and was walking up behind her when a fat man with a shaved head and several double chins suddenly caught up with him. Julie hadn't seen him before.

"Bracken's drunk again. He's making threats." They stood talking low with their heads together and then both turned and took the stairwell down into the hold. Julie hadn't heard either man with the ocean's noise.

Seeka returned with a yellowish waxy looking salve and began to rub it on Julie. She wrinkled her nose at the smell. "What is it?"

"Goose grease. Best thing to use on your skin."

She stared at him a minute, so intense was he at his task, but mostly because of his accent spoken with impeccable English. She couldn't resist. "When you see that goose again, you be sure and thank him. Okay?"

He looked at her after a long moment, then smiled, catching her jest.

•

The chance to rid himself of Bracken and Mallory came quite unexpectedly that very evening. Jerico always carried a small derringer in his boot and the idea came to him that a good game of cards between friends and enemies alike could solve a world of problems.

Bracken had him worried and was drinking way too much. The only thing he found more dangerous than a man with a killer instinct was a drunken one with a killer instinct. Jerico's fingers itched just to shoot them on the spot and be done with it, but knew it would be wiser to wait and catch them unawares.

After a leisurely dinner he invited his two unwelcome guests to his cabin for a game of cards. He busied himself with keeping their glasses full of brandy while pretending to keep up with them.

Four hands later, Jerico drew his ace in the hole. He would often wonder later what their last thoughts were as the cheating pair of fools' eyes dropped to his derringer as it cleared the edge of the table.

Julie had been tossing and turning restlessly when suddenly she sat up, now fully awake. She knew those were shots she'd heard, and then there was running and loud snatches of excited voices. Throwing back her quilt, she stepped onto the cold floor and felt around in the dark for her wrap. Finding it she raced to the top of the stairs, and stopped and listened.

The noise had stopped, so she stood still, barely breathing. Then she saw dim outlines of three men standing down near the rail. Then they bent to pick up two large objects and threw them into the sea.

She recognized Jerico's voice. "Hope they don't make the fish sick."

•

Julie was deathly ill. She had woken three times during the night retching and sweating profusely. She had tried to get out of bed but her legs refused her mind's urging. Disoriented, she couldn't think where she was in the darkness and pounded the wall, but to no avail. Exhausted, she made her way back to the bed, rolled up in a blanket and fell back asleep. The next time she woke, the room was much brighter and she struggled to sit up. There was an odd sensation of floating, but still her legs refused to do her bidding.

Her cheeks felt feverish to the touch and she was perspiring and very hot. Unbuttoning her nightgown, she slipped out of it and lay back down. When Seeka arrived a short time later he left on a dead run for Jerico. When he arrived he quickly assessed the situation; sending the young boy scurrying for warm water and hot broth.

When Jerico made an attempt to move the quilt Seeka was right there. "Please M'souoir, she is shy. She'd never forgive you for looking upon her nudity. It would be better if I ..." his words trailed off.

He knew the boy was right. A fifteen-year-old boy would not humiliate her as much. Nodding in agreement, he left her in his care.

Seeka quickly sponge bathed her and then wrapped her up in a warm soft blanket. Her breathing was shallow and he tried to guess the cause of her sickness, but she only wanted to sleep the rest of the day. Occasionally she drank some thick broth and water.

Once when she awoke, Seeka was sitting by her bed, a look of concern on his face as he bent close for her to hear. "We'll be home sometime tomorrow. Maybe you'll feel better then."

Home? She wondered ... *Where on earth was home?*

She never opened her eyes again until she was being lifted onto a stretcher and down a runway to a pier, and again when she was being carried up a huge stairway in an elegant house. Warm blankets on a large bed were thrown back and then hurriedly placed back over her. She tried to comprehend her new surroundings each time she woke, but was still too tired, so she slept again. Each time Jerico paid her a visit she was asleep.

•

A door slamming somewhere in the house a day later jarred her awake and she took more notice this time. She vaguely remembered a brown-skinned woman trying to get her to eat and fussing over her. She looked at the rich tapestries hung on extra high windows then saw a large fireplace with flickering logs burning low, and just enough to break the chill from the ocean. Woven circular rugs covered a dark paneled floor and the room was richly furnished with damask coverings on the bed and nearby chairs.

For once she was hungry. Her door soon opened and Seeka crept in. His frown was quickly replaced by a glad smile. "You're awake, praise Allah!" he said happily. "How do you feel? Are you ready to eat now?"

"Yes, I feel much better." Her mouth felt cottony and her tongue felt like it belonged to someone else. "Are we at Jerico's house?"

"Yes, this is the island of Martinique." Drawing the curtain aside, he pointed and she could see mountainous greenery and low white fluffy clouds hovering over a high peak. "This is Saint-Pierre and the island is a dead volcano."

She lay back finding she had little strength but still enough to laugh. "You must mean a dormant volcano. How long was I sick?"

It was his turn to laugh. "Okay, dormant. You was sick nearly a week. We thought …" his voice trailed off, "you was going to die."

That would have been too swift a punishment, she thought miserably. Her cross to bear was to go on living and torturing herself forever for having caused Daine's death. She deserved it. If she had stayed away from his ship maybe he'd still be alive.

This was all her doing.

The next day she allowed Seeka to take her downstairs. She was still shaky and weak and her skin was sallow and pale, but she knew she could no longer avoid Trouchet.

He was seated at a large desk and gestured Seeka to place her on the settee next to a large picture window, and then he moved over to a large chair facing her.

"How do you like the house and island so far?" He was tapping some bitter-root into the bowl of his pipe and packing it down before lighting it with the bamboo shoot Seeka had lit in the fire. All the while he was looking at her.

"It's hard to tell since I've only seen my room and sometimes out the windows at the island. I do want to thank you for the clothes that were laid out for me," she said, smoothing the robe over her lap.

"There's more in the closet, and it looks like most of them will fit you."

She wondered which wife they had belonged to but didn't ask. She wanted to get right to the point. "Are you going to hold me here?"

He looked startled at her question but recovered quickly, straightening his cravat then leaning back in his chair. "Do you have someplace you want to go?"

"Yes, I do. I'd like to go to America. I've an aunt there that I'm going to live with."

"Is not this house comfortable? You don't need to be in a hurry to leave, and there are lots of things to do here. You've been pretty sick. There's reading, needlepoint and sewing supplies, and if that's your bag, many servants to wait on you. There's a closet full of gowns and other apparel my former spouses' saw fit to leave behind. I've got all kinds of precious gems in my safe to adorn that lovely neck of yours."

Wife number four was etched plainly on his face as he gazed back at her.

Over my dead body she thought. All along he'd played the perfect gentleman, but his intentions were now becoming clear. She was as much a prisoner here as she'd been on the ship. Her eyes narrowed, just barely holding in her anger.

"Are you telling me you will not allow me to leave?"

He took a deep drag on his pipe before he answered, careful to choose the right words. "I didn't say you weren't free to leave, perhaps in the spring. It's September now, and the start of the rainy season. I'll pick up a load of rum in Jamaica in the spring, and I'm afraid you'll just have to wait until then. We've plenty of time and you need time to rest and gain back your strength. End of discussion."

He rose swiftly to his feet and exited the room. He'd change her mind, he mused to himself as he walked outside. In the spring he'd take her to California and then return with her as his new wife. He could buy her easily with his wealth. After all, he'd been married three times.

Didn't he know women?

Although he allowed her free reign of the house, she was still a prisoner within its walls just the same. She had already been adamantly barred from ever leaving the house to wander alone outside. She also knew that she was being watched. Even Seeka hardly let her out of his sight.

The only thing she could really do was read. She read history books and became quite familiar with maps. The island of Martinique was indeed a large dormant volcano rising up out of the oceans floor. Once owned by France, it exported bananas and pineapples, and was one of the more beautiful islands in the West Indies chain.

Soon Jerico began showing her delicate pieces of jewelry in hopes of gaining her affections. He was no longer relying on his charm alone. At first she just looked at them, but after thinking it through decided she had no resources if she was to find a way off the island, so she became very interested. But he always remembered to return them to his safe. She tried to broach the subject of leaving on the boat to explore other islands, but he always rebuffed her.

On one balmy Sunday he surprised her right after lunch. "If you like; today Seeka will take you for a walk."

She had been standing by a big bay window, looking longingly outside. She turned at his voice, "How generous of you," she said icily, "but are you sure I can be trusted out of your sight?"

Ringing a bell for Seeka, his voice held a warning, "You'll only find trouble if you're looking for it." Lighting up his pipe as she swept by him, he leaned against the door as Julie and Seeka left the courtyard and stopped under a eucalyptus tree. She wound a scarf around her head to ward off the light breeze.

Jerico wasn't at all worried about her walking around the island as he had already left orders at the docks that she was to be returned if she was spotted there. Besides, he trusted Seeka. There was not a man on the island who would chance his wrath by allowing her to escape. He was a very powerful man in Saint-Pierre, and the richest by far, if not the most influential.

Jerico was now hopelessly infatuated with this petite girl. She would be his last. He wasn't used to waiting for a woman to make up her mind. He wasn't an overly handsome man, but with his wealth, his looks always improved considerably. This time it was different. He knew he could change her mind.

Julie had a pressing reason to get off the island and far away from Jerico. She knew now he had no intention of ever letting her leave. She couldn't wait until spring to leave, but she could no longer ignore the signs. She was carrying Daine's child. The sickness on the Ladyluck, the fatigue and soreness of her breasts, and most incriminating, she had missed her second flux.

Letting out a deep breath she smiled back at Seeka when he looked at her. He had already proved he was her friend, and she hoped he could also be loyal to her. "Seeka, can you ever forgive me?"

Stopping in his tracks he looked puzzled. What had she done? "Why do you say this thing?" he asked. They had both stopped in the dusty path that wound around the water's edge. There were no close houses.

"I'm talking about the shameful way I acted when you tried to take care of me on the boat."

"If you mean spilling the tray, forget it." He was relieved that was all that troubled her. "You had many reasons to be angry."

"But not at you, you did nothing wrong. I just want you to know I'm sorry and that I consider you to be a very good friend."

Seeka was happy and grinned broadly as they moved on. "You be my friend too," he stated honestly. He was kicking up dust with his bare toes in his embarrassment.

Julie was quickly growing desperate. Her child had to be born in America and in Daine's homeland. If she didn't get away now then she would have to make her escape with a small child and endanger them both. Knowing Daine would never see his child, or even his family again, she began to cry brokenly.

Seeka was thrown. "Are you not happy? You don't like it here?"

Dropping to her knees in the sand, she forced her sobs to stop. "Oh, Seeka, help me leave! I have to get away from here. Can't you see? I'm as much a prisoner here as I ever was on the ship."

It was the truth. This morning Jerico had instructed him to keep very close watch and not to leave her alone for a second. That she was unhappy was no surprise, but he also knew he would be horsewhipped if somehow she got away from him. He'd been whipped before and that was just for taking some cookies and then forgetting to close a gate and letting a cow loose. He could still feel the welts from the lashes that still scarred his back.

But those two deeds had wiped the slate clean. If those two acts warranted that kind of punishment then what was true loyalty worth? If the truth were known, Jerico probably didn't even remember the whippings at all. Well, that was his first mistake. His second was now taking Seeka for granted.

"But why must you go?" He was shattered she wanted to leave.

She knew she had to tell him, but somehow knew she could trust him. "I'm with child," she said simply. "I have to find his father's family. They have a right to know."

Seeka looked into her misty green eyes. At that moment she looked almost as young as he, but he had no way of knowing she was only three years older. No matter what the cost when she looked at him like that; he knew he could deny her nothing.

With an impulsive shrug, he murmured, "Don't worry. I'll find a way."

•

His chance didn't come until two months later, in mid October.

A large ship had anchored offshore late in the evening, and what he could gather from a crew member, it was bound for Jamaica. This was Jerico's third mistake. He'd been lax on checking new arrivals lately and it would prove to be costly, even much more than losing Julie.

Seeka had nosed around, and then found the first mate onshore and quietly secured Julie's passage with a dozen cases of the valuable Haitian rum he'd bartered from Jerico's stash. He had also thrown in ten wooden kegs of Greek Kalamata olives.

The plan was to make sail at dawn and the passenger was to be at the docks promptly at the stroke of midnight.

Julie was elated when Seeka told her she was leaving that night and she wondered how she could get into the safe and take enough jewels to pay her passage. She had to ask. "How are we going to pay for it?"

Seeka dispelled that problem completely. "Don't worry, it's already been taken care of. They're taking you to Jamaica, and from there you'll have to try and find passage to Florida yourself. You just have to be at the pier at midnight, so have your things ready."

She didn't ask how and he didn't say more.

Retiring as soon as she could after dinner, she was sure her pounding heart would give her away as Jerico bade her goodnight at her door and walked off to his room on the same floor. She needed to pack since she'd had no idea she was leaving so quickly. There was no guilt as she placed extra clothing and toiletries into a canvas bag and set out another change of clothes to wear. He owed her that much. Then she pulled back the covers and lay down to wait.

Time crawled by and when it was finally eleven fifteen, she picked up her bag, and in her stocking feet tucked her shoes under her arm and quietly opened the door. She stuck her head out and looked up and down the hall, and then quietly closed the door behind her. The house was eerily silent as she tiptoed down the stairs.

She almost had a heart attack when a board creaked under her foot near the bottom of the stairway. Sucking in her breath, she listened but no one stirred. She hurried across the floor and chose the side door Seeka had suggested and found it unlocked. Seeka had been very thorough.

Leaving the shadow of the big house, she hurriedly put her shoes on. She hadn't gone far when a small figure stepped out of the trees. Her heart leaped in her throat until she saw it was Seeka and could see he'd been crying.

She gently scolded him. "I told you not to see me off. What if he catches you?"

With a sad look that tore at her heart, he reached up and softly touched her cheek, and then threw himself at her with a giant hug. "Seeka just want to see you once more." He was mortified she had seen his unmanly tears.

They had no more words as they stood and embraced in silence. Knowing she had to get going he followed her until she was safely near the wharf. He waited in the shadows and stood listening a while until he heard the sound of oars and then she was gone.

Chapter Eight

Something was wrong. She'd been whisked aboard a small dingy at the wharf by an unfriendly fat man with muscled biceps and dressed all in black. Then he'd taken up the oars, told her not to talk, and appeared to be in no great hurry. He seemed ever watchful and nervous, rowing slowly in the dark, almost as if he had no direction.

Now they were just sitting dead in the water in the middle of nowhere with no destination in sight. They had been there for nearly two hours and she was now shivering from the cold pre-dawn air and her repeated inquiries only brought short grunts from her strange companion. Finally she heard a far-off horn and he began to row toward it.

Dawn was just beginning to streak across the sky when they pulled alongside a large ship. The man gruffly grabbed her arm and indicated she was to climb up a wobbly rope ladder ahead of him. She stepped to the side of the boat and grabbed at the rough braided ladder, and then felt his hands on her waist, steadying her. When she reached for her bag, he ordered, "Let it be, I'll get it. I'll be behind you after you git up there a' ways."

She placed a small foot on the bottom rung and began to climb. Soon she felt the rope grow taut as he started up behind her. Two men appeared above out of nowhere and they easily helped her over the side. When she stepped onto the rough planks she could see the ship was nearly as big as the Hornet. There the similarity ended.

This boat was piled with all kinds of junk and looked filthy. Raw scratches and chipped wood was everywhere she looked and she saw several mounted cannons, and boxes of gunpowder and cannonballs, along with greasy fittings and leaking oil buckets.

The three men hoisted up the dinghy and soon she was handed her bag. She thanked them, though no one seemed to acknowledge her. One of the men with straw-colored hair seemed more intent on the big wad of chewing tobacco he was wallowing around in his mouth than the young timid girl standing small and still shivering in front of him. Finally he led her below and showed her to a small shabby cabin.

The first thing she noticed was the heavy wearing on the carpet. The once rich Moroccan gold scroll was now barely discernible with its frayed and curling edges. A thin mattress on the bed promised little comfort, and a skinned up commode and worn dresser with the bottom drawer missing was the only furniture she saw. Flickering candles were burning dimly in their insets and he told her to blow them out before she went to bed.

After making sure there was a lock on the door, she slid it into place, stripped to her shift and blew the candles out. There was only the one ragged blanket and a lumpy pillow. She lay there awhile thinking on the last few hours, forever grateful she had escaped Jerico's imprisonment. She didn't know what was ahead for her but she prayed it was better than what she'd just left.

She woke once and went right back to sleep. When she opened her eyes again, it was bright and sunny in the room and stifling hot. She slipped out of bed and stood a moment trying to get her sealegs under her. Seeing a cracked mirror, she crossed to it and stared back at a pale and peaked face. Placing her hands on her stomach, she thought she could feel a gentle swell and was glad she'd brought a dress with a high waist.

Rummaging through her bag she finally found it and pulled it over her head. Then she ran her fingers through her hair and washed her face in cold water from a chipped pitcher, and then smoothed out her bed. She felt a pang of hunger and was debating whether or not to seek out the galley herself when a soft knock at the door hastened her unlocking it.

A large buxom woman stood in the doorway, wearing big hoop earrings and rice powder on her face with a colorful red bandana wound around her head. Her friendly smile faded as soon as she saw Julie. With a grunt, she snorted, "Will ya be wantin' somethin' ta eat now?"

"Yes, thank you." Desperate for female companionship, she motioned, "Come in. Please call me Julie."

With a toss of her long black hair, she came through the doorway and turned with her hands splayed on her ample hips. She wore a flowery peasant skirt and her stained white blouse was low-cut, displaying a deep and daring cleavage. Julie felt some alarm as she read the distaste in the older woman's face.

"Okay, Julie it is. My name's Leela and I'm the only other woman you'll find on board. The captain usually don't take women passengers and I'd advise you to stay as far away from him as you can get. He's not the kind of man you'd like to get close to."

Julie shrugged her shoulders. "Don't worry, I'd just as soon stay in my room if it's all the same to you. Am I to understand my meals will be brought to me here?"

Brown eyes continued to assess her. "Yes, and if you need anything I'm the one to ask."

Julie was curious. There were a lot of questions building up in her, but most could wait. "What's the name of this ship?"

Leela looked surprised. "You don't know you're on The Seeker? Have you not heard of Captain Freedom?"

Julie felt a twinge of alarm. She could vaguely remember something Daine had said about Captain Freedom. What had it been? She knew some type of danger had been associated with it but tried not to show alarm. "No, I haven't heard of either of them."

Leela snorted rudely then left. Fifteen minutes later she returned with a tray of fish, a hunk of cheese and two strips of jerky. There was some tea and crushed cane sugar, fruit preserves and a fairly clean folded napkin.

Finding the fish bony and tasteless, Julie ate only a small portion before going on to the cheese. It had a pungent, moldy taste so she reached for the jerky. Though it was very salty, it was at least edible. The preserves were also moldy and she was left wondering if she could live on tea and jerky alone. Her appetite lacking, she walked to the single porthole and looked out, seeing only endless waves and swells as far as her eyes could see.

Returning to the bed, she sat down on the edge and let her thoughts wander. Loneliness crept in on silent feet and enveloped her, making her shiver. Tears began to roll down her cheeks and soon she began to sob. This was the first time she'd given in to abject sorrow for all she'd lost. She cried for her mother, her father and her lover. Now she had no one.

Then, so faint she thought she'd imagined it, she felt a flutter in her stomach. She held her breath a long moment, and then felt it again. A tiny bird was testing its wings. Placing her hand on her stomach, she soon felt it again. The timing was perfect. She had someone. She'd not forget it again.

•

Leela brought her meals three times a day. The meager fixings did not improve but she was at least able to choose at least two things to sustain her until the next meal. The older girl smiled very little and conversed even less.

Usually she just set down the tray and beat a hasty retreat, but on the afternoon of the fifth day she surprised Julie by inviting her to a walk around the ship's deck. It was obvious she'd been told to by her flippant manner, but nonetheless, Julie was glad for the change.

Once outside, the bright sunlight made her squint. Leela had given her a blanket to wrap around her shoulders to ward off the November chill. There was one man standing watch on deck while the sounds of a concertina and singing below, tinged with raucous laughter, drifted up to them.

She heard a sudden scrape on the planks behind her and turned as a burly form came into view. "Who's the doxie?" he slurred as his lips parted to reveal yellow jagged teeth.

Instantly Leela stepped in front of her to shield her, her massive body barring the groping hands as the big man tried to fondle Julie.

"She's not for the likes of you, Cutter. This here's a real laidy."

Two more men appeared. "Lookee here, me thinks Freedom's been holdin' out on us."

Julie stepped back, forgetting about the first man who suddenly had his hands on her shoulders, and pulling her back toward him.

"I saw her first," she heard him say before she yanked herself away.

Julie felt faint, her knees weak. *Is lust all men crave? How will I protect myself now?*

Leela made a sudden lunge for Cutter, raking her long nails

along his cheek. Her other arm shot out to grab Julie's arm and then pushed herself in front of her as she faced a pack of dogs in heat.

"Don't touch her or Freedom will have your heads!"

The tallest of the three just laughed. "Well what he don't know, cain't hurt 'im."

He reached for Julie's blanket and yanked it away. "Let's see what she's hiding under here." He was not at all deterred by Julie's swift kick to his shin. "Ah...spirit, that's what we like. A little fight in 'em makes fer a tender piece." He had grabbed her, forcing her arms behind her as the other men guffawed behind him. "How 'bout it little girl? Mayhaps a little pleasurin' is what yer a'needin."

Out of the dark stairwell burst a menacing form as she simultaneously heard a loud crack of a whip. She felt a sting on her ankle as it whizzed by and coiled around the calf of her tormenter. In a flash she was released as the startled man was yanked feet-first across the slippery deck, now prone on his back.

A cutting voice boomed and was steel in its authority.

"I hadn't planned on keelhauling anyone again so soon, but it can be arranged." Slitted eyes glared from one man to the next. "Who's first? You Caulie—Sidney?" His gaze rested back on Cutter. "I think I know who started this. You always seem to be my main troublemaker."

Everything had stilled except the sound of waves splashing against the hull. Finally someone muttered low, "Sorry."

All the while Julie assessed what she knew now to be Captain Freedom. He was quite lean but hard muscled, with long dirty blonde hair down to the top of his shoulders. Wearing tall brown boots to his knees, he had a tan colored balloon sleeved shirt and a scarf around his head with the sash hanging nearly to his waist. No doubt he liked jewelry since there were several gold necklaces and bracelets, and a dozen or so rings on his fingers.

One could call him handsome and he would be one of them.

His gaze raked over her then returned to Leela. "Didn't I tell you to keep a close eye on Miss Sinclair? You're nothing but trouble on this ship, servicing everyone from the first mate to the alley cat we keep in the hold. I've a good mind to let you off in the Bahamas and make you really have to work for it!"

Julie could see Leela's face clearly and was surprised to see tears in her eyes as she cowered back against the rail. She felt a wave of pity flood over her and grabbed her hand and squeezed it in support, and then jumped at the resumption of his raspy voice.

"Take her back to her cabin before she catches something you've got," he spat nastily. "And you rake-hells, get your asses down below and don't let this happen again!" He whirled and was gone.

Leela let out a ragged sigh as they all turned in opposite directions, then offered somewhat of an explanation when the two of them stopped at Julie's door.

"What would he know about a woman? That's the only thing in the world I know him to be afraid of."

•

It was a full week before Julie found out she was sailing with the most notorious bunch of pirates that ever plundered the Caribbean. They had broken into Jerico's warehouse the night she'd been brought aboard and stolen his shipment of poppy seeds. Bit by bit Leela had filled in what had transpired on land, even the killing of the big Haitian who had tried to turn a profit by turning on Jerico.

The little island boy that had paid for Julie's passage with rum had unknowingly led them to the Ladyluck.

The pirates then had stolen aboard and gone through the ship's doctored-up manifest, and upon finding some poppy seeds spilled in the cargo hold, found the warehouse on the island that housed the entire valuable cargo. They had taken all they could load on several skiffs docked at the wharf before cutting them free to float away.

While Julie had sat shivering in the boat before being brought aboard that night, a well-executed plan was being carried out. She hoped Seeka was all right; he had only been trying to help her escape. She also hoped Jerico would not link her escape to his warehouse being broken into; thus possibly traced back to the boy. Maybe he would just think she'd been kidnapped. Either way, she was now in a very precarious situation.

After Leela left, she sat dejected on her bed, taking in what she'd just been told. They were murderers, thieves and cutthroats all. What on earth had she gotten herself into? Scarcely sleeping the rest of the night, she got up twice to make sure her door was securely locked.

After breakfast, Leela clucked at the barely eaten tray of food. She'd barely touched the watery porridge but had eaten all of the dried fruit and drank the bitter coffee.

"You eat like a mouse. The food's been worse."

Julie was quite sure of that. "Your captain must not be too finicky. If he's so strict, why would he let his cook try to poison you all?"

Leela laughed, she seemed to have taken a liking to her after last night on deck. "Cutter ain't been our cook long, he was just commissioned as punishment."

"Some punishment," Julie said dryly, thinking of the crew's suffering instead.

"Yeah," Leela chuckled, her wide smile now making her almost pretty. "An eye for an eye. He killed the cook in a fight so he had to take his place. That's the pirate way."

•

Christmas came and went and there was a lot of rain and wind and even some sleet and hail. Her door stayed bolted at all times and she never ventured out of her cabin again, however, the food did improve somewhat. She guessed Leela had something to do with it.

Between Christmas and New Year's, Freedom sent for her to be brought to his cabin. She refused, which turned out to be a big mistake as he showed up at her door a short while later and demanded she open it. She ignored him and he appeared to leave. Emitting a sigh of relief, she felt a surge of triumph he hadn't pressed the issue.

Suddenly the door crashed open from his raised boot and he left it hanging off its hinges. Now she would have no lock at all. Hands on his hips, he filled the doorway with his height. For the first time, she could see a faint scar that ran parallel along his cheek, giving him a demonic look with his squinted eyes staring hard at her as he moved closer. He stopped a scant foot away.

With an angry toss of his tawny hair, his yellowish cat eyes raked her rudely up and down.

"You dare to refuse me!"

With pretended calm, she returned his question with an equally haughty answer.

"I find tripping around your ship has its drawbacks."

He pondered that a moment before stating, "No one will lay a hand on you against my orders. They tend to forget their manners from time to time, but they know who's boss."

His meaning was clear as his hand tightened on the whip he held at his side.

His amber eyes roamed her face more slowly than he had the last time. The island boy had simply said a 'young lady' and he found himself ill prepared for the young beauty that was even more exquisite than he remembered on deck a few weeks ago.

"Are you comfortable? Leela tells me you don't eat enough to keep a bird alive."

"Leela said mouse." When he said nothing, she went on. "I've no real complaints, the food has improved and I'm sure it's her doing," she said tartly. "I'm just anxious to get to America. Do you have any idea when that will be?"

A multitude of thoughts darted through his brain, mainly that she was surely a rose among thorns. His eyes dropped to her bosom but quickly returned to her face. Her eyebrows were arched as she waited for an answer and she had to strain to hear as he picked up the door and braced it back in place.

"Another month or so. I'll have someone fix this door for your safety." He turned to look at her. "But be advised I am master of this ship, so the next time I send for you don't be foolish enough to think a mere barred door will hinder me in any way."

A shrill whistle sounded above just as Freedom went out the door. He took the steps two at a time while Julie stood in her open door with her shawl clutched around her. With the sounds of running and excited voices and loud scrapes from moving heavy objects, her curiosity got the better of her.

When she reached the top of the companionway she stopped and strained her eyes in the direction everyone seemed to be focused on. A ship on the horizon was moving parallel with them. The Seeker made a hard right turn and headed in a direction in which to intercept. When hands flew all directions, donning their cutlasses and stuffing daggers in their belts, she knew. They would run down the luckless ship and steal their cargo.

Cannons were readied and all hands were jacked with excitement but still Julie didn't move. Only when the first cannon belched out its fiery ball did she move to a safer spot down the quarterdeck.

She felt a strange mixture of fear and morbid excitement, then tripped over a coiled rope and nearly fell. A grimy hand shot out and shoved her aside not bothering to ask if she was okay as she pressed against the wall to get out of his way.

Another roar of cannons from the gunwale and the Seeker shuddered beneath her feet. In thirty minutes they bore down on the merchant ship and the pirates surrounding it in their longboats and quickly commandeered it.

Craning her eyes toward the doomed ship, she could see men running, debris strewn all over the decks. Three gaping holes were evident to the naked eye, and as she stared, she could see the pirates climbing over the rails and brandishing their swords. In a matter of minutes men were spread-eagled on their stomachs on the deck and cargo was being lowered into the skiffs bobbing in the water.

She watched in horror as the pursued ship began to list to the left from the three gaping holes in her side as the water rushed into her hold. Protecting the cargo was forgotten as men abandoned ship and jumped in the water. Sounds of screaming reached her ears. Men were drowning and all the pirates could think of was stealing the cargo.

Captain Freedom was in the last boat that pulled alongside the victorious Seeker and also the last man back on board. Julie waited expectantly for lifelines to be thrown out and was aghast when loud guffaws answered the dying screams filling her ears, sending her senses reeling. She was shaking with horror.

When she couldn't take any more, she rushed to Freedom and launched herself at him. Grabbing his sleeve and ripping it away, she left it hanging from one arm.

She screamed. "You must help them! For God's sake, you have to save them!"

He only laughed, and then he reached for her arm and pulled her to him. "So, the little temptress has a heart after all. Don't worry your pretty little head about those poor souls; they'll be picked up sooner or later. By a passing ship, or a passing shark."

She jerked away and ran to the rail. Freedom was laughing with some of his crew and his callousness burned into her brain. He was mad! She watched for several long horrifying minutes, then the bow of the ill-fated boat turned up to the sky and sank slowly into its watery grave below.

The men's cries slowly grew weaker and she could still see arms waving here and there. She turned again to plead with the captain, but when she looked into his evil eyes, she knew it would be useless. His face was glowing with the glory of his victory and the divine rapture of death.

Jamming her fist in her mouth she fled to the safety of her room.

•

Ten days later the Seeker reached Jamaica. Leela told her they'd dispose of some of their cargo and take on more supplies. She was not very generous with her information, and try as she might, Julie couldn't get her to tell her when she'd be taken ashore.

She wanted off the ship now. She'd find another way on to the states. Chewing on her lip nervously, she paced back and forth on the deck.

When she went back to her cabin to get her things, the first thing she noticed was that her door had been straightened and repaired. When it slammed behind her and was bolted from the outside, the small seed of doubt that he'd really let her go burst into full bloom and she ran screaming to pound on it.

"Let me out! I'm to get off here, you promised! Take me ashore!" The sharp click of boot heels grew fainter and then she was alone.

She pounded for a few more minutes and then fell in a heap on the floor. Clutching her dress to her stomach in fear, she lay in a fetal position trying to assess her situation. He had no intention of letting her go. She was still somebody's prisoner.

A little after dark she felt the ship begin to move slowly. She could hear the whip of the sails catching wind as it picked up speed. Hurrying to the porthole, she could see lights flickering in the distance, growing smaller with each passing minute.

Now what was she to do?

She turned at the sound of the lock sliding and sprang toward it. Strong arms grabbed her and pushed her roughly back in the room.

"You can't keep me on this boat!" she hissed at Freedom. "My fare was paid in full. I can get off wherever I want to and I want to get off here!"

She was livid with anger and made to slap him but he seized her hand instead, snarling at her. "But lady, and I wonder if you really are, you're going to Florida. I will take you there myself."

She stopped struggling and looked skeptically at him. She had so much wanted to leave the ship that she was loath to stay on it even a minute longer. "You might have told me of your plans. Where? In Florida?"

"Key Largo. But first, there are riches untold waiting on the reefs of the Florida Keys. A 'salvage' ship such as this," his sweeping hand indicated the Seeker "can make a fortune by anchoring and watching for the idiotic seamanship that lands a cargo ship on their jagged reefs. When a ship goes aground, we'll be there to salvage their cargo." He laughed wickedly. "For a fee, of course."

Julie swallowed. She knew what that meant. Daine's earlier words now came rushing back. Freedom was known for his materializing out of nowhere to relieve a heavily laden ship of its cargo when it slammed into a reef or ran aground.

She let out her breath slowly, feeling a tiny spark of hope. Florida! When she got ashore she could travel by land to the Mississippi River and then on up to St Louis. She felt her baby move and almost put her hand on her stomach before she remembered.

Jutting out her chin, she forced sugary sweetness. She couldn't leave it alone. "Are you saying you'll let me off the ship once we get to Key Largo?"

He smirked as he reached for her. "If you even want to by then." He bent to kiss her with surprising swiftness. His mouth tasted like rum, and with no response from her, he drew back and looked at her. He crushed her to him again, kissing her even harder. This time she tasted blood before she yanked away.

Undaunted, he swung her around to him again and she had to open her mouth to breathe. Smug in his belief she'd surrendered, he felt her teeth bite into his lower lip and he shoved her away so hard she nearly fell.

"You bitch! Do you think to tease me and then walk away Scot-free?" His eyes were narrowed with anger at his thwarted advances. "Those innocent eyes tell me you need someone to awaken you and not some doddering old fool like Trouchet offering you riches in lieu of a night of pleasure in a real man's bed."

"But Leela, she is in love with you," Julie protested, having known this for some time.

"I've no wish to bed Leela! She's a harlot! Fit to be trysted by ten men a night." He pulled her close again and looked down into her face. "I desire a fresh unpicked bud, not a full bloomed dried up old weed."

With that he reached down and pulled off his boots one at a time as a smile spread across his mouth in a sickening grin. He reached back and locked the door and Julie's stomach knotted up in freshly renewed fear.

He took a step toward her and grabbed her dress when she sidestepped away. With a rip, it was torn from her body while his other hand caught her shift and freed it too with a jerk of his wrist. He swung her around to face him then gasped disbelievingly as he stared down at her rounded belly. He stammered and sputtered before he found his tongue.

"Whose child do you carry?" When she could only quake in fear, he shook her. "Who did this to you?" His face was white; his precious flower had already been plucked. When she still remained mute, he continued, "All right, I can guess. It was Trouchet, right?"

Julie's fear was suddenly gone. Let him think what he will, she now felt certain he would never make love to a woman with child. He was looking at her now in such distaste, she felt almost safe.

"Slut!" he hissed as his fingers dug into her flesh. He was torn between wanting to kiss her again and slapping her senseless. Pushing her away, he sat down and yanked his boots back on, looking at her in disgust when he stood up again. "Maybe I have a precious cargo right here under my nose."

Julie pondered his meaning. Precious cargo? What did he mean by that?

As he went out the door he gave her a clue. "A man would pay plenty to have his woman and his child returned safely to him."

So that was it. He would ransom her to Trouchet in his mistaken belief she was carrying his child. She crept to her bed and climbed in, curling up into a tight ball. Determined not to cry, she stared into the darkness and listened to the clunking sounds in the hold as they slowly journeyed on their way.

At least Trouchet had never forced himself on her. She could almost hope Freedom would carry out his threat.

Chapter Nine

Time went by slowly and it was late January when they reached the southern tip of Florida. They had pilfered three more ships and left over fifty doomed crewmen to die in the treacherous waters of the Florida Keys.

Julie and Leela had struck a fond friendship and she spent nearly all her free time stitching little garments for the baby. She used the dress and shift Freedom had torn off her and Leela brought her some bolts of cloth that had been stolen from one of the ships. She was in dire need and closed her mind as to how she'd come by them.

She took special care and lovingly caressed each one of them, folding them away safely in a drawer. She was now starting into her eighth month and getting quite clumsy. She prayed the baby wouldn't come early, therefore making escape nearly impossible. There was also the journey up the river to her aunt's house still ahead of them.

That evening the Seeker dropped anchors a mile or so from the rocky reefs to sit and wait for treasure and treason. Freedom's plan was to falsely guide green ships onto the rocks and steal their cargo and had already duped the commander of a shipment of French cognac, distilled from wine, as well as a new Dutch brandy, or 'burnt wine', aptly named Brandywijn. These import shipments were coveted outside the U.S. where in turn they exported the always-flavorful bourbon derived from corn, dubbed corn whiskey.

Freedom congratulated himself on keeping the poppy seeds. The dried seeds produced the valuable opium and he had only sold a small portion in Jamaica, knowing he could turn a healthier profit by bribing a loaded ship's crewman with them. He planned on making a killing before they moved on.

Two days after they arrived, Julie was awakened by the loud blast of a ship's horn. Looking out her porthole, she could only see a thick blanket of fog all around them. The horn grew louder and sounded as if it were passing only yards from them. Unbolting her lock, she gingerly climbed the steps and looked on deck to see Freedom and Cutter straining their eyes to peer through the thick mist.

Then, there was a terrible crunching sound and she heard shrieks of delight from the pirate crew as they left the ship to swarm over the wreck, a planned accident for profit.

Footsteps stopped next to her and she turned to see the unreadable face of Leela. Julie stared at her and tried to keep the anger from her voice. "Do you condone what these men are doing?" She was surprised to see her eyes full of sorrow.

"No, I do not. But what can I do? I have no say."

Julie made a sudden decision. "Leela, can you help me get off this ship? I'm afraid I'll never get to my aunt's house before my baby is born. I'm terribly afraid for us both."

Leela looked at her and felt a rush of admiration. This girl had guts and stamina, and even more than that, had proved to be a real friend to her. A half smile played across her lips and she took Julie's small hands in hers. "I'll do what I can but we must be very careful. Freedom will kill us both without batting an eye. Have no doubts about that. He won't be made a fool of."

She knew just the person to help them.

Julie felt a fresh rush of hope. "Thanks, Leela. You've only tried to help me and I've done nothing for you."

"Oh yes you have. You've been a friend when I've had none to brag about. We'll have to wait for just the right moment and then you must escape, perhaps in the fog."

They both turned and gazed solemnly out into the mist.

In less then two hours men were scrambling up the ladders, pulling up crates and boxes and bags of various sizes. One by one they climbed back and forth; most of the cargo carried below and some were stacked along the bulwark. Lastly the dripping longboats were hoisted and tipped upside down, then roped tightly back into place.

There were crude shouts and slaps on backs, and then the

celebrating started. Jugs of ale and the stolen Dutch brandy passed through outstretched hands and passed along rows of slobbering mouths while they all drank their fill. The fiery liquid spilled down their chins and wet their shirt fronts as they partied on in gleeful celebration.

Julie felt sickened by the sight and had turned to leave when Freedom came up behind her and reached for her hand. Turning it palm up, he reached in a bag hanging at his belt, and with a wicked smile emptied his hand in hers. Gold coins spilled heavily into it, some dropping to the deck where they rolled to spinning stops while some simply rolled overboard.

She started to raise her hand to fling them back at him when suddenly her face changed expression to smile back falsely, appearing to have changed her mind. She forced a smile and dropped them in her side pocket and even took the second handful he offered. He watched her face with interest, not sure what to think.

Her mind worked deviously. She needed passage fare and though they were stolen she forced herself to close her mind to it. She prayed for forgiveness then glanced upward as if fearing reprisal. Worried eyes met Leela's, then she pulled her shawl tighter around her shoulders and returned to her cabin.

The partying topside grew louder until they sounded like a group of banshees in unison. Now she could truly see how one human being could kill another. Intense hatred for Freedom and his crew consumed her and far out-shadowed her fear of any danger that could befell her, should her escape be aborted by his discovery.

With single-minded determination she found a small scrap of material and hastily put together a drawstring bag she could hide under her clothing. Taking the precious coins from her pocket, she filled it and hid it under her chemise. There was a soft tap on her door and Freedom's voice asked for entry. She had no choice but to open the door, knowing he would break it down if she refused.

Stooping as he stepped in the door, he tossed his tawny hair back and stared indolently at her. She kept her face impassive and his heart leaped. Could she be losing her fear of him? Maybe jewels and coins were the way to her heart.

Suddenly he pulled her to him and kissed her. He felt repulsed by her large stomach for some inexplicable reason, yet at the same time, he was mad with desire for her. She was stiff in his arms but did not fight him.

It took every ounce of her willpower not to scratch his eyes out. She hated him with a fiery passion and forced herself not to gag, finally twisting away. "Leela is on her way, she's helping me stitch baby garments." She hoped this would deter him but what he said next made clear his true intentions.

"Leela means nothing to me. I have decided not to return you to Trouchet. After you have your child you will share my quarters, as my lover." His voice dropped to a serious tone. "Or if you are too delicate for that, I will marry you." No asking, just a statement of fact. He was quite certain he had finally won her over.

Julie's expression never wavered, but a silent shudder coursed through her. Deep down, she had felt this growing need to escape, and now she knew. He wanted her, she had no other recourse.

He bowed to her arrogantly and left. A half-hour later Leela rapped on her door and was quickly let in. She had a look of excitement on her face as she spoke, "I've found someone to help us. If all goes well, tomorrow night he stands watch and can get you ashore. It's the best he can do."

That soon! Julie hugged her, "Oh thank you, Leela. I owe you so much. I've never had a real friend, you're the first." Tears misted her eyes, but she felt deep relief spread over her.

"Just be careful and take care of your baby. I've never had a close friend either, till you. This is the only life I've known. I had a baby once and it was too big. They had to cut it out and I can't have any more." She bit her bottom lip, hoping she hadn't scared her.

Julie was taken aback, never considering a possibility like that. She swallowed nervously. After Leela left she puttered around her cabin and when night fell she slept restlessly. Images of black eyes and raven hair distorted her thoughts and she once again relived every moment they'd had together.

As if feeling her melancholy, the tiny form in her belly kicked and rolled, gradually claiming her thoughts away from its father.

Most of the next day she paced back and forth in apprehension and dogged weariness. Long before evening she had packed her leather valise with her meager belongings, now joined by the little garments she had so lovingly stitched. The drawstring bag was tucked in its hiding place and with added precaution. She'd pinned it to keep it from jiggling.

*

Well after dark she was still pacing when she heard a slight tap. She listened at the door for a second one, and then doused the whale-oil lamp and opened the door a crack. Leela beckoned and she hurried after her in slippered feet, glad to see the thickening fog.

A dark form stepped out of the darkness near the rope ladder and took her valise, lowering it into a boat below. Next he took her arm and indicated he go first and she stay above him so he could protect her should she fall. She had only a moment to reach up and mouth a thank you to Leela before she turned away.

The man began his descent, reaching up to steady her as she followed. Her cumbersome form made her unsteady and she slipped once on the slippery rope, but his strong arms held on to her. In minutes they were seated in the flat skiff and her secret partner reached for the oars, intent on putting a safe distance between them and the ship before he spoke.

"I'm Buck Lischenski, we've no time to spare. I figure I can be back here in two hours before they miss me. I'm glad to help you but my life will be over if I'm caught. When we get far enough away so that I can light a lantern, you'll write a suicide note that Leela will place in your room. Hopefully they'll think you jumped overboard, and the note won't be found for a day or so."

Taking care not to swamp the low rocking boat, they continued to slowly move away from the dark ship. Reaching behind him for a wool blanket, he handed it to her. The air was chilly and their breath could be seen in the darkness.

"These straits can sometimes get rough but it looks rather calm tonight." He reached in his pocket for a small bag and took a pinch of tobacco between his thumb and forefinger, and placed it between his lower lip and bottom teeth while continuing his chatter. "I know'd when I first seen ya, that ya weren't cut out for this kinda life. Yer too much of a lady. But how did ya get caught up with Trouchet? He's a slick one."

"I was kidnapped. He took me to Martinique where I escaped and that's when Freedom wound up with me He wasn't supposed to keep me prisoner. I paid my fare." She bit her lip, that's all he needed to know.

They were far enough out of sight from the Seeker when he stopped rowing. He lit a lantern and reached in his pocket for paper and a stubby graphite pencil. Julie placed it on the wooden seat and scribbled a short suicide note and handed it back to him.

"Jes' remember, girl. There's lots of swamps and alligators, so be very careful when you get onshore. We're getting close so you jes' head northeast. There's a port about four miles thataway," he said, pointing out the general direction. He started rowing again in the darkness.

Frogs were croaking and crickets were chirping, and every now and then an occasional splash broke the monotonous silence. All of a sudden, she heard a loud noise behind them, then felt a lurch as the boat pitched and she was thrown into the water. She became tangled in the tarp and was quickly sucked under. Her lungs close to bursting for air, she desperately kicked the tarp away and fought her way to the top.

Her head struck something when she broke to the surface. She grabbed at a floating plank, her nose and mouth filling with water. Another wave hit her as she tried to keep her head above the churning sea, and then she was floundering helplessly.

Craning her neck around, she saw the back of a boat and knew she was in its wake. She screamed for Buck but no answer. Holding onto the plank for dear life, she screamed again. All she could see was one oar and no sign of the small boat or Buck. Nor could she tell where the shore was.

With her added weight and cumbersome clothes, she was tiring quickly. She was a fair swimmer, and when she saw a bigger board, she quickly swam to it and hung on. She could only rest part of her weight at a time but its buoyancy was better. She feared for her baby in the ice cold water. She screamed until she was hoarse. She heard a faint shout from a short distance away. Not caring whom it might be, she continued to yell.

A longboat with three men in it came through the mist and she choked out frantically. "Here! Here!"

"My God, it's a woman! Half drowned by the looks of her."

They drew alongside and six arms reached out to haul her in.

"Did you see a man?" she gasped as they drug her inside. She was quickly covered with blankets while her teeth chattering noisily.

"Sorry, we found a body a ways back, looked like he'd been hit in the head by a board or something. It looks like your boat split apart after we hit it. Didn't see ya 'til it were too late." One of the men took up the oars. "Sam heard someone yelling so we came back to look. Lucky for you we did."

Yeah, lucky she thought, but not lucky for Buck. It was her fault he was dead. By their association with her, she had now killed two men. Her belongings, as well as her baby's clothes were all gone. Running her hand along her breasts, she felt the bag still intact. She sobbed quietly as they headed for a large boat. Once they were alongside, she was carefully hoisted on board in a flimsy rope chair of sorts.

She was carried down a long passageway and soon they opened the door to a comfortable and very warm cabin. A small oriental man followed them in the door, handing her a large cotton robe. "Put thees' on 'til we find clothes fo' you, I bring you some'ting eat."

"I must speak to your captain at once! You're all in extreme danger."

They all looked at each other in confusion, and then one took off and quickly returned with a pock-faced man with thick graying hair. "I'm captain Tally. How is this boat in danger?"

Still shaking, she managed a smile. "Do you know of Captain Freedom, or the Seeker?"

At his stunned looked, she continued, "I can see you have. His ship is anchored off the reef and I believe he's changed the markers. He waits for ships to wreck and steals their cargo. He even bribes men to ditch their ships, after trading them goods such as opium and cognac."

His eyes narrowed in speculation. "Why should I believe this? Are you from the Seeker?"

"Yes, I was kept aboard against my will. I was escaping when your ship ran us down."

"I'm sorry for that, it was a very unfortunate accident. Thankfully one of my crew heard your screams."

"Thank you for saving me, but you must not proceed."

Her story sounded authentic enough and he was grateful for the news Freedom was in the area. He could lose nothing but time by checking it out. He was quick to act.

"I'll send a boat on ahead to check out the reef. In the meantime, you're quite safe here. Get out of those wet things and into that robe and I'll have someone round up some clean clothes for you to wear tomorrow. I don't know how good they'll fit."

She was in her robe by the time hot tea and small teacakes with honey arrived. Another forty-five minutes and there was a sharp rap on her door. The sober-faced captain stepped in, pulling off his cap and slapping it against his leg.

"Your story is true. My men discovered the channel markers changed and two wrecked ships. We're changing course back to Key Largo where it will be reported to the authorities. Myself and my crew owe you our very humble thanks. You no doubt saved some lives, and our boat."

She gave him a dazzling smile. "I'll get off at Key Largo. I'm going to the United States and thanks again for rescuing me."

He was staring at her oddly, and then caught himself. "Please forgive me but I just noticed you are with child. Where are you going in the states?"

"I'm going to St Louis."

With a wide smile, he stated. "But my dear... you are lucky twice tonight. We can deliver you within six days journey. We are bound for New Orleans."

Chapter Ten

New Orleans
March 25, 1851

Spanish explorers led by Hernando de Soto first discovered the Louisiana territory in their relentless quest for gold. When they found none they moved on. In 1682, LaSalle, the noted French explorer, sailed down the Mississippi River and claimed the large region around it for France. Eighteen years later a group of Frenchmen established Fort Iberville, the first settlement in Louisiana, but finally gave the territory back to Spain.

The French people living in Louisiana did not like Spanish rule and balked, but the Spanish sternly put down the rebellion. Spain eventually grew weaker and Napoleon Bonaparte, then ruler of France, forced Spain to return it to France in 1800. His dream was to build a great French Colonial empire that would bring France huge sums of money and goods, but his plan failed. Three years later he sold the vast territory to the United States, the end of the yo-yoing parcel, hence becoming known as the famous Louisiana Purchase.

Louisiana joined statehood in 1812 and soon became the fasting growing state in the union. It was abundant in raising cotton, rice, tobacco and sugar cane along with the sea's uncharted frontier of shrimp, oysters, lobster and untold fish species. Lumber was booming. Oak, hickory, gum trees and short leaf pine were processed locally and exported abroad, and also shipped upriver to booming towns rising along the shores of the Mississippi.

The farming regions of the south and eastern part of the state were low and flat and dikes and levees were constantly being built to protect cities and farmlands from the often-rising Mississippi and the ever-unpredictable Gulf of Mexico. Lakes and marshes were known as bayous, which produced an endless supply of muskrat furs, coypu, raccoons, mink, opossum and alligators.

Along the waterfront of New Orleans, where the Mississippi flowed into the gulf, was the oldest section of the city, known as the French Quarter. Inhabited mostly by the Spanish and French settlers interbreeding and forming the 'Creole' race, they were a proud people and commanded the highest rank in society. The intermixture created a unique race with generally handsome men and women. Another interesting group was the Arcadians, Cajuns, whose French ancestors fled from Nova Scotia also to settle in Louisiana.

•

The crossing through the gulf had been very rough on Julie. The big cargo ship had encountered another hurricane, not unlike the one she'd endured on the Hornet. She had spent the greater part of the trip in her cabin and had lost an alarming amount of weight. Pale as a ghost, she looked like she had transparent skin and was generally listless and often dizzy.

They reached New Orleans at last in mid March. Julie made a supreme effort to be out on deck where she waited to be taken ashore. The harbor was a beehive of activity and the smells of rotting fish and oil made her queasy.

She couldn't hide the disappointment she felt when she searched the boats lined up for the distinct figurehead and black decks amongst the ships lined down the waterfront. The Hornet had probably been here and gone again. A British frigate was under guard while anchored near a long warehouse and she heard the crew talking about tensions growing in the Far East.

Pelicans circled the new arrivals in hopes of a few tidbits tossed their way. When the neighboring ship dumped a bucket of fish entrails overboard, they spread their wings and dove straight as an arrow into the water and then became airborne again, their pouches overflowing.

A shaky sigh escaped her. She was glad to finally be on firm ground again.

The air had now filled with even more smells. Putrid fish, wet rotting wood, stinking garbage and thick acrid smoke joined the earlier kerosene soaked ties and planks on the wharf she'd already encountered.

She followed the winding trail of smoke snaking through the hazy sky with her eyes, and then continued down the tail as it narrowed into the high smokestack of a sawmill near the wharf.

Tears sprang to her eyes and she hastily rubbed them in an effort to clear her vision. Blinking rapidly, her eyes again focused on the flatboat anchored in the water below the building. The big block letters leaped out at her again. Challenger Mills! She read the words again and again. It had to be! Daine had mentioned owning a sawmill.

She continued to watch as men bustled around the mill where piles of logs spilled into a large holding pond ready to be seasoned, then dried and finally cut to specifications in the mill.

With her knees growing weak, she headed back to her cabin to wait for the ship to dock.

Her entire wardrobe consisted of a dyed flour sack sewn by hand and she was wearing it. On her small feet, she sported handmade Indian-like moccasins, sans the beads. The thin dress was stretched tight over her ungainly figure and was oil spotted and sadly woebegone. She still wore the bag of coins concealed close to her bosom in its frayed drawstring bag.

Twice during the trip through the gulf, she had approached captain Tally and tried to pay him for her passage. He had twice refused, telling her to save her money for passage up the river and to buy herself some new clothes once she reached New Orleans. They had already said their goodbyes.

With a last look around her and feeling a strange kind of dread to leave this safe haven she had come to know, she opened the door and left another home.

◆

Her mind was trying to put in order the things she must do as she was rowed ashore. First, she would get a room for the night then send someone out to purchase her some clothes since she dared not venture out in such a sad state. Then, before she left for Missouri, she'd go to the mill and talk to someone from the Challenger family.

They had a right to know about the baby she was carrying. She wanted nothing from them other than the right for her baby to bear his or her father's name. She owed Daine and her child that.

So it was with her mind wandering, she missed a step and stumbled, falling clumsily to the gangplank. She heard a jingle and felt cold metal sliding across her flesh, and then heard clinks in the water below. Her hand flew to her bosom but she already knew her coins were gone.

A crewman ahead of her turned back and knelt down beside her, concern on his weathered face. "Are ya okay, Missy? Did ya jar the wee one?"

She was still looking down into the oily water with utter devastation. How would she pay for her passage now? How could she buy clothes, or a place to stay?

She didn't say a word, only shook her head as he helped lift her to her feet. His voice seemed a long way off as she struggled to find her balance. Her body flushed hot, then cold, and then back to hot. From out of nowhere, she whispered, "Challenger."

Two other people had joined them, one a woman who quickly grasped the situation. She grabbed the arm of the man with her and pointed to the mill. "Hurry, go get Mr. Challenger."

He took off in a fast walk.

Julie's eyelids closed, if they would only let her sleep. A cool cloth was pressed to her forehead and they helped her to a bench onshore. She was soon shaken back awake and she looked into familiar looking eyes. This was impossible. She must be dreaming!

"Daine. But you're … dead!"

She fought hard to keep her eyes open. He was so young! Why was he so young?

Then she sank into black nothingness.

•

She was dimly aware of a swift buggy ride, and then being carried up a flight of stairs. When she opened her eyes again she was lying in a large feather bed her body engulfed in searing pain. Black faces with huge staring eyes and glittering white teeth floated about the room and she searched among them for a familiar face.

No, it wasn't possible. This was all just a ghastly dream. Some sort of nightmare and she would waken soon and laugh. Laugh? She jammed her fist to her mouth and the laughing suddenly stopped.

Pain shot through her again and she clenched her teeth before she had removed her tongue. She heard a woman scream and it seemed close. Trying to raise up, she felt a warm stickiness between her legs and her gown was yanked off over her head.

The door opened a crack and towels were handed in to a large black woman who seemed to be the one in control. She heard her throw out orders to someone on the other side, "Cain't come in yet. She's nekkid."

The footsteps moved away and Julie sank back down again. Now maybe they'd let her sleep. But it wasn't long before knifelike spasms gripped her taut belly again and the sheet was thrown back as the dark face floated back in view again.

"C'mon honey, let Fannie help's ya. That baby's on it's way, ain't nuthin' gonna stop it."

She went to the door again and yanked it open and hollered, "Whar's dat docta'?" Slamming it shut again, she returned, mumbling all the way. "Masta say he done sent fo'ah de docta— nev'ah could d'pend on dose white folk's city doctas. "

The round black face loomed over her again with a wide friendly smile. Julie relaxed her hold on the blanket before the robust woman threw it back, reached down and crooked an arm under Julie's legs and bent them up where her feet rested flat on the bed. She then parted her knees for a closer view.

"I kin see de' crown 'a de' baby's haid, won't be long," Fannie grunted. Julie felt her stomach knot into another tight ball, and then she reached up to grip the woman's arm as a sharp pain gripped her again. The large woman soothed the frightened girl. "Take's a deep breath honey, 'n don't push yet."

The painful spasm was over and Julie relaxed, but on the heels of that, another soon followed. She was totally wet with perspiration but felt no embarrassment in her nakedness as she grasped the polished dowels in the oak headboard behind her head, bearing down hard even though she tried not to.

"Pant like a puppy, dis baby ain't waitin' fo'ah no docta'. Now push when I tells ya,"

Fannie huffed. "Push!" One last never-ending pain and she felt release as the baby was expelled.

Holding her breath a moment, she leaned up on an elbow and peering over the black woman's shoulder.

"Is it okay? I don't hear anything."

A loud smack and the sudden sound of a lusty wail filled the room and a squirming wet baby was laid on a towel next to her.

"Got's a little talleywacker. You got's a boy. Yes'm, that's fo'ah shore."

Julie's eyes had misted over and she blinked rapidly to clear them, all the time looking into the tiny face of her son. "He's beautiful—and so tiny," she marveled, crooking her little finger into a tiny fist pawing the air.

A young black girl burst in the room. "Masta say the docta' comin' up de road!"

'S'pose now he gonna take all de credit for birthin' this young'un," Fannie chortled, fluffing Julie's pillow. She returned to wiping the baby.

Minutes later an elderly man with a satchel, a big paunch and a kindly face came in and took a quick look at the baby, and then smiled down at Julie. He then handed him to Fannie and began to examine Julie. "Looks like a healthy baby boy and you both came through it just fine. You're quite skinny, I don't know if you can nurse your baby or not. Guess we'll just have to wait and see."

When her eyes kept closing he motioned Fannie out, whispering to her, "She looks exhausted, she needs to rest."

Fannie had already been told to bring the baby to the library when it arrived. Darold, Dayna and the old matriarch were waiting anxiously, all rising when she came in and closed the door behind her.

While they all peered quietly at the baby, Fannie searched their faces for a sign what this was all about but it was not her place to ask. This looked to be quite personal. After several minutes of close inspection, she was told to return the baby back upstairs.

Julie slept for three hours and was awakened by the sound of a baby crying. Her eyes flew open and she rose off her pillow to see Fannie sitting in a chair by the window holding the baby. Seeing Julie awake, she lumbered to her feet and shuffled across the room and laid the baby in her arms.

Tiny fists waved and the small face nuzzled the side of her arm, the little birdlike mouth suckling against her bare skin. She rolled to her side and drew the little face to her breast. Still naked, she had somehow lost all modesty. Grimacing in pain as the tiny mouth rooted and found her tender nipple, a rush of exquisite joy quickly washed over her. This was her baby, hers and Daine's.

The tears that suddenly spilled down the cheeks of this strange young woman moved Fannie. Was she not happy? Who was she? But the strangest thing of all, why was she in the master's bed? Her black face turned thoughtful as she picked up the big pile of dirty sheets on the floor. She was going down to bring a tray up for this girl who had no name. They both fell silent while the baby nursed then fell asleep.

"Where am I?" Julie finally asked.

"This heah's the Challenger plantation, Masta' Darold done brung 'ya here."

Julie's head reeled. How? Why can't I remember?

Memories of the mill and falling as she left the ship, all came rushing back. She heard a tap, made sure she was covered, then said, "Come in." The door opened to a dark-haired man in his late twenties and her heart skipped as she recognized the vivid family resemblance. He was shorter than his older brother and his face looked drawn and haggard as he motioned Fannie to leave, her slippers slapping against the soles of her bare feet as she went out the door.

The man walked to the bed and looked down at her. Even with her hair in wild disarray, she was a beauty even though her green eyes were wide with fear. She was afraid of him? He tried to smile but his face felt frozen. Finding his voice, he asked, more sharply then he intended, "Welcome to Fair Winds. Now tell me who you are and what you know of my brother."

It took a second to gather her thoughts. "I'm Julie Sinclair and I knew Daine Challenger. We met in Crete."

"Where is he and where is the Hornet? He should have returned in November."

She couldn't hide the shock on her face. He didn't know! But, where was the Hornet? Swallowing hard, she brushed the back of her hand across her nose where it still dripped from her tears. "I thought you must have known by now. Your brother's dead."

He sat down heavily on the side of the bed, pulling the blanket away from her when it sagged with his weight.

She grabbed for it and caught it before her nakedness was revealed.

He blushed at his carelessness—he'd been astounded by the clothes she had been wearing when he'd carried her upstairs.

He made no move to get up. "That's what you said at the dock. Tell me what happened."

"We had to return to the Azores Islands for repairs after a bad hurricane, when a man he'd had to put ashore shot him. He was killed trying to keep him from kidnapping me. I'm so very sorry, Darold. He loved you and your sister and mother very much."

His pained eyes locked on hers. "He fathered your child, didn't he?" He already knew but he wanted to hear it from her.

Dropping her eyes in embarrassment, she nodded, "He didn't know, and I didn't know until much later. The Hornet was still docked the last time I saw it."

Rising to his feet, he managed a weak smile. "The important thing right now is for you to get some rest, and then we can sit down and talk some more. We'll try to figure out why the ship or the crew hasn't returned and what they did ..." he stopped himself from going there, now wasn't the time. "I'll have my sister get some clothes together for you, she looks to be about your size. I need to go break the news to them, it won't be easy."

"I know," Julie murmured, "I'm so very sorry and I don't want to be a bother to your family. If you'll just help me get to my aunt's in St Louis, I know she'll reimburse you." She hated having to be beholden to anyone.

Darold only held up his hand to silence her. "You're certainly no bother. I speak for my family when I say we're sorry for all that you've endured making your way here. We'll talk about it later." Then he left her alone.

After he stepped out in the hall, closing the door softly behind him, he reflected a moment on the girl. He believed her story since he'd already examined his nephew. He was the spitting image of his father, and she had known too much about his family.

In the wild buggy ride home, she had cried out Daine's name over and over. The old seaman who had been with her when she fell had stated she'd disembarked alone from his ship and had been plucked from the Florida Keys. That was all he knew about her.

But where was the Hornet and her crew? It had been more than a year since it had been in Italy on its return trip, and surely word would have reached them by now. Bracing himself for the meeting with his mother and sister, a sudden thought struck him. With his mother's frail health he'd simply tell her that Daine had perished in a hurricane and fill in his inquisitive sister Dayna later. He'd return to her room and ask Julie to go along with him when he had finished.

His mother and sister were still in the library. Pulling up a chair, he set it down in front of them. Their eyes were both fearful and it quickly became a tremendous effort to speak. Dayna read his look and nervously sloshed her coffee onto her lap. Then he swallowed hard and looked from one face to the other.

"It seems we have bad news. The Hornet went down in a hurricane and all were lost." He had emphasized *all*.

Dayna gasped and dissolved in a flood of tears while his mother simply closed her eyes and hung her head, her lips mouthing a silent prayer. He quickly squatted down in front of her, taking her frail birdlike hands in his.

When she finished her prayer, she raised her eyes to his. "How is the girl? Who is she and where did she meet him?"

"She'll be all right, she's very weak and very undernourished. Her name is Julie Sinclair and they met in Crete. She traveled here on another boat and we all know the child is Daine's." He reached for Dayna's hand and squeezed it. "Let's not question her until she's a little stronger."

Dayna indicated she was going to the kitchen to have them hold dinner a little longer.

When the servants saw her red face they spoke in whispers, knowing it had something to do with the frail girl upstairs. She ordered another tray be sent up with lots of fresh milk to be coaxed down her.

After Darold had left Julie lay staring around the beautifully furnished room. The wooden floor gleamed from many coats of beeswax and on the east wall a cheery fire was burning in a stone hearth. Thick green velvet draperies were pulled away from the large window where she could see tall trees swaying in the light breeze, their leaves only having recently budded out. The walls were papered with decorative flowers and the bed and dressers a rich polished mahogany. Double doors opened onto a terrace. The four-poster she laid in had a delicately scrolled headboard and two wing-backed leather chairs were placed on either side of the fireplace. It was definitely a man's room.

A sudden thought struck her that this was Daine's room. On the dresser, probably just like he'd left them, was a pewter of shaving cream and a straight razor. She blinked back hot tears. *Am I to see him everywhere I turn?*

The doorknob turned and Fannie entered with a steaming tray of baked chicken, mashed potatoes and gravy, vanilla pudding and a pitcher of milk. A young black girl followed behind her, giving Julie a timid smile.

"This heah's Soonie, she be heppin' ya. Masta Darold say so." The girl was already fussing over her, setting up the tray and cooing at the baby. Julie felt ill at ease, she didn't know what her role was. They were all extremely kind to her but she was self-conscious around so many strangers, her mind was already on how long she'd have to stay before she could go on to her aunt's. She hoped just a week or so.

Leaving his mother and sister to comfort each other, Darold climbed the stairs back up to his brother's room. He wished he could cry just to relieve the tight hurting ball in his chest, but he knew of a better way. After everyone was settled in for the night, he planned on getting roaring drunk. There was nothing like a few belts of strong Irish whiskey to knock one on one's ass, thus rendering their thinking blessedly incapacitated.

Julie had just finished eating and was nursing the baby when Darold knocked and Fannie let him in. He smiled at her when she quickly pulled the sheet up to her chin to cover herself.

"We must see to your privacy immediately. Sorry, I've been lax," he offered. He then asked Soonie and Frannie to leave until he sent for them; Frannie picked up the baby and took him with her. "I must ask a favor of you. I would like for you to go along with my story. I've told my mother and sister that the Hornet and the crew perished during the hurricane you spoke of, close to fact but much easier for them to bear."

She understood. "I'll tell them the same thing, t'would be a kinder truth."

Her green eyes were enchanting and he could see why his brother had been taken with her. "My mother can't make the stairs but my sister is champing at the bit to meet you. She'd like to come up right away, and when you're up to it, you can go downstairs and meet our mother."

Julie told him to send his sister up, and after he left, she lay back on the big fluffy pillows and tried to make herself presentable. She had become so used to the constant pitching and rolling of being on a ship that it was hard to get used to a solid floor.

The door suddenly opened as a dark haired girl who looked almost identical to her twin brother stepped in. She was holding a blue cotton nightgown, fresh sheets and several white fluffy towels.

"I'm Dayna and I'm quite positive you'll want a bath," she smiled, as her eyes took in the frail girl in the bed. She was much younger than she'd pictured since she'd only barely seen her when she was rushed so quickly up the stairs. "Your water is being readied and Soonie will help me change your sheets while you're gone." She set the sheets down in a chair. "Tomorrow we'll find you some of my clothes and we'll send for a seamstress to come fit you for new ones."

Julie was embarrassed. "Don't go to all that trouble, I can make do with just a couple of things."

Dayna felt her self-consciousness. "I've got plenty of clothes and there's scads of baby clothes, so don't pay no never'mind." She moved closer to the bed, assessing her. "You sure are little, you must weigh ninety pounds wringing wet. Did they tell you the baby is five and a half pounds?" She rambled on. "Have you a name for him? Where are you from and how did you meet my brother?"

Suddenly at ease with the friendly girl, Julie reached out and lightly touched her arm. "Hold it, I can't think that fast. The answers are no, no, Crete and Crete."

Dayna laughed, realizing now how she'd sounded. "They sometimes call me jabber-jaws. They say I didn't talk until I was three and I would say I haven't stopped since."

Julie haltingly told her the agreed upon story of how she had been kidnapped and the Hornet sailing into a raging hurricane. Hating to lie, she kept it short. They both were crying before she was through.

They were already fast friends by the time Julie bathed and returned to nurse the baby all the while answering more of Dayna's questions, even asking some of her own. When it was time for bed, Julie drifted off right away while Soonie and the baby bedded down in the room next to hers.

Bright and early the next morning, Dayna brought in a couple of dresses and some fresh underthings. They were close to the same build, although Julie was much thinner and Dayna was three inches taller. There was also a pair of soft-soled shoes, a hairbrush and several personal hygiene items. She'd thought of everything.

"I sent one of our people into town to get a clothier here as soon as possible to fit you for a new wardrobe."

Julie was shocked. "I can't accept all these things from your family! I'm going to leave as soon as the baby's able to travel, so I can find my aunt."

Dayna didn't bat an eye. "Hush, we'll talk about that later. Right now, we'll concentrate on your getting your strength back, and the baby's too little to travel anyway."

Julie felt a rush of uneasiness but let it pass.

Dayna spent the rest of the morning running in and out of Julie's room making sure she had everything she needed. Julie was a little steadier on her feet and no longer needed to be helped to the privy, a small private room that held a commode and a large brass tub for bathing and a dressing room of sorts. It was the first time she'd ever seen a room expressly for this purpose.

The baby began to fuss a lot and took up most of Julie's attention the rest of the day. Two more days passed with little variation. He was cranky and wore them all out holding him and alternately rocking him.

Late in the afternoon of the fifth day Darold returned from town. After checking on his mother first he went up to Julie's room. She was rocking the baby and wore a flowered dress, her hair curled loosely around her shoulders. Her natural beauty was startling and she finally had some color in her cheeks.

"Are you feeling well enough to come downstairs and meet my mother?" he asked. She felt a rush of panic and it showed. Cupping her shoulders with both hands, and knowing the reason for her hesitation, he went on, "It's time she met you. She's been quite anxious."

Dropping her chin, she relaxed. "Yes, I'm ready. No doubt she has questions for her son's ..." She looked up into his face, not knowing how to finish it.

He reached for her hand, leading her down the corridor to the stairs.

"How about the mother of her grandchild?"

Chapter Eleven

Descending the long curved marble staircase for the first time, Julie was awed at the splendor she saw around her. Crystal prisms hung from the huge chandelier catching beams from the afternoon sun, and tinkling softly as they struck against one another.

She could see her reflection in the highly polished floor in the main hallway as she walked behind Darold. Opening two large double doors into a large library, she could see rows upon rows of books on neatly arranged shelves. Timidly slowing her pace, she saw a frail figure seated in a reclining chair covered with a blanket, even though she was seated in front of a large working fireplace.

She looked up at two large portraits on either side of the mantle, acknowledging where the family's looks had originated. Eyes black as coal looked down at her from the male counterpart, then on to the quiet beauty of the original matriarch. She was drawn back to the woman seated before her. For what seemed minutes they stared quietly at one another, then a small shaking hand covered with brown age spots slowly reached for hers.

Extending her own without hesitation, she was surprised at the firm grasp as she clasped the thin bony fingers. The smile that met hers was very warm.

"My son always had an eye for beauty. A trifle skinny I see, but hearing some of the horrors you've been through, it's quite understandable." She motioned for them both to sit. Julie sat right down but Darold went over to the sideboard and poured himself a drink of bourbon. He then returned to pull up a chair near them.

Julie was already deep in conversation with his mother, relating the same facts she had told Dayna. When she'd finished, Darold cleared his throat and asked, "Julie, have you picked out a name for your son?"

"I thought perhaps a combination of my father, and his father. Nicholas Daine Sinclair, we weren't ..." her face reddened at the new direction this had taken.

Darold reached in his side pocket for a document he'd had prepared, handing it to her. "Why don't we change it around a bit and call him Nicholas Daine Challenger?"

She stared from one to the other. "But I have no right ..." She skimmed down the document seeing blanks for the first and middle, then followed by Challenger.

"You have every right, my dear," Darold's mother said. "A mere formality and you will be introduced as Mrs. Daine Challenger. You must think of his child. He wouldn't want his son labeled a bastard." Julie noticeably reddened at the word. "The Challenger name must be carried on and only your child can do it for certain at this juncture."

She looked over at Darold who smiled at them grimly, then borrowed his nephew's mother's brogue. "Since I have no prospects in sight, 'tis your duty."

"You can accept my story so easily? How can you know for certain I haven't concocted this story just to get some of this?" Her hand swept around the room.

"Your son has the same French Creole features. But most revealing, he has the same birthmark on his shoulder that all Damien's offspring have, except for Dayna. She was overlooked. But she raises no doubts, since she is a twin."

It took only her signature to give her son a name and herself a husband by proxy. The dates had been changed accordingly and Daine's signature forged by the family's trusted lawyer only this morning. She faltered a moment when Darold slipped a plain gold band on her finger. Her eyes were misty when she kissed her new mother-in-law's cheek and graciously accepted a small goblet of wine for a toast.

Before she left the library to return to her room, she was invited to begin taking her meals with the family downstairs. When she got back to her room, the baby was still fussing in the room next door where he'd been the last three nights with Soonie. She picked him up and carried him back to her room.

He was especially cranky and nursed hungrily, and then refused her altogether. No amount of coaxing could get him to suckle. By late afternoon, Julie's nerves were frazzled and shortly after dinner Soonie brought a young golden-skinned mulatto girl into her room. She stood there fidgeting, her bare feet dirty while she sniveled quietly.

"Miz Julie, yoah so thin 'n woah down, they's no nurish'ment in yoah milk. Fannie sent up Hallie, she jest lost her young'un, n' got's lot's a'milk. She kin wetnurse yer'n."

Julie looked at Soonie dumbly. Fannie had correctly guessed her watery milk held no substance for the baby and she acknowledged the old Negro woman knew what she was doing. The baby's wailing went up another notch. Feeling inadequate and frustrated, she handed the baby to the young girl and they all followed after Soonie into the next room.

Fannie arrived and followed after them with a wet towel and basin to wash Hallie the best she could. Hallie then took the baby and in moments the crying stopped and she could hear the baby sucking noisily. When he was done, she took him and returned to her room where she changed his diaper. Her eyes were drawn to the birthmark she had somehow overlooked.

When the baby slept for six hours straight, she knew that her nursing him was over.

The next day the clothier arrived. She was a hefty blonde woman with a strong German accent. Bustling around with a tape measure, she spun Julie around and around until she was dizzy, then poking pins and needles and jotting down measurements all the while talking nonstop.

"And to think Daine Challenger had a wife and a baby all this time, n' nobody knew it," she said, then expressed her sympathy, "Too bad what happened to him n' his crew. He used to set heart's a'twitterin' in this town. Many a girl around here set their caps for him. There was one ..." She caught herself and changed the subject. For the next two hours she talked incessantly while Julie had no choice but to listen.

Her new clothes arrived three days later and soon one day blended into the next.

After she'd been there for three weeks, she finally ventured outside. The house had a veranda on three sides with several tall white pillars across the front. A large sloped lawn reached down to the river with carefully tended flowers, vegetable gardens—all recently tilled and expertly planted.

Huge magnolia trees were in full bloom and Spanish moss hung like white spider webs from their many branches and she could see a large mounded underground cellar. To the east, there were several rows of small-whitewashed cabins.

Dayna had suddenly caught up with her. "Do you like to ride horses? I forgot to ask."

"I do, but I'm afraid I might need some practice. I rode some on Crete, but it was just an old plowhorse," she laughed. "But she did have beautiful big brown eyes."

Dayna grinned. "We've lots of horses here and Darold said he'll pick you out a mount when you decide to ride. He doesn't want you getting hurt. Now that he's head of the family, he's got lots of responsibilities." She saw a look of sadness flicker on Julie's face, then it was gone.

Seeing her looking at the rows of cabins and children playing in the dirt, Dayna said, "Those are the slave cabins. Most of the adults are out in the fields planting corn and potatoes, some are hoeing cotton and others work the sugar cane." Some of the children had moved closer, seemingly fascinated with Julie's red hair. She had never seen so many black faces.

"Do all of them work for you?"

"Of course, they're slaves. They're ours." Dayna looked puzzled.

"You mean you actually own them?" She had heard astonishing tales of white men owning black men to work their fields and care for their fine houses but had thought at the time some might have been stretching the truth.

Dayna laughed at her naivete. "Yes, silly. My grandfather bought or traded for them."

"Traded what?" she asked.

"He traded slaves for slaves, or traded goods or else bought them outright at auctions."

Julie was aghast, how could one human being own another? Horror gripped her. Owning them meant they could buy or sell them at will. Maybe sell their babies and break up family members if they wanted to?

Dayna's eyebrows shot up, seeing the stricken look on Julie's face. "They have a good life here. Most are happy and they're not mistreated. There are a few troublemakers but they usually wind up getting sold. The rest have roofs over their heads and food in their bellies. We make sure a doctor checks them all out regular. Everyone in the south has at least one slave, that's just the way it is."

Julie was silent a long moment, pondering what she'd said. *Just the way it is?* Her mind ran rampant. *Sold to the highest bidder? Men, women, and children alike?* She looked around at the children playing and running around barefoot and seeming quite carefree. They all looked happy and content.

They were now moving slowly back toward the house but her mind was still in a quandary. This was all very foreign to her. She'd heard about slavery, surely no one she had ever known had owned any.

When she got back upstairs, she looked in the next room to see her baby nursing. She went back and lay down on her bed to think. Fear gripped her; she had no control over her own baby, just like these negras. Just as soon as her baby was able to drink from a cup, and they could travel, they would leave. But she was trapped here for the time being. Her milk had mostly dried up and she had no money for passage up the river. The best thing for her to do was to stay on guard and watch Nickie, as everyone now referred to him

Later, dressing for dinner, Julie studied herself in the mirror. Her arms were still much too thin but she had lost the dark shadows under her eyes and the rest of her skin showed more color. Her damp hair from her bath was pulled back and caught with purple ribbons to match the lavender and white sundress she wore. Peeking in on her now sleeping son and a napping Soonie, she went downstairs.

Dayna was sitting on the bottom step waiting for her. Julie joined her.

"Do you do a lot of entertaining here?" Julie asked.

"Oh yes, and very soon we hope to have a ball to introduce you to our friends. This room is mostly where the women gather. The men congregate in the library where they talk and rant endlessly about politics. The main foyer is cleared out for dancing." Pointing to the balcony curving both ways from the top of the stairs, she couldn't contain her excitement. "The orchestra sits up there above the dancers. We must plan it soon. There are so many people we want you to meet!"

A horse galloped up and stopped outside the front door, then was led away. Darold swept into the room, tossing his hat on the nearest chair and ceremoniously removing his jacket. He looked at the two faces pointed in his direction then crossed unsteadily to a recessed cabinet and removed a corked bottle and three glasses.

"Drunk as a lord," Dayna whispered.

"Yes I am," he grinned, obviously having heard her. "And I intend to get a whole lot drunker." He handed each girl a glass and poured them all some red wine, nearly spilling it.

Dayna read his mood. "Darold, I was just telling Julie that we must have a ball. When she's stronger of course."

He dove into it with both feet. "By all means, let's have a ball." He snickered then pulled up a hassock and seated himself on the floor in front the girls. Loosening his collar, he grinned, the action taking Julie's breath away. He looked so much like her husband. Just thinking of Daine as her husband made her dizzy.

"Julie, Dayna, I want you both to know I've sent out messages to ports looking for the Hornet and the crew." Julie looked at Dayna, who didn't seem surprised.

She looked back at Julie. "Darold told me what happened, we just haven't told mother. I don't think her poor old heart could take it."

Little by little Julie filled in the blanks and answered their questions, telling them everything but the first time she'd met Daine. She had forgiven him long ago and it was just between them. She felt a growing family connection, yet she knew she still needed to leave when she and the baby were able. She wanted to make her own way.

After Darold left them, saying he had work to do, Dayna saw Julie frowning. "Darold will be all right. He finds running the family business harder than Daine ever did. I keep the books for the house and crops, but the shipping has been at a standstill, and Darold runs the mill. I hope he's not taking on too much. This is the first time I've seen him tipsy in a while."

Julie was curious. "Daine seemed to have something bothering him at first but gradually his personality improved. He wasn't so … sullen and cross."

"I know. Something happened before Daine left to sea. He stayed drunk for a week. Nobody could get anything out of him."

When Julie got back to her room later, the baby was still awake. She excused Hallie to go get some fresh air and rocked her son, marveling again how much he looked like his father. The old familiar lump in her chest was painful knowing they'd never know each other. His tiny fist bopped her chin and she kissed the top of his fuzzy head, her heart swelling with love.

After he left her to nurse, she stared out the window. She acquiesced she would likely run into opposition with leaving but an unreasonable fear still gripped her. What kind of fear she knew not, but it was always there, lurking in the background. One day blended into another.

•

The tenth of June was a Sunday and Darold surprised her at the breakfast table.

"Why don't you come riding with me this morning?"

"Okay. But I'm a real greenhorn. You'd best pick a tame one out for me."

With her promise to meet him in the stables in an hour, she returned to her room to find Hallie just getting up. Nickie was cooing and making smacking sounds. She hadn't heard him cry in quite some time and he seemed quite contented now.

She hadn't worn her new riding habit yet. It was forest green velvet with black silk frogs cinching the jacket snugly down the front, a stylish two-piece with the long skirt sewed together between the legs.

Studying her reflection before the mirror as she worked the frogs in place, she noted in the two and a half months since she'd had the baby, she'd filled out nicely. Sitting down on the edge of the bed, she pulled on her brown lace-up riding boots, and then stood to plunge her feet in place. There was also a small brimmed green velvet-riding hat she pinned in place on one side of her head.

Ten minutes later she strolled into the stable. She spied Darold standing in front of a wood gate. She walked up and looked past him into the stall. A beautiful black horse was in the corner tossing its head, snorting its agitation and restlessly pawing the straw.

"He hates to be pinned up, but he'd just run himself to death. We only turn him loose once a week and that's about it. He can't be ridden." Darold turned, looking her up and down. "You look fantastic. Green is a good color for you."

She blushed self-consciously before turning her attention back to the horse. "Isn't he broke?"

"Yes, he's Daine's horse, Sultan. He raised him from a colt and he won't let anyone else on his back."

Julie reached out to touch him but he yanked his head back, then backed into a corner and shook his head. "He's a splendid animal," she murmured, and then spoke low to the animal. "I know how you feel. I miss him too."

They moved on and stopped again when a groom led a trim white mare with gray dapples all over her out of a stall. Her head was small and finely chiseled and her mane, tail and lower legs were black.

"This is Felina. She's yours if you want her."

Patting her neck, the mare dropped her head and rubbed her cheek against her shoulder, stamping a front foot impatiently. Julie rubbed the velvety nose and then kissed her muzzle. "She's beautiful, thank you. Like I said, I haven't ridden much. Do you think she'll notice?"

"I won't tell her if you don't," Darold laughed. "You won't have any trouble with her. She's as tame as a kitten."

He stepped aside as another groom led a large chestnut gelding up to them. "This is my horse, Duke. Duke, meet Julie."

Julie curtsied, drawing Darold's laugh, then they both led their horses out into the courtyard. The groom boosted Julie into her saddle while Darold swung up onto his. She had took a quick look back at the two grooms' faces, who were obviously surprised when she straddled the horse rather than the customary feminine sidesaddle practiced by that era's cultured women.

"Well, they won't be the same again," Darold laughed as they moved out. "Did you see their faces?"

A short while later they turned off onto the trace that eventually met up with the Louisiana and Natchez crossroads snaking through Texas to end up in Mexico.

The El Camino Real was originally an old Indian trail followed by the early Spanish conquistadors. The pathway was worn deep by the wheels of weighted wagons and pony express riders and countless feet trudging their way from Mexico, across Texas and

Louisiana. Then it traveled along the Mississippi River to meet up with the Natchez Trace flowing into Kentucky and points east. Darold was proud to share the history.

Hoof-beats suddenly sounded behind them on the hard-packed road, and when Darold reined in, Julie followed suit. A smartly dressed couple drew up. One was a good-looking brown haired man in a smart cutaway suit, and the blonde girl riding sidesaddle alongside, was quite beautiful. They were both studying her quite intently.

"Julie," Darold finally spoke as the horses calmed down. "This is Felina Beaumont and Kip Fontaine."

Julie made mental note of her horse and this woman having the same name.

The man tipped his hat. "We stopped by the house to meet Miss er, I mean Mrs. Challenger. She's all the neighbors around here have been talking about. Dayna told us you were both out riding so we hoped we could catch up with you."

Fontaine was looking only at Julie, and when she glanced at Darold, she saw his jaw clench tightly. Again she was struck at the resemblance of he and his brother. She'd seen that look many times.

The girl spoke. "I hope you're finding New Orleans quite agreeable."

Julie stared back into the honey-colored eyes. "Yes, I like it just fine. You can both call me Julie."

The blonde tossed her head, then said with an edge of bitterness in her tone. "So sorry to hear about your husband. Tell me, just how did the two of you meet?"

Feeling oddly uncomfortable, and somehow on trial by circumstance, Julie spoke carefully.

"We met on Crete. It was a whirlwind romance." Then she added for good measure, "We were introduced by a mutual friend."

"I see," she returned icily, "It must have been a whirlwind, to get married and have a child so quickly."

Julie was quick to respond to what she recognized as an insult. "The minute we met, we just couldn't seem to keep our hands off each other."

Felina's icy blue eyes sliced into hers and she reminded Julie of a cat twitching its tail before a mouse hole. She was certain that

Daine had meant something to her and maybe she to him.

Darold made a turn into the lane leading back to his house. Then, remembering his manners said a little gruffly. "I'm afraid I must get Julie back up to the house to rest, she's still not fully recovered." Hating to say it, he continued, "Do stop by soon for tea."

Fontaine could hardly tear his eyes away from Julie before he looked back to Darold, then said, "Oh, but we shall. We've been invited to the ball at the end of the month. June 28th I believe."

•

In the middle of June, Dayna and Julie decided to go into New Orleans to pick out their costumes for the ball. The house was already beginning to buzz with activity as the servants began cleaning and polishing and endless list making. The invitations had already gone out, and there were close to one hundred people that were expected to attend.

It was hard to leave the baby behind but she and Dayna had no way to take him and Hallie with them in a two-seated buggy with a driver. The ride into town was pleasant even though her thoughts returned again and again to her son. Since she'd been unconscious when she'd first been taken to Fair Winds three months ago, she was seeing the countryside and New Orleans for the first time.

Wide cobblestone streets were lined with tall black streetlights and Dayna explained how lamplighters lit them at dusk. They passed through a section of stately old homes and when they reached Jackson Square she showed her a huge imposing stone cathedral. Next, she pointed out an opera house, two hotels, a feedstore and a large general store.

Madam Clovis' dress shop was next to the general store.

Julie and Dayna had sketched a general idea of the dresses they wanted, and having three employees all having helped with Julie's previous wardrobe, they were assured they would have them in plenty of time. Julie had decided on a Greek empire-style gown and Dayna chose a French princess style, the current rage of Europe.

Just before six PM they pulled up in front of Fair Winds. Julie was out and halfway up the steps before Dayna even got a foot on the ground. She hurried up the staircase, her feet barely touching down.

When she went through her room and into the baby's nursery,

no one was there No bedding, no Hallie and no baby. She felt light headed, then a sudden buzzing began in her ears, and she slumped to the floor.

She was aware of being shook, and then someone lifted her and laid her on her bed. Darold's face hovering above her was flushed and he patted her cheeks. Dayna had raced to the room and also looked alarmed.

"My baby! What have you done with my baby?" Julie shrieked.

A moment later Hallie came in carrying a gurgling baby in her arms while Soonie followed behind with her arms loaded with fresh laundered bedding. Julie only looked dumbfounded while everyone else looked at her strangely. Darold shook her gingerly.

"Julie, get hold of yourself. Hallie took him out for some fresh air while his room was being aired out and cleaned. He's old enough to be outside now."

Julie hoped she didn't look as foolish as she felt.

"I'm sorry, but I thought," She wrung her hands. "Oh, nothing. I don't know why I reacted like I did. It won't happen again." Even as she said it, she still felt lingering fear.

Chapter Twelve

The day of the party dawned. As usual, Julie was up before the crimson streaks of dawn dissolved into bright sunlight. Overnight guests had begun arriving the afternoon before and she had met some cousins, aunts and uncles as well as the new governor of Louisiana.

She slipped quietly down the stairs and into the kitchen for a fresh cup of coffee, as was her daily habit. Fannie was throwing orders, shooshing girls hither and yon, back and forth to the pantry and springhouse, a bandana twisted around her head to keep her hair out of the food.

"Whut I tell's ya, Soonie girl? I done tole' ya, bring fo' hams, ya done brung me two."

"But Fannie," Soonie wailed, "I already brung t'other two, they's on the larder, lack ya say-ed."

Fannie spied them, spewing out even more orders. "Git yo'self on back out the'ah, n' git me dem turkeys, 'n I bett'a not find one single pinfeath'a or singed hair anywhar's." Her massive arms picked up a pail of milk. "They bett'a be slick as a newborn baby's butt."

Julie chuckled, but thankfully no one noticed.

More guests from town and the surrounding area began arriving in the late afternoon. Julie went the back way down to the kitchen for a late lunch, trying to avoid the crowd as best she could. By four o'clock the house was buzzing with activity. Dayna checked on her once then left her alone to finish dressing for the party.

Soonie was kept so busy in the kitchen that she called on Hallie to help her with her hair.

Dressed only in her shift, she relaxed while Hallie arranged her hair in a beguiling style atop her head with cascading ringlets draping down one shoulder. Helping her into her dress, the younger girl stepped back and voiced her admiration.

"My, ain't you da pretty one! Jes' ain't nobody kin hold a candle ta you, not even dat prissy Miz Beaumont. No siree."

"Thanks Hallie, but I fear if I eat one more ounce of anything, I'll bust right out of this dress."

Hallie's eyes swept her length. "Mayhap jes' don't bend down, else you'll fall out. I know's how deez gentlemen's are. Dey point dey heads one way, while dey eyes look t'other."

This didn't quench her fears as she moved hurriedly to the closet. There wasn't anything else in it she could use as a costume. She picked up her silver cutout mask. *Good, this will help me some.*

The orchestra was tuning up and she again took the back stairs for a short walk in the garden before she went on display downstairs. She felt a new wave of dread, but the cloying smell of chrysanthemums, portulaca and exotic roses worked to calm her senses as she moved among the large variety of flowers. The lights from the big house illuminated the yard as she moved deeper into the maze. She was glad to finally be alone.

But she was not alone. She heard a shoe strike a stone on the walkway, then a shadow moved a few feet away. A red glowing ash struck the ground and she watched as a shoe ground it out. Then the shadow moved closer and she saw it was Fontaine. His disguise was foolhardy. Anyone could have guessed he fancied himself Napoleon Bonaparte.

"Thank goodness it's you," she breathed gratefully.

"Were you expecting someone else?" he answered wolfishly.

"No. I was just startled, that's all. I thought I was alone."

He had moved closer until he was looming over her, looking down in her face, faintly lit by the house lights. "You aren't disappointed, are you?"

"No," she answered uneasily, cautious of his bold stare.

"You're a very beautiful girl, or I should have said... woman. You are all of that, you know." His hazel eyes swept down her length, then returned to her bare shoulders and cleavage, and then finally back up to her face. He was disappointed when she turned away.

Her impulse was to leave but she stood rooted to the spot. He was nice looking but she'd seen the blatant yearning in his eyes. She distrusted him and had no desire for romance. Leaning close, his lips closed on hers before she suddenly twisted her head away. He grabbed her arm, pulling her back around to face him.

"Damn it, Julie! I'm mad for you!"

"Please Kip, let me go back inside. I'm not ready for a relationship."

He had long ago given up on ever winning Felina. She was still in love with a dead man. So was Julie. He wanted to hurt her for rejecting him as he himself had been hurt.

"Felina and Daine were to be married when he returned," he blurted.

He bent toward her again and she yanked away, scurrying away in the darkness. He watched her fleeing figure, and with a rush of anger at his own stupidity, slammed his boot deep into a hedge.

•

The lights of New Orleans twinkled in the distance. A big dark ship eased into a wide berth where lines were being thrown out to dockworkers gathering on the long wharf. The sounds of angry gulls wakened from their perches filled the night air, then gradually quieted. After more than a year away from this familiar port, The Black Hornet was not just another ship arriving in the dark. It had been gone a long time, and this was home.

On deck, a man of sixty-plus years limped with a crooked wooden cane and the thump heard below was eerie to the ears. He stopped near a gangplank being lowered and rubbed his aching knee, taking the weight off his bad leg as he leaned on the rail.

He had taken a ball in his already injured ankle as he'd rushed to the aid of his best friend and captain that long ago night in the Azores. Lead fragments, combined with long chilly nights like this, brought on a never-ending ache in his weary old bones.

Drawing on his gray goatee, he stared out over the wharf at the familiar mill, mostly dark now, and breathed a sigh of relief they'd finally made it safely home. Soon a much younger man joined him.

"Walters, I have to go now. It's been so long. Will you check us in?" Already they were being tagged by port patrol for inspection in the morning, as was the custom.

A trio of men were quickly gathering on the wharf, recognizing the ship and waiting for an explanation about their lengthy absence.

"Yes, you git. Your family surely believes you dead. And by all that's holy, you should be."

Daine clasped his hand then ran down the gangplank, avoiding the group and pointing to the ship's coxswain behind him for an explanation. He stopped a short distance away, taking a long deep breath and looking around him.

Home at last! He took in the dying embers and sparks shooting intermittently from the tall smokestack at the family mill, and then hurried on. The night was as black as coal and he found it hard to keep from running, soon forcing him to slacken his pace since he was still out of shape from his long siege in bed.

After renting a horse at the livery, he galloped through town barely taking in any changes from his lost year away. He didn't want to stop and see any of his friends, concentrating only on getting home to his mother, Darold and Dayna. His mother! She had been aging rapidly even before he left and he hoped she hadn't given up on him, or even worse, maybe it had all been too much for her!

On the long ride through the darkness, his thoughts once again turned to Julie. Where could she be? If it hadn't have been for the medicinal supplies she'd gotten that day, or if Bracken had been a better shot, he wouldn't be alive to even think about it now.

He'd been in a coma for nearly four months and owed his life to a Chinese man stranded after the hurricane the very day before he'd been shot. The bullet had exited cleanly and the little man had stopped the bleeding, but had told Walters that he didn't stand much of a chance for survival. He had suggested he be taken to his brother in China, a master in Chinese medicine.

After Daine stabilized, the Hornet had set sail for China with the stranded brother aboard. Upon arrival there, the older brother had performed his magic (or voodoo as Walters preferred to call it) and had brought him out of his deathlike sleep using Chinese herbs, ginseng leaves and water baths using ancient oils.

Daine had slowly gained his strength back, and in the meantime, Walters had managed to sell their remaining cargo to an empty ship headed for Boston. But before they'd left the Azores, Jeremy had nosed around and discovered the name of the ship that had sailed away that fateful night. When Daine had recovered, he'd been aghast to learn it was the same man that had smuggled opium out of Turkey and he had run afoul of in Greece.

They had learned Trouchet lived on the island of Martinique. But when they'd docked there, they found out the Ladyluck had sailed for San Francisco in the month before they'd arrived. Julie, according to Trouchet's housekeeper, had already escaped the island. No one knew where she'd gone or if anyone had helped her.

Walters and Jeremy had headed back to the dock when a young island boy had caught up with them. He'd told them that the men who had kidnapped Julie from the black ship were dead and that he had helped her get passage to Florida, and that was the last he saw of her. He couldn't give them the name of the ship she left on, only that it had been sometime in the late fall.

Daine had been devastated. Her trail was now cold.

Now, as he rode through the familiar countryside, he renewed his vow to find her once he made sure his family members were all right. His biggest concern right now was his mother, plus his men badly needed the rest. They needed to see their own families as well.

Once he saw his family he would travel to the ends of the earth to get her back.

•

It was nearly ten o'clock when he loped up the drive. He stopped his horse short in surprise when he saw dozens of carriages and heard music coming from the brightly lit house. They were having a party? He tethered his panting animal to the hitching post and circled the house to get a better look.

Buggies and carriages of all kinds and descriptions were parked outside. Hitched horses stamped their feet restlessly, some munched feedbags strapped over their muzzles, while others hung their heads to the ground and dozed.

He looked down at his worn trousers and rubbed a trembling hand over his beard, deciding he didn't want to be seen in this badly rumpled state. Slipping stealthily around to the back of the house, he could see through the windows; clowns, gypsies, princesses and the like, all laughing and dancing. A costume party? This was June. What were they celebrating?

The thought of scaring his mother half to death never once

occurred to him.

Her window was slightly open and he could see a yellow shaft of light shining down on the grass. He knelt down below the shade to look in, then sighed in relief when he saw her sitting alone in her wheelchair. She had a blanket covering her frail legs and reading a book with a magnifying glass.

She was quite deep in whatever she was reading. With her growing hearing loss, she didn't hear the window being shoved up in it's casing, nor did she hear the slight scrape of someone climbing through. Only when a shadow fell across the page did she look up.

When she opened her mouth to scream, Daine gently covered her mouth with his gloved hand, easily lifting her up into his arms.

She yanked his hand away. "Oh son! Daine! Daine! Oh my Lord, is it really you?" She was shaking all over, afraid to believe her eyes.

"It's me, mama. Your number one son."

His eyes were moist as he kissed her, then he gently set her back down into her chair.

He drew the warm blanket back over her thin trembling legs. She started to say something, then buried her face in her hands, sobbing uncontrollably, unable to talk.

Lowering himself to eye level, he rested back on his heels, quickly removing his gloves and taking her cold hands in his. He rubbed quickly to warm them between his rough ones, and then reached for her chin, raising her face back on a level with his.

"It's me, mama. I know I've been away much longer than we planned. Did you think something had happened to me?"

A log exploded in the fireplace and a shower of embers shot onto the hearth where he quickly brushed them back with his glove. Her next words stunned him.

"We had word you were dead. Lost in a hurricane."

He twisted around to stare at her. "How did you know about the hurricane? Who told you I was dead?" His mind raced. As far as he knew, no one here knew anything.

"Why, your wife did."

This was absurd. He rocked back on his heels, studying her and wondered if her mind had finally slipped. "My what?"

Of course, he didn't know he had a wife! What was she saying?

Drawing herself up to her full height, which was already small indeed, she filled him in. "You don't even know you have a son." Stated as gently as she knew how.

He stood up slowly.

As her eyes followed him, her maternal eyes took in the lean gauntness of his face and body. There were fine lines around his eyes, dark circles underneath and he looked like he'd been to hell and back.

His eyebrows were still arched in puzzlement. Yes, she'd lost her mind but she seemed serious enough. A wife? What the hell?

"Daine, did you hear me? You have a son," she repeated. "He's upstairs this very minute and born right in your very own bed." She could see the pulse now pounding hard in his neck.

"Listen to me! Julie has borne you a son."

His face blanched white as he grabbed her shoulders and shook her before he thought. "Julie? Julie Sinclair?" No, not possible. Godalmighty, was she daft? "Mother did I hear you right? Julie is here? She had a baby?"

She was deliriously happy. "Yes, they're both here, but please don't frighten her like you did me. She thinks you're dead too. We're having a costume ball to introduce her. Go up the back stairs to your room, the baby is there and so are your clothes. Julie wouldn't think of throwing them away." Her shaking hand went to her cheek. "Oh, blazes, I can't think!"

Daine bent and kissed her again. Then, when he was sure she was okay, he left her to sneak up the servant's stairway to the second floor. Hurrying into his room, he closed the door quickly behind him and looked around.

It was still a man's room, but now feminine ointments and brushes adorned his dresser and a thin filmy nightgown was draped over a chair. He stopped long enough to pick it up, rub it against his cheek, and then laid it back down softly.

Not seeing a crib, he tiptoed into the adjoining room to see a sleeping mulatto girl laying on a cot. Next to her was a wooden cradle he recognized as his own when he was a baby. Tiptoeing across the floor, he peered down into the small reposed face bearing his likeness.

The tiny mouth was puckered in sleep, sucking at intervals at some unseen treasure. His chest tightened in pride. Julie had given him a son! How had she ever managed?

Daine moved silently back to his room. For some reason his mother had the mistaken impression that he and Julie were married. No worry, he'd remedy that as soon as he could get the necessary license and no one would ever be the wiser. He'd not shame her. His son would bear his name.

His mind whirling as he undressed, he poured lukewarm water from a copper kettle into a crockery basin then scrubbed himself hurriedly all over. His thoughts returned again and again to Julie. She was right here in this house!

He shook so badly as he pulled on a white ruffled shirt, he had to stop three times, unable to fasten the pearl buttons on the cuffs. He was as clumsy as a mother bear trying to thread a needle.

Suddenly he stopped in the middle of his dressing. A costume ball? He couldn't go down there and scare all his friends. Or even worse, Julie and his brother and sister!

Then an idea struck him.

•

Julie had hardly sat out a dance. She was growing tired and with every song that ended, she was instantly grabbed by someone else. Felina seemed to be everywhere. She had bumped Julie's arm deliberately at the punch bowl but luckily the drink had missed her dress. Someone had trounced on the hem of her dress and pulled the ribbon loose on her head. Felina was always near when those things happened and she knew the spiteful girl was responsible.

Julie danced by with Fontaine when she happened to glance toward the stairway and saw a tall swarthy figure leaning nonchalantly against the wall. She couldn't remember having seen him earlier and her eyes kept returning to the landing.

He was dressed like a roguish pirate with tight fitting black trousers and a flashy shirt opened to the waist. His bare chest was brazenly exposed. A bright red bandana was tied around his head and he wore a black mask. A saber hung at his side and he looked to be in his element with his cocky stance and arms folded casually in front of him His booted feet were crossed at the ankles.

His eyes were glued to hers as she moved about the room. He'd spotted her the minute he stepped out onto the balcony. Her fiery red hair had caught his eye while she held her mask up to her face in one dainty hand, and holding her long skirt up with the other. He'd immediately felt a sharp stab of jealousy when Fontaine claimed her and swept her around the room in a close waltz.

Julie kept being drawn back to the dark mysterious man. As she stared up at him, she heard other people whispering around the room. Who was he? Did anyone know him?

Everyone seemed to be staring at him.

Remaining slouched, he was afraid his height might give him away. Good, he had her attention. Hell, he had everyone's attention!

Julie looked away, trying to focus on her dancing partner.

She was smiling up at Fontaine, who hadn't taken his eyes off her. Then she was suddenly spun around into strong arms, her cheek brushing the thick mat of hair on his chest, but somehow never missed a step. Looking up into the masked face, she smiled but was embarrassed that everyone seemed to be now looking at them.

This wasn't a tag dance. Why had he humiliated her by breaking in?

Thankfully, an intermission was called. Julie took advantage of the pressing dancers and quickly disappeared into the crowd, heading straight for the veranda.

Daine saw the back of her dress going out through the door and had nearly caught up to her when Fontaine stepped out and stopped him in his tracks.

"Going somewhere, mister?" He pointed to where Julie had stopped a few feet away. "The lady is taken."

Dumbfounded, Daine watched as Fontaine walked to Julie and led her away.

This is not going well, he thought. He spotted Darold also staring after them, then figured he'd better let him know who he was.

The music soon started up again and Julie excused herself from Fontaine. He'd been monopolizing her all evening and she wanted to return to some of her other guests. She didn't see the bold pirate anywhere, so evidently Fontaine had succeeded in getting rid of him.

She had just started the second dance after the intermission when she found herself once again in the arms of the tall swarthy pirate. Taking in his hastily trimmed black beard, she couldn't help but stare entranced at his bare chest. His skin was deeply tanned from the sun, and when he pulled her close, her heart began to beat in an uncontrollable fashion.

Knees suddenly weak, she listened as he spoke to her in a low French accent while marveling at the evenness of his perfect white teeth. Then staring helplessly at his lips, she had an overwhelming and sudden desire to feel those lips covering hers.

He reeked with masculinity and she could feel the steady beating of his heart, so close he held her. What is the matter with me? I haven't felt this way about a man since ...

She pushed herself back, but he only held her tighter. The low soothing French words of endearment continued and her pulse skyrocketed. His head was bent low and then he lightly brushed her lips with his in a brazen kiss.

She jerked to a stop, yanking her hands away. "You ... you!"

"Pirate. Does that sound familiar? You have called me that before."

"I have called you that?" she asked incredulously. "Who ... are you?" As she spoke those words, his hand reached up to slowly pull down the mask.

She stared into familiar, though never truly forgotten, black piercing eyes.

Then she fell forward in a dead faint.

Chapter Thirteen

The music had stopped and all eyes were on them as Daine swooped Julie up in his arms before she hit the floor. The whispers grew until it sounded like a swarm of locusts had been let loose in the room.

Felina was the next one to react, following Julie's lead and swooning into Fontaine's arms, whose face bore a stricken expression. But no one noticed them as all eyes were still on the first couple moving toward the library. Daine kicked the door open and they could see Dayna inside before she closed it. Darold stepped out just long enough to signal to the orchestra to resume playing.

Depositing Julie on the settee in the library, Daine asked Dayna for some of their mother's smelling salts. Opening a drawer, she found it and poured some on a hanky and gently placed it under her sister-in-law's nose.

Julie's eyes fluttered, then opened. They fastened again on those smoky eyes she thought she'd never see again. "It is you," she breathed raggedly. "But how?" She began to cry.

He reached for her hand and brought it to his lips, kissing her fingers. Dayna was suddenly beside him and threw her arms around his shoulders. Tears were running down her face too. She never thought she'd ever see this day again either.

The door burst open and Felina and Kip burst in, neither waiting for an invite. Felina was oblivious to all but this handsome man she had loved for more than five years. She wanted him to know she had paid for her mistake a thousand-fold and could think of nothing else but him at the moment.

"Oh Daine, I can't believe it! We all thought you were dead."

She could see Julie on the settee and couldn't stop herself, "You would be the kind of man to do the honorable thing."

Her words were lost on Daine but the family knew her meaning. Darold could see where this was quickly heading. It was a volatile situation that could turn into an eruption and he neatly maneuvered himself between them.

Felina recognized the move for what it was and brought herself under control. She moved back to stand next to Kip, accepting his handkerchief and quietly blowing her nose. All eyes turned again to Daine when he spoke.

"I seem to have crashed a party." It was about all he could manage.

Darold and Dayna reacted and shooed everyone out, leaving Daine and Julie alone together at last. When the door closed, he reached for her and hugged her close.

"So, I have a son."

Julie looked surprised. "How did you know?"

"My mother told me. I've seen him. He's beautiful." His eyes crinkled with sudden mirth. "Can one say that about a boy?"

"Of course. All babies are beautiful. But tell me, what about you? You were shot! They told me you were dead!" She ran her fingers through his hair lightly near his temple, looking for a scar or telltale mark. She discovered a faint line behind his ear, looking as though it were a natural part. "Tell me what happened—"

Her words were cut off when his lips claimed hers in a dizzying kiss.

Her lips parted beneath his and she felt a tremor pass over her body. When she gasped for air, he reluctantly broke his hold and looked at her knowingly.

"Let's go to our room and we can fill each other in. But we must at least say a word to our guests. It would be rude to just run past them in our haste to be alone together." He grinned down at her. "Are you okay now? Can you make the stairs?"

"Yes, I'm fine But one thing I need to tell you. Your mother doesn't know you were shot, only Darold and Dayna. She thinks you were lost in a hurricane. We thought it would be easier for her."

Daine agreed, glad he hadn't said anything. When they reentered the ballroom again, the music stopped and everyone clustered around them, asking questions and slapping him on the back. Any plan of escaping to their room flew right out the window. He stuck to Julie's story of the Hornet being badly damaged in a hurricane after Julie's kidnapping, and of taking many months to fix it to return home.

Every time he turned around someone shoved another drink in his hand. The festive mood earlier had changed to an explosive celebration of life. Julie had danced three dances and still hadn't seen Daine when she finally met up with Kip.

"Have you see my husband?"

Kip was feeling no pain and was totally annoyed that he had no chance now with Julie. He decided to dig the knife in a little deeper. "Yes, he went out on the veranda with Felina. They must have had a lot to say to each other since they were both in a big hurry."

Julie's heart gave a sickening lurch as Kip's words from last Sunday returned with new clarity. He would have married Felina when he returned from the Mediterranean. He led her outside to show her where he'd last seen them. He stopped near a trellis of thick ivy, but she still didn't see them anywhere.

Julie had just turned to say something when Kip pulled her into his arms, kissing her hard. She raised her hands to his chest to push him away when a voice drawled sarcastically behind them.

"I see I must be missing something here. Perhaps I returned a little too late."

Julie looked over Kip's shoulder into twin daggers as Daine's angry eyes bore into hers. Stepping back she could see a triumphant smile on Felina's face just before Daine whirled and disappeared back inside.

She swung on Kip, looking from him to Felina.

"I don't know which one of you planned this, maybe both, but it won't work. Right now Daine thinks I've betrayed him but not for long." With that, she walked off while they were both left looking sheepish.

She skirted the dance floor and then hurried up the stairs. Checking on her son, she was relieved to find he and Hallie were both sleeping soundly. An old grandfather clock in the hall struck midnight and she was about to go downstairs when Daine sauntered in.

Crossing to the bed and avoiding her eyes, he yanked off the bandana from around his head, then unbuckled his belt and pulled it from the loops. She could see the hard line of his clenched jaw as he sat down on the bed, then he pulled off his boots. When he finally looked at her, they both searched the others face.

Daine spoke first. "Well, am I too late? Are you in love with Fontaine?"

She was taken aback. "Of course not! I didn't know he was going to kiss me."

"Would it be the first time?" He needed to know.

Her hesitation was damning, picturing the scene earlier in the garden now cost her.

"He's tried, but tonight he took me outside to find you."

He looked skeptical. "Felina told me you and Fontaine—"

"Were what? We're nothing!" She was suddenly quite furious. "While we're on the subject, were you or were you not, going to marry Felina when you returned?"

Black eyes narrowed dangerously. "That's beside the point. I want to know what Kip means to you!"

"Beside the point? You make love to an innocent girl and get her with child and you were planning on marrying another when you got home? What about the horse? The one you named Felina." She was horrified to find she was on the edge of bursting into tears.

He stood up. "I never even gave her the horse. I had...changed my mind."

She blinked back the tears. How could he stand there half-naked and talk to her like she had no feelings at all? What manner of man was this?

He suddenly walked to the closet and removed a robe, unaware why it was even still there. "I'm going downstairs. Most of the guests have gone except for a few that will be leaving in the morning." Yanking the sash around his middle, he gave one last shot. "I'll be back to continue this discussion after you calm down and can be rational."

Me be rational? She stood there a moment and seethed. After a long moment of staring at the closed door, she quickly removed her dress and reached for her nightgown.

Pulling back the top cover of the bed, she slid between the sheets and punched her pillow angrily until she found exactly the right indention for her head.

Her pink tipped nipples were outlined under the thin bodice and she smiled smugly to herself. A virile man like Daine that had been at sea for almost a year, without a woman, would surely listen to reason, his abstinence flung aside like the wind. She could forgive his wrong assumptions, and he could forgive hers, but first she had to get his attention.

She lay curled up on her side and waited. One hour went by and she was near to falling asleep when the door opened and Daine walked over to the bed. He stopped and looked down at her and she opened her eyes to meet still angry ones as he swayed on his feet.

Drunk! These Challenger men seemed to look for their courage in a bottle.

His eyes traveled over her and he said glibly, "I'll sleep in my father's room, that way we can both think first before we each say something we may both regret." He started for the door.

Julie jumped up onto her knees, covering herself with the sheet. "But, what will everyone think? You and I not sleeping in the same bed? We're married!" The thought of everyone knowing in the house that they had shared separate beds his first night home was humiliating.

"Married? That's what my mother said, that you were my wife." He had returned to stand at the edge of the bed. "I'm afraid you're mistaken, my dear. I am married to no one."

"Oh yes, but you are," she said smugly. "I am your wife, by proxy."

Daine looked stricken. His heart had lurched with gladness, but at the same time his stubborn Challenger pride had suffered a setback.

She looked a little fearful, and in truth, she was. She was afraid of losing him, but trapped animals usually bit dangerously.

After what seemed like a long time, he slowly untied his robe and tossed it onto a nearby chair. Standing naked, with no show of modesty, he drew the covers back as she rolled over to let him in.

"Married, eh? You managed just about everything, didn't you? Well, don't just lay there and shake with fright, you're perfectly safe with me. The whole house will know we slept together. So go to sleep!"

He turned his back to her and left his astonished wife to stare at the proud and unrelenting back of his head.

•

When Julie woke the next morning, after sleeping late, Daine was gone. She felt an impulse to lie in bed and sulk for the rest of the day but then thought better of it. She wouldn't give him the satisfaction.

She helped Hallie bathe her son and was surprised when she told her Daine had taken the baby downstairs earlier to visit his mother and show him off to the last of their guests. When she went down to breakfast a little later she had the kitchen to herself and learned he had already ate in his mother's room.

Deciding just to keep busy, she helped pick up after the party mostly just to occupy her mind. Later in the afternoon she changed into some walking shoes and set out on the main road. She'd gone nearly two miles when she saw a horse and rider kicking up dust as they came toward her.

A prancing black horse, she recognized as Sultan, drew close and was reined to a stop beside her. Shading her eyes from the bright sun, she looked up into unreadable eyes as Daine leaned across the saddle horn. When she started to walk on, he reached down and lifted her up easily to ride sidesaddle in front of him. Flicking the reins, Sultan started off at a brisk walk.

Daine's warm breath against her neck was disconcerting as she sat stiffly, but soon the animal's rocking gait forced her to lean back against him. His chin lifted to rest on the top of her head and she could feel his hard chest against her shoulder. Though leaner than she remembered, he was still remarkably solid and even more charismatic.

Neither spoke of personal things as she listened while he pointed out landmarks, and he dutifully answered if she inquired. When they reached Fair Winds, Daine rode right up to the steps and held her under an arm as she slid to the ground.

She turned to thank him, but he said, "Since I had just passed Three Oaks and saw Fontaine hitching up his team, I thought I'd save you the trouble of running into him."

With a curt nod, he wheeled his horse and put the spurs to him.

Julie stared at his back a long moment, and then flounced into the house, ignoring the buggy that came up the drive.

●

Whoever invited Fontaine to stay for supper that night was never revealed, since no one took credit for what later proved to be a disaster. Much later, all surmised that Fontaine had simply brazened his way into staying, uninvited and hoping each would think another had invited him.

All during dinner, Daine, Darold and Kip had exchanged scowls while the atmosphere crackled with underlying tension. Daine and Darold indeed both thought the other had invited him to stay, while Fontaine steadily grew more obnoxious.

Julie was at a loss trying to figure out their strange attitudes. She gave most of her attention to Dayna, who seemed oblivious to her brothers' behavior. Her blue eyes glowed as she talked about a young man recently moved from Kentucky.

"He's a doctor and is just setting up his practice. He bought the old Dickens house and brought his widowed mother here to live with him." She was quite excited, leaning closer to Julie who sat next to her, then whispering, "He was the one I danced with mostly at the ball. He wants to call on me."

Daine was at the head of the table, Darold at the other end, while Kip sat across from Julie and Dayna. Daine watched her like a hawk and she was very careful not to look Fontaine's way unless he spoke directly to her.

Daine addressed his sister having overheard her conversation. "When do we get to meet this young man?"

"His name is Monty Calder. I invited him out next Sunday, after church."

Daine gave her a brotherly smile. "By all means, a doctor as well as a Christian. Now if he was a lawyer on the side, we'd really be in business." Fontaine opened his mouth as if to speak but wisely thought better of it. He was a lawyer himself but had yet to do any real business with the Challengers. This was a bone of contention he had given up on ever rectifying.

Dinner was brought in. There was roast beef, mashed potatoes and a thick brown gravy, string beans with onions and bacon, and steaming hot roasting ears fresh from the fields. This was followed by warm raspberry rhubarb pie and a pitcher of heavy cream.

When they were all through, Daine invited everyone into the library for an after dinner drink. While he poured the two girls a glass of wine, Darold began telling them all of the possibility of a new tobacco growing plan he was undertaking. The men opted for corn whiskey and the two brothers talked about the lumber business and how things had fared in Daine's absence.

Julie knew nothing of these things and she and Fontaine just listened quietly.

"Some of the clearing has begun already but the rainy season is starting soon. I'm thinking of taking a room in town, commuting back and forth to the mill on horseback sometimes gets tiresome," Darold announced after a few minutes.

Daine was still leaning against the brick fireplace watching Kip watch Julie.

Kip's eyes had seldom left her and he'd brushed much too close to her a couple of times. All the while the brothers had talked about business, Kip had seemed mesmerized by his wife and clearly had no desire to even enter into the brother's conversations.

Clearing his throat when he heard Darold's plan, Kip finally spoke. "Personally, I find staying in town a bore with nothing to occupy my time but an occasional night at the opera and dreary business matters. In fact," he went on, moving ever closer to Julie, "recently life in the country seems to have its advantages."

Daine's outward calm betrayed his inner conflict as he watched Kip pour Julie another drink, again lingering way too close to her for his liking. His grip tightened on his glass until his knuckles turned white, staring at the biting amber liquid swirling on the bottom.

When Julie turned away he watched her graceful movements and was once more inflamed with jealousy.

His thoughts returned to Kip's words, then he added bitterly, "The opera you speak of seems to be located in the tenderloin, which can be quite outstanding in itself. Clearly the business matters you speak of only benefit yourself, since you totally ignore your family's welfare. You forgot to mention how your family's fortune has dwindled to almost nothing with your nightly spread of a deck of cards."

Kip's mouth dropped open and then Daine walked to the liquor cabinet and splashed his glass full. Tossing it down in one motion, he saw Julie out of the corner of his eye as she stumbled toward the veranda.

For no clear reason, other than abject embarrassment, Julie had an overpowering desire to flee. Faintness had zeroed in on her and she shook her head blindly as she slowly moved to the door.

Daine anxiously stepped forward but Kip had reached her first.

Pushing open the double French doors, he took her elbow and steered her out onto the veranda. "I'll see to her," he said back over his shoulder. "She looks like she needs some air."

Daine's already questionable patience ran out. With Kip's manhandling of his wife and his all too familiar attention to her all evening, stuck in his craw like a snifter full of sand.

He reached the doorway in two giant steps and jerked Kip back inside, where his face connected with Daine's iron fist dead center. Stepping over Kip's now prone figure, he took Julie's arm and led her down the steps into the dark night.

Darold stood over Kip and stifled a yawn as he sat up slowly, withdrawing a handkerchief to staunch the flow of blood pouring from his nose.

"Touchy son of a bitch, ain't he?" he said as he rose painfully to his feet.

Chapter Fourteen

Descending the steps with Daine close behind, Julie didn't jerk away when he grabbed her elbow. They were both silent and the only sound heard was the crunch of gravel beneath Daine's boots. Walking the sloped lawn down to the river's edge, she stopped at last, fighting the nausea rising from the mixture of too much food and drink.

I don't think I'll take another drink, ever! She thought to herself. Look at the trouble it causes. Maybe Daine hadn't learned his lesson back at the Azores. A clear mind or pay the price?

After a moment, Daine turned her around to face him. "Are you all right?"

Swallowing hard, she was determined not to test his mockery if he saw any tears and she forced herself to look unblinkingly at him. He had the power to hurt her so, but he might just as well have thrust a knife through her as effectively as his words last night hurt her.

"Yes. I guess I drank too much wine." She wished he wouldn't look at her so tenderly. Suddenly quite flustered, she blurted, "Is Kip hurt?"

There was a sharp intake of breath and she wished she could take back her words.

He smirked, then yanked her close, his fingers digging into her flesh. "Don't worry yourself. I didn't mar his pretty looks, although he won't be doing this for a while ..."

His mouth came down on hers, hard and hurting. She winced as he ground his hips against her and she could tell he wasn't as unaffected by her as he'd like her to believe.

She pushed at his chest but he caught her wrist in one hand

while the other moved down her front and sought the opening of her dress. One hand slipped inside her chemise and he tipped her head back with his other, a look of animal passion on his face. He rubbed his thumb over her nipple while a slow smile played over his lips.

Unreasonable anger flared and she drew back, slapping him hard across the face.

"I'm not a whore!" she hissed. "Don't you dare treat me like one!"

He quickly released her and she ran around the back of the house into the night. He watched her go, and then moved away silently with self-loathing dogging his heels.

Back in her room, she undressed in the dark. Feeling drained of all emotion she tried to close her mind to all that had gone on since his return. They couldn't go on like this, taunting and hurting each other. Turning over on her stomach she buried her face in the pillow and sobbed quietly.

She was still in this position, but sound asleep when Daine entered the room much later, and only slightly drunk this time. Her red hair was spilled over the pillow and her golden skin glowed when he lit the small bedside candle. Reflections of the flame danced on her smooth skin and he fought the desire to ravage her on the spot.

Then images of her and Fontaine darted across his mind's eye, he saw them lying together in the aftermath of frenzied lovemaking. Dropping down in the wing chair, he stared at her in the bed. Felina had done her job well, and he was now totally convinced of her secret affair with Fontaine. After all, he had trusted her, hadn't he?

After several minutes of his mind running rampant, he rose to his feet and retreated back down to the library. Not trusting himself to climb into bed with his wife, he found he could face a few more drinks. He succumbed to the urge and ended up spending the night in the big easy chair, pulled up to the window with his feet propped up on the casing.

He avoided breakfast and lunch with the others the next day.

Right after lunch, Julie developed a throbbing headache and returned to her room for a nap. She slept for nearly three hours, and when she woke she still had it, though not quite as severe.

After running a comb through her hair, she went into the baby's room finding he and Hallie both gone.

She went downstairs and searched the house, but soon discovered Daine and the baby were both gone. Fannie told her he'd taken the baby somewhere with him in the buggy. She was in a volatile state—he'd taken the baby without telling her.

Dayna caught up with her with a concerned look. "Julie, what's the matter with you? The minute that child's taken out of the house, you go all to pieces."

How could she explain her fear? This kind of life was still foreign to her. She would never understand how one human being could own another. She was convinced Daine meant to hurt her through her child. Would he hide her baby away just to keep her docile?

Julie paced and paced. Then, just before dark she heard the sound of a horse and buggy as it drew up outside. She sprang to the door and opened it and was down the steps before Dayna even left her seat.

Outside, Daine had Hallie by the hand to help her to the ground, when Julie flew at him, her small fists pummeling his back.

"Where is he! What have you done with my baby?"

Daine had a look of surprise on his face before he grabbed her hands and pushed her back, then leaned back inside the buggy to pick up a blanketed bundle. With a loud gasp, Julie made a grab for it then opened the blanket to inspect the grinning infant. Satisfied he was all right, she hurried back to the house.

Daine looked at Dayna with raised eyebrows and she shrugged her bewilderment.

Once in her room with the baby, she laid him down on her mussed up bed. He was cooing and gurgling with all this attention, kicking his legs happily at her while her mind raced.

The time had come for her to leave. She felt she was losing control. She'd have to be very careful and wait for a day when Daine had to be gone. Hallie would have to go with her, but she couldn't risk telling her ahead of time. Her mind continued to race.

What will I do about money? I've got nothing!

Daine walked in and took in the sight of Julie lunging for her baby. Her eyes were wide with fright as she cowered against the dresser with the baby who had now started to cry.

"I'm sorry, Julie, but I can't understand for the life of me why you would be so upset with me taking my son for a ride."

"Ride?" she screeched. "You were gone for six hours without telling me! Don't you think I deserve some consideration? I'm his mother, he's mine! Where were you when I needed you?" she went on mindlessly. "Your family took me in and cared for me and gave my child your name. They did, not me."

She stood proud, yet ridiculously small, it crossed his mind. But she had never looked more innocent and appealing than she did at that moment. He cursed himself silently as he moved to her and pulled her head down to his chest. They stood thus for a few moments, each mind in separate torment while he felt her trembling.

"I took him to the mill and the Hornet to show him off. While I was there I found out there's a huge labor dispute and I need to leave for the county seat in Baton Rouge tonight. Darold is tied up with the tobacco contracts and the like, so it looks like it has to be me." He released her. "When I return, we'll have this out. I want things settled between us."

Julie stepped back, her face devoid of emotion. Daine opened a drawer and removed a change of clothing to take with him. From his breast pocket he removed a folded wallet and withdrew several bills and placed the rest in a drawer and closed it.

"I don't need all this on me. Will you see to it Darold puts it in the safe?"

Returning to her side he placed a bronzed finger under Nicholas' chin, smiling down at him. "He's wonderful, Julie, and perfect in every way." Then he bent down and lifted her chin, kissing her long and hard.

Refusing to submit so easily, she hardened herself to a response. Her pride too had suffered, though the embers of love were still there. His lips burned against hers, and despite herself, hunger leaped like a flame as she leaned hard against him. She was nearly lost when the door opened and Darold walked in.

"Your horse is ready. You should make good time." Looking from his brother to his wife, he was unsure if the volatile situation between them had improved any or not. "Daine, are you sure you don't want me to go instead?"

"No, I'll go. You've got your hands full here. If this carries over to a real problem, you'll be needed at the mill too." Brushing his lips across her cheek, he shot her an unreadable look and quickly followed Darold out.

Julie watched out the window until she heard him gallop away, then she flew to the drawer. He'd forgot to say anything to Darold about the safe! There was more than enough money to see them to St. Louis. Removing only what she needed, she replaced the rest and looked around the room.

She chose three outfits to take with her and then gathered the baby's things. The time had come much sooner than she'd expected, but it was perfect.

She'd just stuffed the valise under the bed when there was a tap at the door. Frantically, she looked around for telltale signs of her leaving. Finding none, she smoothed back a loose wisp of hair behind an ear and opened it.

Darold walked in still sporting a look of concern on his face.

"Julie, may we talk a minute?"

She nodded.

"I know it's none of my business but I know something is terribly wrong between you and Daine. I feel I have a right to pry, being the nosy brother-in-law I am."

If she didn't feel so sick inside, she'd have laughed. After a long moment, she said softly, "Maybe we overwhelmed him too soon. It had to have been a shock for him to return home to find himself married through no fault of his own and a father all at the same time."

"He's hardly a young man, nor did you accomplish this all by yourself." He chuckled. "It takes two to dance, you know."

"I hadn't thought of it that way," she smiled back. "But I wonder if perhaps he had other plans when he returned."

"If you mean Felina, forget it. That was over before he left."

"But Kip said ..."

"Hang Kip! He knew better more than anyone else. It was finished. It is finished. She knew it too by the look on her face when she left here this morning."

"She was here this morning?"

"She was visiting with him in the library while you were asleep." When her eyes reflected her confusion, he put his hands on her shoulders, forcing her to look up at him. "Believe me, lying has never been my nature. Daine can't see her for dust. She means nothing to him. I don't think she ever did."

He hugged her. He knew his brother was deeply in love with Julie and she'd already told him how much she loved him. Whatever their obstacles, he was sure they could overcome them. Maybe a couple of days apart would cool down their tempers.

Even after Darold left, her doubts still lingered. Fear soon overrode reason and panic took control again. She needed to leave. Thinking it best to wait until the household was asleep for the night, she went over everything again in her mind. She'd go to the stables after it got dark and have a horse and buggy readied. She would tell Hallie last since she couldn't trust her not to blab to anyone.

She took off her gold band and laid it on the dresser then wrote a note while she waited. Brief and to the point, as if to a stranger, it read:

Dear Daine:

I have taken my son away. I can't bear for him to grow up in a home where love doesn't live. I thank your mother, Darold and Dayna for their friendship and caring when I needed it most. They took me at face value. Your son will only hear good things from me about his father. I leave my signature on the enclosed blank paper for your annulment of our 'so-called' marriage. I had no choice but to borrow enough money to get me where I'm going and to take Hallie with me. Rest assured, I shall return the money when I secure employment.

Julie

It was close to ten o'clock when Julie wakened Hallie. She had her get some clothes together and they tiptoed down the servant's back stairs. The baby was sleeping peacefully and she'd told Hallie they were going to meet Daine in town for a cruise down the river on a belated honeymoon trip. It was to be a big surprise for him.

Seth was waiting by the buggy, rubbing his sleepy eyes with the back of his hand, and quieting the impatient team of horses. He helped them in, then placed their valises in the storage place behind the seat. Julie carried her baby, making him comfortable for the brisk ride ahead.

"Yo shure Fannie knows I'se goin' too?" Hallie questioned her for the third time. She'd never been farther away than New Orleans and was more than a little apprehensive. "Yo say Masta Daine done say it okay? But whut 'bout Fannie?"

"Fannie knows. We can't go anywhere without you, you know that." She poked Hallie in the ribs, making light of it. "You've got something Nickie needs."

The girl relaxed, smiling now.

Soon they were on their way. Julie looked back at the house when they pulled away and she heard a dog barking somewhere in the distance. A pang of regret formed a tight lump in her throat as the house quickly faded in the background. Determined to carry out her escape, she turned and hugged her baby tight to her. No one would ever take him away from her again.

Slightly more than an hour later, they pulled up at the darkened wharf. Seth also believed she was meeting up with Daine later for a belated honeymoon and she hoped he would arrive back home and no one would be the wiser.

She left Hallie and the baby behind with Seth and headed down the docks to the large white double-deck riverboat with a large paddle-wheel in the stern. In no time at all she had secured them a stateroom. Then she hurried back to the buggy, finding all three asleep.

Shaking Seth awake, he carried their baggage to their new quarters and asked, "When's Masta Daine goan be he'ah?" he asked.

"He's going to catch up with us upriver. He didn't know for sure how long his business was going to take in Baton Rouge," she lied.

It seemed to satisfy him as he waved and left the ship.

There were two bunks and a large canopy bed, a small round table with three chairs, and two red velvet upholstered chairs with a thick plush red carpet. Heavy cream-colored draperies covered the windows and a red and cream striped bedspread, trimmed in a shiny gold braid, richly enhanced the decor of the interior.

It looks like a floating house of ill repute she'd once seen in a journal somewhere!

Julie had given a fictitious name in hopes Daine would be unable to track where she got off. They would arrive in St. Louis early on the sixth day. She was a little nervous about the departure time of six am, but hoped they'd be well on their way upriver by the time the family discovered them missing.

She opened her eyes at dawn's break only when the loud steam whistle blew their departure.

At exactly ten o'clock on the sixth morning, they arrived in St. Louis where a new life for her and her baby was waiting to begin. When the baby was weaned, she'd make sure Hallie was returned home.

•

The labor dispute had proved to be no big thing. Daine had straightened out the grievances to everyone's liking and had the support of several mill and other business owners, as well as the three hundred or so workers attending.

There had been talk before he'd left the year before of workers uniting with a single representative entity for improving their economic status and working conditions through a collective bargaining with employers. He'd heard support all around for the forming of such a union and Daine was the one they had chosen to represent them.

He'd also sparked an interest in the growing of the tobacco and had several landowners expressing a desire to meet with Darold. That meeting was set up in New Orleans as early as next month.

Now, as Daine rode through the darkening shadows of early nightfall the third evening after he'd left, he recalled his last conversation with Felina. She had contemptibly revealed her blatant lie only after he'd threatened her, then he'd had to sit through her crying jag while she begged him to forgive her. But he had not. He finally saw just what her vicious lies had cost them all.

It was well after dark when he arrived home to find the house strangely quiet. Dayna met him at the library with a grim look and thrust a note in his hand. He skimmed through it quickly, shoving it in his pocket and shook his head.

"When do you think she left?"

"Sometime Tuesday night. She took Hallie with her. Darold checked with the grooms and Seth admitted taking them and the baby to the wharf in New Orleans. She had told him she was meeting up with you later." She nervously wrung her hands.

"Darold went into town and found out that a woman, baby and mulatto girl had indeed booked passage upriver. He's in the library waiting for you."

Daine's mind reeled with self disgust. He was every kind of a heel and fool to have believed Felina, or Fontaine. After all, Julie had thought he was dead. What would he have her do? Forever remain a spinster? Hell, she was his wife! She had run away because of his rotten unreasonable temper and imagined infidelities. She wasn't like Felina. She'd never …

He rushed upstairs with Dayna hard on his heels. He wanted to see for himself that she was really gone. Darold came up the steps behind them two at a time. Catching up with his brother, he said, "She told me she had an aunt in St. Louis. Do you think she went there?"

"She had a letter from an aunt in St. Louis she'd left aboard the Hornet in her belongings when she was kidnapped."

"Good, you stop by and get it. There should be an address on it." He pursed his lips, seeming to choose his words. "But first, you damn fool! You're gonna sit down and listen to your little brother for a change."

•

When the big side-wheeler finally docked, Julie couldn't help feel a little reluctant to leave this safe haven she'd enjoyed on-board to strike out again on her own. All she could remember was her aunt's name since she'd left her letter with her address behind when she'd been taken so quickly from the Hornet.

As far as her mother could remember, her sister had remained a spinster. If she had decided to remarry these past few years then she'd probably never find her. Only the maiden name of Adele Linder was all she had to go on.

Upon leaving the ship, she hired a hack and asked to be taken to the city courthouse.

In less than an hour she had located an Adele Linder at 230 Westwood Avenue. Giving her driver the address, she twiddled her thumbs nervously. Presently her mood lightened when he finally turned down the marked street.

There were rows upon rows of older colonial style houses, most in need of a coat of paint and their lawns manicured. Craning his neck to both sides of the street, the driver finally stopped in front of a once-white small frame house.

"Here 'tis," he pointed, jumping down to unload the baggage onto the wooden walkway and helping her out of the hack.

The house looked vacant with the yard overgrown with weeds and a queasy wave of apprehension washed over her.

"Could you stay a minute so I can see if anyone lives here?" she asked.

"Yes ma'am," he said, beckoning Hallie to just stay put inside.

Out of the corner of her eye as she approached the house, Julie saw a curtain move slightly at a window, and then a grating sound as something was moved away from the door. A small white-haired lady opened the door a tiny crack, peering out at her over wire rimmed glasses which had slipped down her nose.

"Who might ye be lookin' for?"

"I'm Julie Sinclair and I'm looking for my aunt, Adele Linder."

The little old lady opened the door wide. "I'm sorry honey, but your aunt passed away just six months ago. I was her companion for many years. Go get your friends and come on in."

Julie worked her mouth but no sound came out. In all her imaginings, she'd never considered this possibility. What was she to do now? She just stood there a moment in frustrated sorrow.

"My my, did you come all the way from Greece?"

The real story would have to come later. It was too complicated. "Yes, and you don't mind if we come in?"

"Lordy no, I don't mind. Looks like you have a baby out there, bring your bags in too."

She hurried back out and paid the driver after he lugged their baggage in. Hallie carried in the baby, who was now beginning to fuss with the heat.

The wrinkled little forehead furrowed in a frown as she peeked at the squirming baby then looked at Julie. "I'm Lucinda, but they call me Lucy. It looks like you folks need a place to stay. But I'm going to warn you, I talk to myself. Your aunt's room is empty and she'd have just loved having you here. She talked about you a lot." Her worn slippers slapped against her feet as she moved to a door and opened it, revealing a cozy bedroom. "I don't have much but you're welcome to share it."

Instantly Julie felt welcome and comfortable. She had no other options with a baby and a young girl both totally dependent on her.

Smiling into the kindly faded blue eyes, she was confident she'd made a new friend.

"I'll look for a job tomorrow. I can sew quite well and I've got a little money to tide us over until then. We don't wish to be a burden, we can find a bigger place when I'm on my feet."

"You can stay here even if you don't find work," Lucy said. "There's ample food in the icebox and we'll worry about tomorrow, tomorrow." She leaned over and patted Julie's hand with a kindly smile and Julie suddenly choked up. "I have some homemade potato soup on the stove and your girl can help me dish it up."

Hallie was eager and in no time at all they were all seated at the small kitchen table and conversing like long lost friends.

Lucy and Julie still talked nonstop after dinner while Hallie bathed the baby and took a bath herself. Lucy gave her the names of several millinery shops and clothing stores that might be able to use her services. And later, when she finally climbed into bed with Hallie and the baby between them, she found she was totally exhausted.

When a tap presently sounded on her door, Julie whispered for Lucy to come in. She was dressed weirdly in a long white granny gown with a sleeping cap atop her snow-white hair. Padding softly to the side of the bed, she whispered so not to wake the baby.

"Thanks for giving an old woman something to look forward to in the morning," then she left. But not before she saw a glint of tears.

Julie was deeply moved.

•

The next day Julie found a job at the second place she inquired. She was to start work the following Monday. It was a general type store that sold everything from food to clothes to hardware. It even had a feed store in the back. She returned in the early afternoon to the house with both arms loaded with foodstuffs, and a tiny rattle for the baby, his first store bought toy.

The next few days flew by quickly and on Friday, Lucy surprised her with some jewelry and a miniature of her Aunt Adele. "She wanted you to have these. She always had a feeling you and your mother would come looking for her someday. She knew your mother had been sick and finally guessed she must have died, but still she worried a lot about you."

Julie was again moved. There was a string of pearls and three beautiful brooches, one a cameo and the other two were diamonds. She had no idea what they were worth but vowed to always treasure them. The picture of her aunt bore a striking resemblance to her mother. If nothing else, she'd be reminded of her each time she looked at it.

Bright and early the next morning, Julie was up and puttering around the kitchen before anyone else was up. She'd made the coffee and had it steeping gently on the back of the old cast iron stove while a frying pan of bacon sizzled on the front.

The wood stove was sweltering as she cooked in just her shift. She had small beads of perspiration forming on her forehead while some ran down between her breasts. Hallie soon joined her having already nursed the baby and left him cooing in their room while Lucy fussed and cooed over him.

They all heard a loud clatter outside and Hallie rushed to the window while Julie stayed to turn the bacon. At Hallie's loud gasp, Julie peered around the partition.

"It's him!" Hallie turned wide eyes to Julie, choking, "and his face looks like thunder!"

Julie stood frozen when she heard banging on the door, and then recognized Daine's voice as he hollered, "Julie! I know you're in there! Open the door!"

Hallie immediately opened up and stepped aside with her nervous fingers covering her mouth.

Resplendent in a dark suit with a white ruffled-front shirt, he ducked his head down as he stepped under the low doorway, stopping dead still in the center of the room. His eyes raked Julie in her immodest attire as she held a long handled fork in her hand.

Looking around the room, he growled, "Where's my son?"

At the intrusion to her home, Lucinda stepped around a doorway with the baby in question and marched straight up to him. David before Goliath.

"And just who might you be? You've scared these poor little girls to death, charging in here and bellowing like a bull!"

Daine looked down into flashing blue eyes that showed not one ounce of fear, and suppressed a smile at her daring.

"I happen to be the lady's husband," he said, nodding in the direction where Julie stood quaking. "And she's coming with me!"

Looking over Lucy's head, he glared at his wife.

Julie's heart sank. She'd have to obey. There was no question about that as she quickly wilted under his authoritative gaze. Laying down her fork, she nodded at Hallie who'd already made up her own mind.

Daine insisted they finish their breakfast, since they'd be on the road for several hours before they stopped for the night. Lucy sniveled all the time Julie packed and when Julie carried out their valises into the living room, he took them from her, his look unreadable. He watched in silence when Julie kissed and hugged the old woman.

"I promise to write," she murmured. "Aunt Adele was lucky to have you. I'll keep in touch. Thank you for everything."

So, Daine thought. *This isn't Julie's aunt after all.* She seemed to have a knack at finding loyal friends and this included his own family. Even Fannie had berated his haughty attitude.

He must have been confident in finding them since he had brought the carriage, Julie noted as she moved up the walk ahead of him. Seth took the bags and put them in the storage area while Daine boosted them all inside.

Julie was last. When he suddenly drew her close, she stiffened.

His dark eyes held hers a long moment, then he whispered huskily, "Don't you want to come with me?"

"To what end?" she answered, barely above a whisper as conflicting emotions washed over her. "You do own us all, do you not? My debt to you already far exceeds any payment you've received, is that not right?"

He smiled at her strangely. "We could leave that one open for discussion, but I always keep what's mine. Don't ever forget that."

His hands circled her waist and he lifted her in with ease. Leaving the door open, he stepped around to give Seth instructions before climbing in himself.

Hallie eyed them both as they started off. She had always liked Daine, he'd always been nice to her and was a fair and caring master. With the same toss of the coin, she greatly admired Julie. Everyone liked her and she'd captured all their hearts with her quaint musical voice and European accent. These two seemed perfect for each other. What could be the rub?

Daine had stretched out his long legs and was looking out the window on his side as the last of the city fell behind a short while later. Tall cypress trees and rolling hills were lined on their left while bushes and buck scrubs were intermittent along the banks, and next to the lazy current of the river on their right.

Laying his head back on a cushion, he watched Julie play with the baby on the seat next to her. He was laughing and grasping at her finger as she teased him. The love on her face was starkly apparent and he was hard put to keep his hands to himself. But he was soon astounded at the pain he saw on her face when the baby started to fuss, and Hallie took him and withdrew a barely concealed breast whereupon the baby nursed noisily.

•

Julie always felt a stab of regret that she could not nurse her own child, and it showed plainly on her face. She looked up once and met Daine's smoky gaze with a strange mixture mirrored deeply in her green ones, and he felt an overwhelming desire to pull her onto his lap.

Looking away in desperation, he made small talk. "We'll stop tonight at an inn I visited briefly last night. We changed horses there and we'll switch again."

When no one spoke, he closed his eyes. So much for that.

In no time at all he was snoring softly while Julie watched him warily. Hallie and the baby soon fell asleep too with the carriage's swaying motion and presently Julie closed her own eyes.

Sometime later, the buggy hit a sharp bump and she found herself in Daine's arms. His hand slipped around her shoulders while his face changed from bafflement to amusement when he realized what had happened.

Then the baby squealed, breaking the spell, and Julie pulled away after tossing him a stormy look. She reached over for the tot. After helping Hallie right herself, seeming more grateful for his help than Julie was, he settled himself in again.

This time he watched Julie under lowered lids while feigning sleep. His eyes traveled down the length of her, stopping back up at her small waist. No cumbersome corsets for her. Her gray traveling suit was cut superbly, with a mauve under-blouse, made of India silk. It was stretched tight over her rounded breasts and with her red curly hair pinned up in a style he hadn't seen her wear before.

But ah, the skin beneath. That, he remembered well.

His desire surged like a bursting flame and he flushed guiltily while he untangled his cramped legs. Her icy look thrown his way wilted any thoughts he may have harbored in that direction.

Shortly before noon they stopped at a halfway house to eat a light lunch. Daine let the two girls eat alone while he watered the horses and kept watch on the carriage sitting in the shade with the sleeping baby.

When they returned Seth and Daine ate a quick bite and soon they were on their way again.

The rest of the afternoon was spent trying to hold onto their seats as they traveled over the deeply rutted trace. Daine and Seth took turns as the horses constantly fought their restraints and their arms gradually grew tired with the strain of holding back their tossing heads.

A little after dusk they pulled into a brightly lit inn and they were all very glad to leave the bouncy carriage. A light rain was falling, wetting down the dust and they all felt dirty and grimy.

"All I want is a bath," Julie said, lifting her skirts from the mud as they tiptoed through it.

"I'll see to it," Daine promised. A man suddenly appeared beside him, handing him two skeleton keys. At Julie's wondering look, he smiled, "I had no doubts of finding you."

He took the lead and then stopped at one of the cabins. He inserted a key and the door swung open. Then he lit a candle and turned to Julie. "This is Hallie and Nicholas' room, ours is next door."

She didn't know if he had expected her to try and escape or if he thought the baby would only get hungry in the night. Either way, she knew she was still a prisoner.

A young boy appeared at Daine's elbow. "Mrs. Challenger would like a bath and also the girl and baby next door," Daine said, and followed the boy back outside.

Removing her gloves, Julie laid them on the dresser and then shook off the jacket to the traveling suit she wore. The room was quite small, but tidy. Candles burned in sconces on the wall with a large brass bed. The door opened again and Daine toted in a dented tub, which looked like a confiscated horse trough. Two young boys followed, carrying four buckets of water.

With a look of apology on his face, Daine stood back while the boys emptied the steaming water.

"It's the best I could finagle at the moment, but it's clean." He left.

She quickly disrobed and stepped into the small tub. She sponged herself and washed her hair, rinsing herself with the last bucket. Finishing in record time, she stepped quickly out and put on her robe. She was brushing her hair when he came back.

He'd changed his clothes and his hair was wet and she knew he'd also bathed. Eyeing her still in her robe, he questioned, "you're not dressed for supper?"

Startled, she turned to look at him. "You didn't say anything about going to eat."

"For God's sake, woman! Do you think me such an ogre that I would send you to bed without your supper?" What the devil was wrong with her? She tortured his mind and wrenched his soul and warmed his blood with just the sight of her. Yet, she trembled like a frightened child whenever she was in front of him. He moved closer, looking down into her face.

Intimidated, she turned her back and reached for a dress and pulled it on over her head.

His hands were warm as he touched the back of her neck, seeming to linger as he buttoned it for her. "Is Hallie going to join us?"

"Have you forgotten, she's a slave? I already took a tray to her."

Her mouth opened in disbelief. "Of course, she is but a lowly slave, how could I be so stupid?" Her eyes sparkled with anger. "Tell me, is that what I am to you? A slave?"

For the first time he guessed some of her discontent. The ways of the south was still foreign to her. To him, it was just a way of life—a life he'd inherited and had never once questioned.

"Would being 'shackled' to me, as you put it, be so bad? Have I ever laid a hand to you?"

He both terrified and fascinated her. Her skin still tingled where he'd touched her but she obstinately refused to submit to her inner yearnings. His eyes had turned smoky again and his sensuous mouth curved into a slight smile. It was that same smug smile that infuriated her so, one that she refused to succumb to.

He tried to remember. She had something still eating at her and it had to do with the baby, something deep and oddly emotional. He vowed to find out once they got settled in back at Fair Winds. Reaching for her shawl, he drew it around her shoulders and led her out the door.

They ate at the inn, which was connected to the livery stable down the road, and dined on roast duck and squab. They managed to stay civil to each other throughout the meal, and even garnered a few stares from other patrons as they sat sipping wine.

Returning to their room, Julie found herself yawning. She half expected Daine to leave and give her time to undress, but he stood quietly looking out the dark window. She slipped into her thin nightgown and climbed into bed, pulling the covers up to her chin.

Turning her back, she faced the wall and waited.

To Daine, she looked like a canary trapped in a lion's cage, and it cut him like a knife. Dropping into a chair, he pulled off his boots and removed his shirt and pants, and then blew the candles out and crawled into bed.

Julie felt the bed sag beneath his weight and braced herself for his touch. But it never came.

Chapter Fifteen

Dawn was still hours away when Daine again opened his eyes. Sleep had eluded him for nearly two hours as he stared unseeing at the ceiling and listened to the low steady breathing on the pillow next to him. Turning his head he could see her profile in relaxed repose as the full moon shone in through the window.

His movement stirred her and she suddenly turned on her side facing him where the blanket slipped down off her arm, revealing creamy breasts spilling over the side of her gown. In haste, he drew the covers back up to cover her but her eyes opened and she made a quick grab for his hand.

"Wh-what's the matter?"

Looking like a small boy with his hand caught in a cookie jar, his voice faltered, "I was just returning your covers. I must have pulled them off you."

To her relief, he rolled away a safe distance. They both lay quiet a moment, and then Daine spoke softly, "Do you mind if I get up and take a walk? It's impossible for me to sleep."

"Go ahead," she whispered, aware of the thin wall next to Hallie's room.

Somewhere is the deep recess of her mind she felt a smoldering desire, so remote she would never have guessed its existence. She had a sudden impulse to fling herself into his arms and bury her head in his furry chest and forget all the rest of the world. Then a tear escaped, and she turned her face so he wouldn't see.

This was an obvious dismissal to him, so he rolled out of bed and reached for his pants and shirt. Feeling around for his boots, he found them, and then skimmed the top of the dresser for his cheroots. He jammed one between his teeth and opened the door.

It wasn't her fault sleep refused to come his way the remainder of the night.

•

Morning saw them well on their way again. They had eaten breakfast in strained silence again, and he'd left when Julie went to pack their things. He sent Seth to carry out and stash them in the carriage well.

They spent three more nights on the road without incident, and by mid morning on the fifth day, the skies had opened up sending torrents of driving rain all around them.

The carriage had bogged down in deep mired mud three times while Daine had to climb out and lead the frightened animals through, all the while shouting orders to Seth. They were jostled and bounced every which way and Julie was left wondering if any of them would make it through the rest of the trip without any broken bones.

Finally, in mid afternoon of the fifth day, they were forced to take refuge in a small decrepit wayside inn, having no choice but to wait out the storm. Julie, Hallie and the baby were sent on to their rooms while he and Seth rubbed down the horses and got them fed and sheltered.

He had just started to his room when he met Julie coming down the stairs.

"You can take the first bath, you're covered in mud. I found some dry clothes for you, they're on the dresser." She was actually smiling. "I'll stay down here."

"No, you can take yours. I'll use the commons out back." He ascended the stairs to get his clothes while Julie stared after him. She was still there when he passed her on his way back down.

Forty-five minutes later, he returned.

Julie had taken her bath and was seated in a chair still wearing her robe, her face scrubbed clean and nose shiny. Reaching for his bundle of damp clothes he'd rinsed the mud out of, she shook them and hung them over a chair in front of the little heating stove in the corner. He set his damp boots near the fire, he'd not thought to throw in another pair.

Failing to see Julie back up, he turned and bumped into her in the narrow space between bed and chair. In the squeezed confines,

Daine's mood quickly worsened as the rain continued to pelt the windows. Feeling ill at ease in the close confines, he plopped down in the overstuffed chair and reached for a journal to read.

Julie sat back down, her hands in her lap and looking out the window at the rain.

His eyes lifted to fix themselves on the gap of her robe where he glimpsed the soft curve of a breast as she bent over to slide her foot back into a slipper. With an effort, he returned to the paper in his lap.

She rose again to her feet, refolding the same clothes she'd folded only a short time before. Brushing by him, her faint perfume assailed his senses and he moved his legs for the umpteenth time. Reaching down for his boots, he stuffed paper in the toes so they wouldn't shrink and tried to give it his whole attention. Try as he might, he couldn't extend his project for more than fifteen minutes, and when he leaned back in his chair, his eyes sought hers like a magnet once again.

She was standing with her arms raised in front of a mirror, brushing her hair with her back to him where the stance had drawn her robe tight across her buttocks, revealing a slender ankle below an exposed calf.

Completely unnerved, Daine threw down the dog-eared journal he'd been thumbing through, grabbed up his boots and headed for the door.

"Where are you going?" she asked, seeing his sudden action in the mirror. "You'll catch your death, it's wet out there." Her pivot when she stepped back, collided her with him.

He growled something inaudible as their bodies molded for only a fraction. As if pursued by the hounds of hell, he flung open the door and slammed it closed behind him.

When he didn't come back for several hours, she admitted she was worried. Was it something she said?

A generous tray arrived for dinner and still he didn't return. In slow degrees the realization hit her that she longed to see him. No matter how strained their relationship was, she still felt protected and safe with him.

Long after dark, she finally lit a candle for him and decided to go to bed.

She had just removed her robe and slipped into her nightgown when the thin strap on it broke. Standing next to the bed with one breast exposed, she didn't hear the door open when he stepped in.

He sucked in his breath seeing her so revealed with her head down and fixing something but he couldn't tear his eyes away. Then, with a low muttered oath, he grabbed up a towel and backed out the door just as she swung at the sound of the door's closing.

Seth had been out back of the barn performing his ablutions when he saw Daine moving toward the little shack that served as a bathhouse. When he saw him stop and pick up a bucket of water from the well, he couldn't help but holler out.

"But Massah Daine! That wata' is ice cold!"

Daine turned at Seth's voice, flung his towel over his shoulder, not missing a stride.

"It sure as hell better be!"

•

The rain was still falling in the morning when they got up. Daine went out to gather what information he could from passersby about the road conditions ahead.

Julie found Hallie and the baby in a little alcove off the kitchen where she was spooning warm porridge into the baby's mouth. Some of it had dripped down his chin. When he saw her, he gurgled, working his little hands and legs in excitement.

"My goodness, Nickie, your table manners need tending to," Julie laughed, picking up a cloth and wiping his fingers, ears and mouth. "You even got it in your hair."

Seeing how good Hallie was with the baby, she asked the question that had bothered her for some time. "Hallie, what happened to your baby?"

"Fannie say she was—still birthed."

"It's stillborn. But what about the baby's father? He must have been devastated."

"No ma'am, he was Cora Mae's man. She had the curse so I pleasured 'im, didn't mean nuthin', 'ceptin' I got kotch'd," she quipped nonchalantly.

Julie was flabbergasted at this insouciant attitude in lying with another's mate and her feckless response in losing her baby. She made a sudden silent vow. If she was going to have to participate in this way of life she must try and bring a little education to these colored folks. She suspected most, if not all, couldn't even read or write.

"Has the Challenger family ever sold any of your family, Hallie?"

"Lordy no, miz Julie.   Masta ain't sole no blacks long's I ra'memba."   Frowning, she went on. "But one'st I ra'memba' hiz sellin' two boy's 'bout sixteen, n' that's cuz they was trouble maka's. Nope, Masta Daine n' Darold mighty good ta' us.   Nev'ah whup's us, less'n some smart aleck needs it bad."

"Then he does have some of you whipped," she asked suspiciously. "For what reason?"

A deep voice at her elbow answered for her. "One reason might be for asking too many questions.   Have you done something wrong that you might be expecting retribution? Or is it still in the planning stages?" His face looked oddly perplexed.

"No, of course not," she answered hurriedly. "I was just curious, that's all." Quickly changing the subject, she asked, "Are we going on?"

"Seth and I just spoke with a driver who said he was going on through.   Someone traveling the other way told him it was muddy, but that the river is up, though it seems to be handling the overflow. We think we'll give it try."

He suddenly chuckled as his son reached out and wiped some porridge left on his finger on his sleeve. Bending low to his eye level, he tickled his chin making him giggle. Then he told the girls they would leave as soon as they all had breakfast.

At the last minute, Daine decided to ride on top with Seth and had the girls wrap blankets over their legs. Julie watched the river on her right and from time to time she could see groups of people shoring up the levees with rocks and shovels full of dirt.

The inn had prepared a basket of food for them in case they got stranded. If all went well, Daine told them they should be home by early evening.

Julie gave a huge sigh of relief at that news.

They were only an hour away from the inn when they came upon a buggy stuck crossways in the road. The back wheels were buried in the mud. The horse was bleeding about the head and looked ready to drop. Foam bubbled under the harness, and its back withers were also crisscrossed with bleeding gashes.

Julie felt a lurch as Daine bolted to the ground, and she looked open-mouthed at Hallie when she heard shouting, followed by a woman's high pitched scream. Opening the door to get a better look at the commotion, she was in time to see Daine plant his foot right square in someone's behind. Telling Hallie to stay put, she leaped onto the bank.

Her foot slipped and she went down to one knee, catching herself before she fell the rest of the way. Wiping the mud from her hands and ignoring the slosh in her shoes, she hurried to Daine, hearing part of his rant at the stranger.

"Any numbskull knows a dead horse pulls no load! Beating the hell out of a spent animal is not going to free that carriage!"

The stranger just glared back, obviously not wanting to look foolish in front of his female companion. Daine, nevertheless, kept up his ranting.

"I wouldn't lift a finger to help you out of this mess you've got yourself in, but we can't get by you. Besides, I feel sorry for this girl and the horse!" He had turned to holler at Seth when he saw Julie standing there. "Dammit."

"You may swear at fools, but cursing your wife is hardly a gentleman's way, now is it?" Her eyes were teasing, a far change from the past couple of weeks.

He shook his head, taking her arm and leading her back to their carriage. "It really frosts my ass to see an idiot like that owning a nice animal and mistreating it. We've enough to worry about without some knucklehead blocking the road."

It took longer than Daine had planned, but they were finally able to free the coach. When they'd hooked onto the sunken axle, they'd pulled it completely out of its drive-line. Hesitant to leave the girl behind, Daine offered to take her to Fair Winds and see that she got home. He also promised to send help back for her now very docile friend.

Once inside, and on their way, she introduced herself as Regina Pendarrow.

"Actually I live in New Orleans with my aunt and uncle, and Foster, that's my friend's name, was bringing me back from school in Baton Rouge, where I just graduated." She was a quite a tall girl with skin the burnished color of a Georgia peach. She had deep dimples, blonde hair and strange sapphire eyes.

Julie liked her at once and was glad to have her company. "Have you lived in New Orleans long?"

"Since I was nine. My parents both died and my aunt and uncle took me in." Her attention dropped to the baby and asked if she could hold him. The baby was soon cooing with all the attention and soon fell back asleep. His little head rested on Regina's shoulder and she opted to continue to hold him, patting his back and enjoying herself.

When they reached the small settlement of Grays Corner, ten miles from home, Daine summoned help for Regina's friend. While they fed and rested the horses, they ate their lunch from the basket the inn had prepared and watched the unrelenting rain.

Topside, Daine and Seth shook the rain from the tarp covering them, noting the water had already filled the trenches in the road around them.

Deciding to ride inside for a while, Daine took off his wet jacket and laid it over the back of the seat, trusting Seth's judgment. They had only gone four miles before they were stuck again. Using a small log, the men pried up the mired wheel and wedged rocks under it, finally allowing them to pull the horses forward and on their way again.

When they at last dropped down the last hill near Fair Winds, Daine heard a shout from high atop the carriage. "Massuh Daine! Massuh Daine!"

Julie was holding the baby and moved her legs back as Daine leaned over her and opened the door. Gray muddy water was rushing toward them from a broken levee at the river.

"Hold on Seth, I'm coming!" He shouted as he leaned out and grabbed the railing along the carriage top. The carriage rocked as he hoisted himself up and onto the seat beside the groom.

Ankle deep water was filling the swale they had just dipped into and Julie heard the crack of a whip as the carriage lurched through it. Churning muddy water with large pieces of driftwood was letting loose from the bank, and men with shovels and axes fought to close the rest of the weakening banks.

Julie could see the house in the distance and see livestock being led to higher ground with people milling about on the road ahead. She already knew the house sat high on a hill and was thankful they were nearly home.

Hearing a shout from far-off, she couldn't quite make it out.

The carriage had just crested the last hill when he saw Darold waving his hands and yelling at them, but the warning was too late. Water rushed in from nowhere and in seconds was pouring in the door, filling the floor of the carriage. Julie heard wood cracking, then both doors were suddenly torn away. She held on to her baby as Regina and Hallie were pulled outside and thrown into the swirling water.

"Julie!" Daine shouted as he leaped on the side of the twisting carriage.

Inside, Julie was struggling to keep the baby above water. She grabbed the side of the door but was knocked back against the seat, still holding him tight against her.

Daine could see the two girls in the water but where was Julie and the baby? He shouted again. "Julie, for God's sake! Answer me!"

Hearing shouts behind him, he saw Darold riding hard on horseback and two slaves running pellmell down the hill behind him.

Darold leaped off his horse near the girls in the water as the water rose even higher. The carriage tongue had twisted off and he saw the horses dragging it as they swam away in the current.

As the rolling carriage came around again, Daine reached in but felt nothing. From far-off he heard a weak cry. Several yards away, and in this frightening new river that used to be a road, he saw her.

Never had she known such terror, it was worse than when she'd escaped the Seeker. She had a baby now, which she was fighting hard to hold above water while trying to swim with one arm. At any second he could be torn from her grasp, and it was even harder with trees and debris in the water, all crashing into her. She kept an eye on the bank but it seemed to be getting farther away.

She was tiring very rapidly, but still she held on to her baby. She could hear shouting close to her but it was too much of an effort to answer. The blanket had ripped away and the baby wailed, then choked on a mouthful of water.

Oh God! Take me, not my baby! He's just an innocent ...

Daine had nearly reached her when he felt something kick his ankle. It was the blacksmith, Silas, who had moved alongside with long powerful strokes, cutting through the water like a messenger from God. His black face glanced sideways at him, then stroke for stroke they narrowed the gap just as Julie went under.

Silas' brawny arms closed around the baby just as Daine dove.

Chapter Sixteen

When the rains hadn't let up, Darold had had all the livestock moved to higher ground. The house, stables and slave quarters had been built on Metairie Ridge and boasted some of the best well-drained land in the area for crops. Running parallel to River Road, it was the only route to Baton Rouge, and was the only mainland route into New Orleans from the east.

Darold had worried all morning about Daine. He should have been back by now with his family. He'd had no doubts of his finding them. He'd ridden his horse Duke up and down the river all day, checking the banks for signs of weakening. Just before six, he'd finally seen their carriage coming up the road.

At just that precise moment, he'd heard a loud roar when a huge floating tree struck the levee, and it gave way. He'd stood up tall in his stirrups and waved frantically for them to stop but apparently they hadn't seen him. The rushing of the water had been too great, in seconds the carriage was churning in the water. He'd saw Seth dive off the seat and then a door flying off taking a woman with it. No, there were two women!

Spurring his horse into a fast run, he circled the rim of the hill meeting two slaves also running down toward the water. He could see his brother on top of the carriage so he leaped off Duke and dove in after the two girls. The two men were right behind him.

When he reached Hallie, he hollered, "Take her, I'll get Julie!"

She was thrashing about in circles, her heavy petticoats dragging her down. When he grabbed her and turned her, he found it wasn't Julie at all. Blonde hair streaked across her face, and when she felt him, she thrashed around even more.

"Stop fighting! You'll drown us both!" he yelled.

Still she kept pulling at him, hanging on for dear life. Heaving himself away, his hand shot out and he struck her a hard blow to her cheek. She fell against him and he sidestroked with her to the bank. Seth was at the water edge, reaching out to help him drag her ashore. Then Darold fell onto his back next to her, taking in big gulps of air.

A few seconds went by and he sat right back up and searched the flowing current, but Daine and the carriage had disappeared. He yelled at Seth, "Have you seen my brother?"

"Ain't seen 'im, or Miz Julie. Silas got's da baby, dat's all I know."

He looked down at the girl, her eyes were still closed and breathing hard. "See to her and tell Silas to get the baby on up to Fannie," he wheezed, then put his thumb and index finger together and whistled to his horse. Duke came at a lope, then he pulled himself into the slippery saddle and headed down the bank to look for his brother.

•

Daine knew the exact spot she had gone under and had dove twice but couldn't find her. On the third try, his hand tangled in long hair, then he quickly slipped an arm under one of hers and dragged her up to the surface.

They were a ways downstream when he finally got her onto the bank. She was limp and he couldn't feel her breathing when he laid her down in the wet grass. Rolling her over onto her stomach, he pushed on her back with a slow push and pull motion, then let out his breath when water spilled out of her mouth.

He rolled her onto her back again and patted her cheeks lightly, then a little harder. With panic rising in his throat, he bent and put his mouth over hers to blow in it.

She was floating high on a cloud, then warm lips closed over hers and she opened her eyes and slowly lifted her arms to encircle his neck. It was he! The man she always dreamed about. The kiss deepened and she was aware of strong arms wrapped around her tightly.

"Here I thought I was going to find two drowned rats but instead I find the two of you making love in the sand." Darold's voice sounded close. He was sitting astride his horse on the bank above them.

Daine released her only long enough to lift her in his arms, turning to face his grinning brother. "You're timing stinks," his dry reply.

Darold hoisted one leg over the saddle-horn and slid to the ground. "You take her on Duke. You both look like the walk would do you in." Reaching in his saddlebag, he took out a jacket and put it around Julie's shoulders.

She was very groggy, then suddenly jerked her head up. "Where's Nicholas?" Horror washed over them both as she turned and looked pleadingly at him.

Daine felt sick, but his brothers' words quickly dashed that.

"He's okay. He's up at the house with the two girls. Even the horses escaped with no injuries." He looked puzzled. "But who was the blonde girl I pulled out of the water?"

"We picked her up near Bower's landing. Her name is Regina Pendarrow. She and a friend were stuck in the mud and she came on ahead with us. She'll stay with us tonight and go on to New Orleans tomorrow."

More than once as Julie sat sidesaddle in front of Daine, she felt his lips press her temple in light kisses. By the time they got up to the house, Fannie had placed warm rocks wrapped in towels in the bed to warm it, then helped get her out of her wet clothes. Hallie, Regina and the baby were already snug in dry warm clothes and had already eaten.

In no time at all, Julie was fast asleep.

It was mid-morning the next day when she heard the door open and looked into a familiar jolly face with deep crow's feet near his merry blue eyes. He looked a little older since she'd seen him last.

"Walters!" She exclaimed, sitting up and reaching for him. He walked over to the bed and sat down, giving her a big bear hug. "What are you doing here?"

"I came out to see how you'all were faring. Heard there was some flooding. They tell me you nearly drowned. Sounds like they worked all night to get things all shored up."

Her eyes misted. "Daine risked his life to save me." Quickly, she brightened. "I'm so happy to see you. I have a surprise. We have a baby."

"I know. Daine brought 'im to the Hornet a couple of weeks ago, to show 'im off. He was proud as punch. You'da thought no one else had ever had a kid, the way he was showing 'im off."

So, Daine had told the truth when he 'stole' the baby and took him to town. She felt foolish. Had he been merely showing him off? His next words puzzled her. "And you, lass! When you were missing, he drove the crew half-crazy trying to find you. He was wild—"

Daine had just stepped into the room and caught the last of Walters' words. "Always yappin' off at the mouth, you old son of a gun," he chastised. He moved to the bed and looked down at her, glad to see color in her face. She'd been so gray—

Walters went down to eat while Daine went outside to check with his overseer. Julie wanted a bath and told them she'd be down as soon as she could. Darold had just sat down when Walters joined him.

"Fannie's coffee tastes like poison this morning, you could remove a coat of paint with it," Darold laughed. He filled a cup for Walters and handed it to him.

"Long as it's hot, I could drink most anything."

"Thanks for coming out, but you'd better stay a few days. You know your room's always ready for you."

"Nah, the guys're paintin' the Hornet's hull, n' I have to git back. We didn't get all the repairs we needed while searchin' fer Julie. We limped back home with only three quarters of her sails."

"Listen," Darold leaned close, talking low in case his brother came in. "I want to ask you a couple of questions about that idiot brother of mine. For some reason he and Julie fight like a couple of hound dogs. He's been acting like an ill-tempered bear and she acts like a little banty rooster, both going after each other every chance they get. Whatever happened on the Hornet to make them act this way?"

Shaking his gray head, Walters chuckled. "Ya got me. When he was thinkin' she was a boy, they sparred like two Greek gladiators. Then, when he found 'er out, they backed off twenty paces and eyed t'other, neither givin' an inch." Turning serious, he went on, "Then she saved 'im from a fall durin' a 'cane, after that we could all see they were stuck on t'other. They must'a not fought all the time, seein' as how they somehow begot a kid."

"Beat's me how they ever quit snarling at one another long enough for that to happen," Darold said disgustedly. "But something's rifted them. Guess it's up to me to find out."

Dayna and Regina came in just then, seating themselves across from Darold and Walters. Julie walked in behind them. This was the first time Darold had seen Regina all dried out and at close range. He filled their coffee cups and then settled back to admire her face.

"I usually don't slap pretty girls until I'm properly introduced, I hope you'll forgive my liberty," he smiled at her crookedly.

Dimpling at him, Regina's eyes met his. "I think the situation called for drastic and immediate action on your part." She looked around the table. "I can't swim."

Darold's eyebrows arched in surprise. Then, copying his sister-in-law's European accent, leaned across the table at her, "Tis fate then that the river chose such a spot to jump its banks."

"Yes, tis fate," she copied, setting her china cup back in it's matching saucer and blushing. She liked him already.

•

Darold was quick to offer to take Regina home. After they left, Julie returned to her room and lay down with the baby while he napped. Daine had still not returned, and she became quite anxious when he still hadn't returned by suppertime.

She had thought of little else but the undeniably loving kisses he had bestowed on her while they'd laid on the riverbank after her rescue. If he hadn't been in love with her before, she was certain he was now. She knew she still loved him.

Julie had just reached the bottom of the stairs in the late afternoon when Darold returned from town. Merrily tossing his hat on a hook, he started to tug off his boots at the boot-jack by the entry, grinning up at her.

"Is Daine back yet?"

Too quickly to mask concern, she answered, "No. He's been gone ever since he went to talk to the overseer before breakfast and I don't know where he is or if he's had anything to eat."

One boot nearly off, he stamped it back on. "Maybe I'd better go look for him." He turned to go. "Regina has agreed to go to the opera with me on Saturday. She's a really nice girl."

Julie was happy for him. "Yes, I like her too and she's well rid of that nitwit she was with."

Darold thought a moment. "Daine's a good man, Julie. He does right by his workers, his neighbors and his family. I think he's finally figuring things out, just give him a little time. I know for a fact he loves you." He gave her a quick hug and she watched him from the window as he mounted his horse then rode away.

Then, needing something to occupy her mind, she went to her mother-in-law's room to read to her. After an hour she fell asleep and Julie quietly tiptoed out. Hearing horses stop outside, she opened the door just as Darold and Daine both dismounted.

She was appalled at Daine's appearance. He had mud from head to toe and looked utterly exhausted with his several days' growth of beard and he was leaning tiredly on his brother as he moved up the steps.

"I found him at the county schoolhouse, helping pack books and supplies upstairs. God knows what else he's done. He'd been at the Willoughby's, Doc Morgan's and the widow Shuster's. Damned if I know if he's had anything to eat or not!"

Julie grabbed Soonie in the doorway, "Please have Maxwell fix some bath water for Master Daine, he needs to get out of those wet clothes. Then ask Fannie to fix Master Daine something to eat."

She followed the two brothers up the stairs and found a set of clean clothes for Daine. When she heard the troupe of servants coming down the hall with the warm water, she hurried to the bathroom with clean towels and gave no sign of leaving after the servants left.

Daine wasn't as tired as he looked. He still had his wits about him and he sure as hell wasn't going to let his wife help bathe him. He was in no mood to be placed in such a vulnerable position quite yet.

"Darold can manage quite nicely, my dear wife. But if you like, turnabout is fair play. You can scrub my back tonight, if you'll let me do yours in turn." His infuriating mocking smile was once again evident.

Her spine stiffened as she gazed back at him and she gritted back, "You delude yourself, dear husband. I will not deem you the pleasure you so arrogantly seek." She moved to the door and jerked it shut behind her with a bang.

Daine's black eyebrows arched in surprise at this peppery retort, then he was nearly bowled over as his brother yanked his pants down around his ankles, then flipped them off in a corner.

He yanked the rest of his clothes off and then pushed him down roughly into the water.

"For Christ's sake! Can't you two be civil with each other for even five minutes? What's the matter with you Daine? She didn't deserve that from you!"

Daine's sheepish look didn't deter his brother's harsh scolding as he pushed his shoulders down in the tub. Grabbing a washcloth, he dunked him down in the water, lathered his head with the bar of soap he held in his other hand, then swiped the cloth angrily across his back and up and down his arms.

As his anger increased, so did the pressure. When he started for his face, Daine grabbed the soapy rag.

"I'm not that helpless."

"You can't prove it by me!" Darold growled as he reached for a bucket of water and poured it all at once over his head.

Sputtering, Daine choked, "All right, all right! You win this round!"

Darold threw the dry towel in his face, then reached for a chair and straddled it and looked eye level at him. This was the second time in a month he'd scolded his older brother.

"Would you please explain to me why this little redheaded pint-sized spitfire of a girl reduces you to a mass of quivering jelly when she oversteps those invisible boundaries you've put up around yourself?"

The need to confess was strong, yet when he started to shrug it off he knew he couldn't sink any lower in his brother's eyes.

With a long sigh, he said at last, and almost too low for Darold to hear. "Guilt. I met her even before she ever set foot on my ship. I tried to rape her."

Darold's eyes narrowed, trying to imagine such a thing. "That's hard to believe when you've had all the willing women in the county hot on your tail."

"I was drunk and still brooding about Felina. Julie stopped me before—well, she stopped me before it happened. But every time she looks at me I know she remembers. I can't seem to forget it." With a grunt, he rose dripping to his feet, dried himself off, and then wrapped the towel around his waist.

They were both silent as he walked to the dresser, lathered his face and picked up his straight razor. With quick sure strokes he shaved, and then wiped his face clean with another wet towel. Even when he combed his hair, they stayed silent.

All the while, Darold had studied him and plotted. How blind could one person be?

"She loves you," he stated simply.

Daine turned, looking mystified at him. "What makes you say that? She ran away from me."

"No, you drove her away with that rotten temper. She mourned you right along with the rest of us. She thinks you still love Felina. She told me so."

"You know how I feel about Felina. How I ever considered marrying her is beyond me," he said as he laid the comb down.

"But does Julie know? Have you ever told her how you feel? Have you ever once told her you loved her, or even talked to her about Felina? How you found her with Fontaine? How he even broke Dayna's heart?" He ranted on. "For God's sake, man! Tell her anything, but at least talk to her!"

Daine couldn't believe his ears, his brother was chewing his butt royal and still chewing.

"Don't bury your head in the sand and think everything will work itself out, because buddy, unless you do something about it pretty soon, it'll be too late." Moving to the door, he calmed down somewhat. "If you're smart, and I know you can be, you'll get some sleep and then talk to her after some of what I've said sinks into that thick skull of yours. Goodnight!"

Bloody hell! Daine thought after his brother left, yanking back the covers and climbing into bed, and totally forgetting about eating.

Maybe I've misjudged Darold after all. He does have a mind of his own!

·

Something awakened him. It couldn't have been the clock, as just now it rang two bells, signifying two in the morning. Raising his head off the pillow, he could see Julie standing on the widow's walk just off the bedroom. Her face was illuminated and the warm breeze had billowed her flimsy gown around her bare legs.

From his vantage point he could see her in silhouette between himself and the moon, affording him a revealing, yet unknowing, interception of light.

Moving with catlike grace across the room, he stood in the shadows only three feet from her. When she turned her head at the distant sound of a dog's bark, the tears he saw on her cheek shook him. A dam burst in his chest and he stepped out and reached for her.

Muffling her cry of alarm with his deep kiss, he pulled her close feeling her warm body melt against his own. His hand slid inside her gown and moved down her satiny spine. He tasted the saltiness of her tears on her soft yielding mouth.

She started to struggle as he dragged her back inside.

"No!" she cried out. "I won't be your slave—or your whore!"

His look was thunderstruck and he drew back and looked down at her. "What do you mean by that!"

She lost herself a moment as she stared into the luminous depths of his eyes and fought to resist the tremendous attraction he still held for her. He was an enigma, and he had been from the first moment she'd met him. She'd not fall into his arms in the darkness of night and loathe herself on the morrow when sanity returned, thus wrenching her soul and mind asunder.

"You figure it out, you're supposed to be so smart," she said as she yanked her arm back. "If that's all you want from me, just the satisfying of your animal instincts, then surely there are those more willing in the bordellos on Bourbon Street. But," her green eyes flashed, "This time know this well. I will not give myself freely only to have you throw it back in my face."

"Oh, my dear Julie, how you lie," he said huskily as he slowly pulled her close again. "Do you think to deny me my rights? You were never a whore to me, certainly never a slave. I have never thought that. Have you forgotten how it was between us? I have forgotten ... nothing."

His head lowered and he kissed her lips firmly, one hand lifting her chin, the other cupping the back of her head. It took only that, this burning kiss rekindling the flame she had tried to fan away. Scooping her up in his arms, his lips stayed glued to hers as he moved to the bed.

His skilled hand loosened her sash and it fell to the floor seconds before the bed sagged with their weight. His hand raised to brush his palm over the soft tip of a breast, teasing it into instant hardness and she squirmed, pulling his head back down to hers to kiss him deeply.

Their overpowering love was quickly revealed to each other, no matter how hard they'd both tried to deny it.

He was deliberate in his slow seduction and her earlier protestations faded in his ears, and soon she was in his arms, her body twisting from side to side in sweet agony. His low moan of pleasure patented his own pent-up torture.

When he parted her legs she moaned, her body having been denied too long this exquisite pleasure. He gathered her close as she took him in. They began a slow rhythmic motion that slowly built in intensity, their lips burning hot together. She welcomed his probing tongue creating a whole new delicious sensation. Her hips arched to meet his and soon they both found blessed release.

In mere minutes, he rolled from her but still held her tight. She buried her head in his shoulder, unable to speak.

His words caught her off guard, but stilled forever her doubts.

"I love you, Julie." When she didn't answer, he turned on his side facing her. "I've loved you from the moment I saw you coming down those stairs in Crete. I tried to take my hurt out on you that night and I'll regret it forever. You own my heart."

She started to speak but he stopped her with a finger over her lips.

"Shush. It's incredulous to me that I ever considered marrying Felina. She tried to sway me from leaving on the Hornet when I went to Europe by trying to make me jealous. She kissed Fontaine in front of me at a party the night before I left. It didn't work, I only laughed at them.

"Later that night I caught them together in a compromising situation upstairs. She thought I'd left for home, and I had, but I'd forgot to tell her about the horse."

Julie took it all in, her heart growing lighter while Daine poured out his heart.

"Fontaine was angry that I'd caught them and he'd blurted out it hadn't been their first time. While I'd been traipsing all over the seas, I learned she'd bedded every eligible bachelor from Fair Winds to New Orleans. I was mostly angry with myself that night, not Felina. If I had cared for her, I'd have beaten the hell out of Fontaine."

Raising up on an elbow, he cupped her chin in his hand and

kissed her long and lovingly, sending a tingle through her again. When she lightly kissed his neck, he talked on.

"I'm sorry for a lot of things, Julie. Mostly the near rape, then poking fun at you on the Hornet, then comparing your imagined infidelities to Felina, and my silence in declaring my love for you. I don't deserve your forgiveness, so please don't give it. I'd rather try and earn it."

Remembering something, he released her and leaned over the side of the bed for his muddied charcoal jacket he had worn to St. Louis. It was the one he'd been wearing when he'd saved her from the river. Running his hand down the front, he slipped his hand in the side pocket and found what he was looking for. He settled back down next to her and reached for her left hand, slipping the gold band back on her finger.

Lifting her eyes to his, she could see only genuine love and her breath caught in her throat.

His voice was very husky. "With this ring, I do honor, love and cherish you forever and ever. This is your home, yours and Nicholas'. And a daughter." His eyes twinkled. "And maybe another son ..."

His arms encircled her again. "I want you to love it here as I do. It's a great place to raise a family."

"Stop," she laughed, "I love it here too and for the first time in my life, I feel like I belong somewhere—and with someone." She knew what he was waiting for.

His eyes changed half a dozen expressions before he asked, "Okay Julie, say it now or never say it at all."

It was worth the wait.

"Oh God, if I'm dreaming then let me sleep forever. I love you too, surely you know that by now."

"Darold hinted as much but it sounds much better coming from you. I'm sorry for all you had to endure when you were kidnapped, then enduring my stupid accusations. Pride is a crippling thing. Soon, I want to hear all about every minute you went through on your miraculous journey here."

Her eyes were misty and he leaned over and kissed her tenderly, their passion rising again. His palm caressed a breast, watching her eyes change to a smoldering hue.

Pulling back, she looked him in the eyes. "Did you mind when you found out we were married?"

"Why in the devil a woman wants to talk when she'd being made love to is beyond me," he said hoarsely. "Does it look like I mind?" She followed his gaze and blushed. "If we'd both spoken our feelings before, we'd have saved ourselves a lot of misery," he said, propping himself back up on his pillow. "I need to tell you that the Hornet will be seaworthy in September." Seeing the frown she tried to hide, he rushed on. "I'm not going, and Walters is getting too old, but I made Jeremy the new captain. I've been appointed the representative of a new collective bargaining committee, formed when I went to Baton Rouge. I'm hoping it won't take me away from you and Nickie too much."

"Looks like I married a busy man," she said, fingering the curls at the nape of his neck.

There was still a problem that needed to be solved. "Would you tell me now what bothers you so about Nicholas? Why you get so frantic when he's out of your sight?"

She was silent a long moment.

"Dayna told me that the Challengers buy and sell slaves. This was right when I had to quit nursing and Hallie took him over. It all happened so fast, removing him from my room and then bringing in a wet nurse. I didn't think your family would ever separate us but I really haven't wrapped my mind around slavery yet."

"Good Lord! You thought …" It all made sense now. "We raise crops here. I'll admit there are a few plantation owners who buy and sell slaves, some just to make money. We very seldom buy slaves, most have grown up here and die here." He had a feeling Dayna had embellished a little. "This is the south, Julie. I don't expect you to understand our customs. We certainly don't break up families; we feed, clothe and give them shelter. They work for these privileges and most are loyal and happy with this long standing way of life. A doctor comes regular to check them out."

She wasn't quite convinced. "What about marriage, are they allowed that?"

"They have a wedding of sorts, it's called 'jumping the broomstick.'" He fell silent a moment knowing how ridiculous that must sound to her. "Look here, Julie, we've never had a 'runner,' they have their own church and nobody works on the Sabbath. We reprimand for stealing and haven't had any major problems to speak of."

He became thoughtful again, thinking of the purported rumblings of his abolitionist sympathizing neighbors upriver in the North. It was still only hearsay but things could get volatile in the next year or so it was best to keep quiet for now—or it may not even amount to anything.

Julie had a sudden thought.

"What about schools? Why can't I teach them? I've been wanting something productive to do. With you in Baton Rouge a lot on business it would be something for me to pass the time, unless you plan on keeping me busy with all those babies," she laughed.

It was a merry sound that delighted him.

"Okay, but you might get run out of the county," he sighed, pulling her close.

"I'll take that chance. And another thing," she added, a sly smile on her face. "I'm going to rename my horse."

He was certain his life would never be the same.

• • •

Judie Kleng

Judie Kleng was born and raised in the Pacific Northwest. She worked as a 911 dispatcher until she retired and followed her dream of writing romance. She also enjoys songwriting and performs in local area clubs. Judie says she's married to her soulmate—with whom she raised two wonderful sons and raced thoroughbred horses. Judie currently lives in beautiful eastern Oregon and continues to follow her dreams.